BUCK

A Survivor of the Shut Down

W. R. FLYNN

ISBN-13: 978-1470092238
ISBN-10: 1470092239

This book is a work of fiction. Names, characters, places, and incidents either are products of the author's imagination or are used fictitiously. Any resemblance to actual events or locales or persons, living or dead, is entirely coincidental.

First Edition

Correspondence for the author should be addressed to:
wrflynn54@gmail.com

Manufactured in the United States of America
CreateSpace, Charleston, SC

ALSO BY

W. R. FLYNN

SHUT DOWN

Acknowledgements

These are the people who contributed to make this project a reality. I hope I haven't overlooked anyone.

First, I want to thank my dear wife, Deborah, who kindly gave her inspiration, proofreading skills and patience. Without her support, writing this novel would have been impossible.

My sister, Patricia, performed the final editing making the work publishable.

My daughter, Alison, meticulously edited the manuscript from start to finish.

My daughter, Kelly, corrected numerous punctuation and grammatical errors as the work progressed and helped create the maps.

My son, Casey, who proofread an early draft and kindly edited several critical points, deserves special thanks.

My good friend, Jerry Kalapus, proofread this work and offered priceless encouragement. The advice he provided was essential to the successful completion of this novel.

My wonderful friend, Angel Williams, generously reviewed the final draft providing key suggestions granting me a green light to submit the manuscript.

I must also thank the fantastic Multnomah County Sheriff's Department for keeping the hard working people of Corbett safe every minute of the day.

Lastly, I give thanks to the other good people who helped make this work a reality: Tina Tebbens, Aaron Throop, Jeff Fauth, Jerry Stitzel and all the rest. You know who you are and I thank you.

So that there should be no division in the body, but that its parts should have equal concern for each other. If one part suffers, every part suffers with it; if one part is honored, every part rejoices with it.

Paul the apostle
1 Corinthians 12:25-26

... when one being suffers, it becomes the suffering of all. The happiness of any one, becomes the joy of all! None can exist in isolation from the other!

Shakyamuni Buddha
The Sutra of Compassion

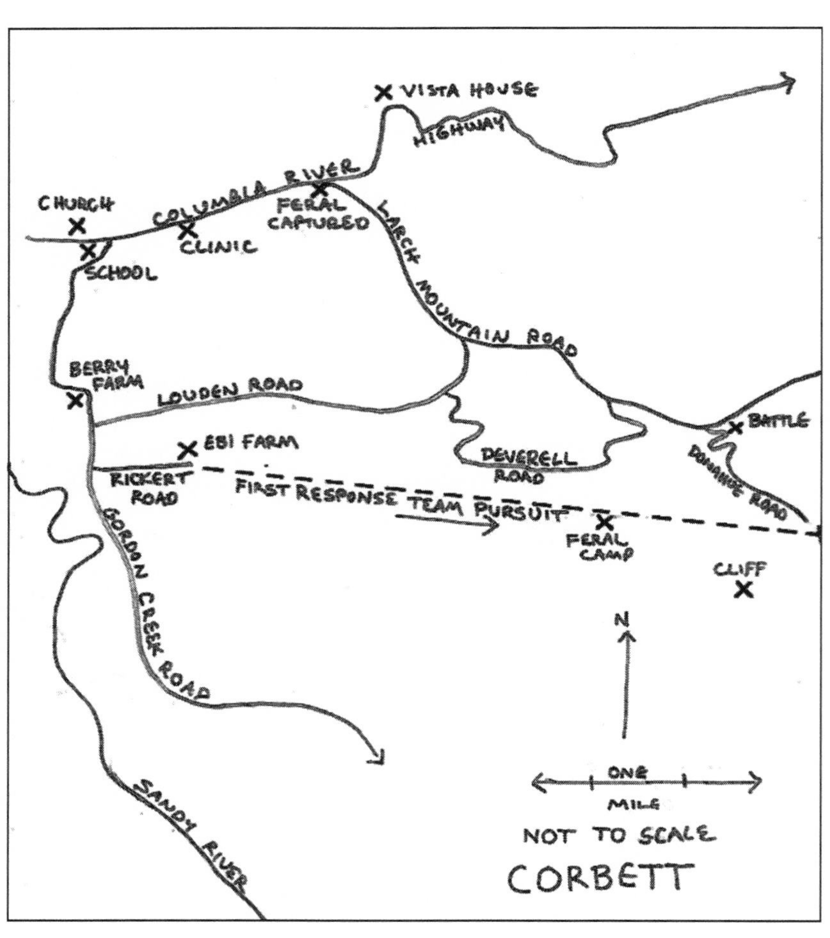
VISTA HOUSE
HIGHWAY
COLUMBIA RIVER
CHURCH
FERAL CAPTURED
CLINIC
SCHOOL
LARCH MOUNTAIN ROAD
BERRY FARM
LOUDEN ROAD
EBI FARM
BATTLE
DEVERELL ROAD
RICKERT ROAD
FIRST RESPONSE TEAM PURSUIT
FERAL CAMP
CLIFF
GORDON CREEK ROAD
N
ONE
MILE
SANDY RIVER
NOT TO SCALE
CORBETT

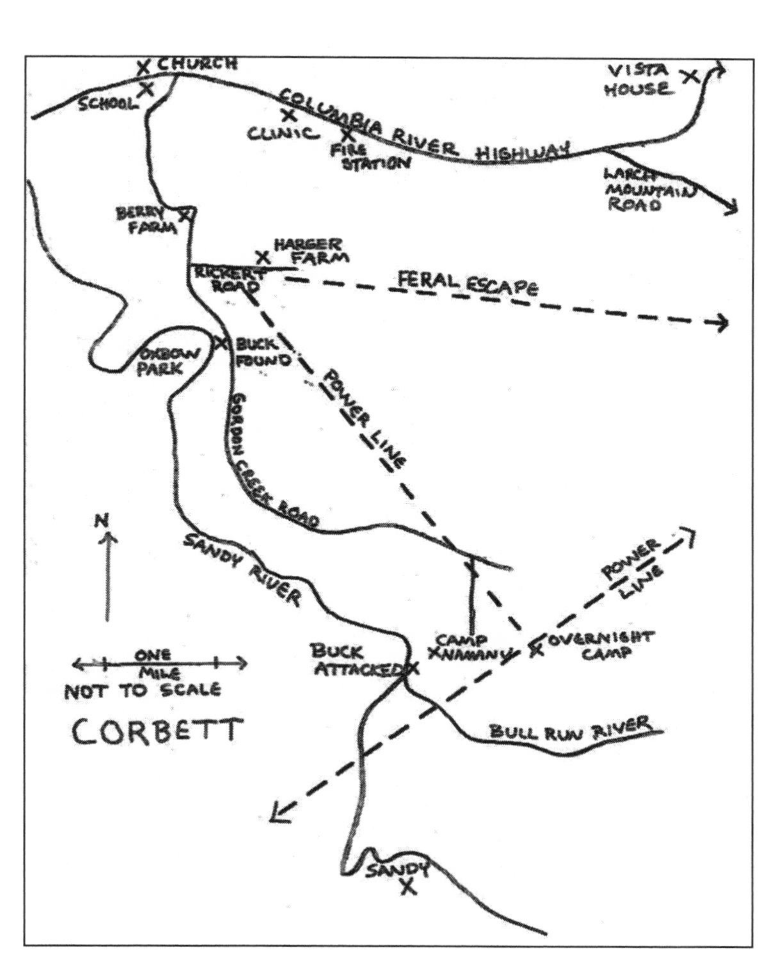
CHURCH
SCHOOL
COLUMBIA RIVER HIGHWAY
CLINIC
FIRE STATION
VISTA HOUSE
LARCH MOUNTAIN ROAD
BERRY FARM
HARGER FARM
RICKERT ROAD
FERAL ESCAPE
OXBOW PARK
BUCK FOUND
POWER LINE
GORDON CREEK ROAD
N
SANDY RIVER
ONE MILE
NOT TO SCALE
CORBETT
BUCK ATTACKED
CAMP NAWANY
OVERNIGHT CAMP
POWER LINE
BULL RUN RIVER
SANDY

Chapter One

"Joe, look!" Chris Saunders said, as he nervously drew his handgun for the first time in nearly two years.

"Whoa," replied his friend, Joe Hancock. It was the last thing they expected as they tried to catch a few trout or an early-running summer Chinook salmon.

It was late morning, warm, and would soon get hot as they fished along the shore of the snowmelt-swollen Sandy River. The river was still flowing fast, but in two weeks, by mid-July, the river level would drop and, as the summer Chinook became more numerous, they would become easier to catch.

The two men had been up since early morning working on Joe's family vegetable garden, getting their hands dirty in the early cool air. Summertime meant long hours of hard work but they didn't complain. Everyone in town pulled their weight working on farms, fishing or hunting with bows to make sure they had enough food to feed everyone.

Prior to the sudden economic collapse, Joe's family farm grew blueberries, selling them to local markets and overseas wholesale buyers. For years, as a hobby, Joe's mother, Mary Kay, tended a small vegetable garden alongside her family's well-maintained early-twentieth-century Sears Craftsman farmhouse.

Since the disaster struck, the Hancock vegetable garden expanded. It grew from a few hundred square feet of tomatoes, peppers and zucchinis to five acres featuring dozens of assorted organically grown vegetables. Next year they planned to grow corn, which meant cultivating ten acres. The blueberries still grew in nice straight long rows meandering over the easy rolling hills of western Corbett. They would soon ripen with little help, but their vegetable plot needed constant coaxing, especially during the annual spring and early summer planting period. It was one of many small vegetable farms that had sprouted up in Corbett over the past two years. Work crews would be tending the crops every day all summer and well into fall. As the morning grew warmer, a walk to the river was a welcome break from the backbreaking farm labor.

Chris and Joe began fishing for the summer Chinook a few weeks earlier when the first ones arrived. When fishing line grew scarce, the way people fished had to change. There were still plenty of quality, pre-disaster fishing poles to use, but many now preferred the short, simple, birch-branch pole, like the one Chris made during the past winter. Since fishing line was in short supply they no longer casted. Instead, they dropped short lines along the shore, always bringing the lines home afterward.

Since midmorning they had caught only one, a twenty-pounder, so they tried their luck downstream. They moved to a point where they could look across the river at the trees and aging picnic areas of Oxbow Park along the opposite shore. Each time they fished along this beach they felt the ghosts of the dead. The shore they stood on was the site of the old battles. Thinking of the hundreds of dead, Joe usually became misty-eyed as he walked nearer and today was no exception.

As they settled in and went to work preparing to drop a few fishing lines, Chris glanced downstream a short distance and saw him first. The man was barely visible, lying prone on the riverbank partially shaded under a low-hanging birch tree branch. He was facedown and motionless between a few large river rocks, barefoot, both legs in the water. His scraped and bruised feet stuck out of badly tattered pants. Two dirty hands reached out through the sand toward the trees. His long, greasy dark hair and filthy grey t-shirt were wet and bloodstained. He was an outsider; someone they didn't know. And that scared them.

"He looks dead," Joe said, whispering back to Chris while clutching his well-worn fishing pole near his skin-tight tan sleeveless t-shirt.

"Yup."

"I don't recognize him," Joe replied.

"Me neither," Chris said, "but I don't know everyone. With over three thousand people in town I still meet new people all the time."

"He looks like a stranger," Joe said.

"Yeah," Chris said.

"We better check him out," Joe said.

"His pants're wet. So's his shirt. Looks like he just washed up," Chris replied, as they both moved cautiously closer along the shore of the river.

"I dunno, Chris. He may've been here all night. Hard t'tell. It's been a few years since we've seen a dead body on this beach," quipped Joe, referring to the ferocious battles fought along the banks of the Sandy River one terrifying afternoon two summers back.

"It's been a long time since we've seen anyone at all," Chris said.

"Let's hope it stays that way. But when there's one…."

"True," replied Chris, as the two of them carefully scanned with their eyes in all directions, barely moving their heads.

Chapter Two

Two hundred and fifty men had been killed that day two summers ago when a small Corbett foot patrol stumbled upon and quickly slaughtered a battalion-sized invasion force of freed jail inmates. Their guards had waited helplessly as they sat for days in their cells and dormitories slowly starving to death. Food shipments had stopped when the nation's trucking system ran out of fuel and collapsed. When the inmates were finally turned loose by good-hearted jail guards, they quickly organized and set off on a manic search for food, drink, drugs and women.

A massive Monday morning wave of bank closures, which shut down the world's fragile financial system, released humanity from its once-powerful social bonds. The sudden unraveling of human civilization was worldwide and struck without mercy. Within a few days everything had fallen apart in a historically unprecedented orgy of death and destruction. Riots and looting exploded unchecked in nation after nation as social order vaporized and the Four Horsemen saddled up for yet another ride, their best ever.

Immediately after hitting the streets of northeast Portland the newly-freed, rag-tag army of thugs went on a brutal rampage, looting, raping and burning their way east during two intoxicating weeks of pure mayhem. They were on a winning streak and optimistically thought Corbett would be easy to take, too. After all, northeast Portland, Fairview, Wood Village and Troutdale fell with little resistance. However, when it came to terrorizing Corbett they were dead wrong. Two weeks after the collapse nearly all of them were slaughtered moments after crossing the Sandy River along this shallow stretch of riverbank.

The attackers were giddy with excitement as they waded across the Sandy River and clambered over thick logs deposited by past floods. Their anticipation grew as they danced and joked their way to Gordon Creek Road, which meandered near the river at this point. They carried little other than a crazy assortment of looted rifles and handguns, some of which were unloaded. Few knew how to shoot the ones that were. Nevertheless, they were an intimidating force made up of violent wannabes, social outcasts, toothless drug addicts and other assorted Multnomah County rejects.

During the two weeks of looting they had shed their jail clothes and were nicely dressed as they strolled north up the road and prepared to attack. After weeks of rummaging through abandoned suburban closets, most looked like they had climbed out of a Columbia Sportswear or an Eddie Bauer catalogue, while others wore casual business attire, some for the first time in their lives. Their meager possessions were carried in colorful convenient daypacks that once held schoolbooks. Many packed sharp knives pilfered during their two weeks of freedom, knives littered with the DNA of their countless victims.

A well-armed, well-trained, six-member Corbett foot patrol spotted them. They knew the terrain very well and they knew their weapons even better. After silently taking solid cover positions alongside the road, the local militia waited, hidden in the bushes behind logs, boulders and trees until the noisy mob drew near, then all at once they opened fire. Moments after the shooting started, five members of another nearby foot patrol heard the gunshots and rushed to join them. The one-sided battle lasted only a few minutes. One defender died on this particular beach: Steve Nelson. He had taken a stray bullet in the forehead. He'd died during the first of two one-sided battles fought near the same beach where the filthy barefoot outsider just washed up.

Chris had been shot, too. His friend, Alison Lee, also took a round, but she was saved by her father's Kevlar vest and remained in the fight, bruised but otherwise uninjured. Chris had nearly lost his left arm during that battle along this wooded stretch of beach, but he kept fighting, firing away with his good arm until the battle ended. He'd taken a bullet through the bicep. If not for his inner determination to recover and the loving care of Denise Song Bird, the Native American town veterinarian he later married, he would probably now be fishing one-armed.

At five-foot nine and a lean one hundred and fifty-five pounds, Chris now sported a shiny black, foot-long ponytail. A few dozen short wispy black hairs sprouted randomly from the chin and cheeks of his round unscarred face. He once scaled in at a chubby, yet clean-cut, one-ninety. However, with a primarily vegetarian diet and the loss of junk food he, like nearly everyone, lost his body fat. His new weight left him lean and muscular: ripped, in fact. Barefoot and shirtless in his orange-brown deerskin pants, the baby-faced former soldier now looked like an adopted Indian child standing alongside his much larger, light-skinned, bald-headed and blue-eyed friend, Joe.

At the time of the collapse, Joe had been packing nearly two hundred and fifty mostly fat free, muscle-bound pounds on his thirty-something superhero frame. Premature baldness had slammed Joe hard, leaving only a stray hair or two on his squarish, sun-reddened head. Always standing straight as a totem pole and well over six feet tall, he was once a mighty presence wherever he went. Heads would turn as he passed by with his nineteen-inch neck and twenty-one-inch arms.

However, with the daily foot patrols and hard labor, combined with the limited diet following the disaster, he had lost fifty pounds, reaching a weight he hadn't been since he graduated from the Navy's BUD/S training ordeal over a decade earlier. Others had lost even more, but a hardened, intimidating two hundred was how Joe stood since. Along with his father, Joseph, who likewise lost a wheelbarrow full of body fat, he nevertheless continued to hit the weights hard, so Joe and his dad, now nearly sixty, were still considered among the toughest men in Corbett.

Sadly, as the months passed, walking was gradually becoming more and more of a minor annoyance for Joe, but when asked why he would always brush it off. Over the last two years he had developed what Denise simply called a nervous disorder. It caused him to walk with a slight rhythmic limp reminiscent of those suffering from a mild case of cerebral palsy. She told him it could worsen over time but, although running fast was no longer possible, he could jog slowly and otherwise get around just fine. Still, if folks needed something heavy lifted or someone friendly to talk to, they often turned to Joe.

Chapter Three

Joe and Chris quietly moved closer, then stood staring at the stranger from about ten feet away. They once again silently scanned around a moment, listening to the nearby woods and looking in all directions to see if anyone else lurked nearby.

"There's no trespassing," Chris said. "What should we do?"

"He isn't trespassing. Just washed up on our beach. Look. His head's bleeding," said Joe, pointing at the blood on the man's face and in his hair.

"Maybe he hurt it crawlin' outta the water," replied Chris a bit louder, as he set down his homemade fishing pole alongside Joe's tackle box and much longer, fiberglass pole.

"I doubt it, it's partly scabbed up, but he looks harmless. Skinny. Bony, like he hasn't eaten much in weeks. I think he's hurt bad. You have your gun. Cover me. I'll roll him over, check him out," Joe said.

Chris still held his Glock nine in his hand, careful to always have it ready after what occurred two years back. "Wait. What if he's sick? Maybe we shouldn't take the chance. Remember the old rule about newcomers? We aren't allowed to go near anyone 'til we find out if they're sick," explained Chris.

Joe had stopped carrying his handgun long ago, but he always felt safe as long as his friend Chris carried one. After hearing the man's story, he'd never again go out without it strapped to his faded baggy blue jeans. "Okay. Let's find out if he's sick. Poke him with a stick, Chris. See if you can wake him up. We'll ask him."

"Let me look at him first," Chris said, as he approached closer. "Let's see here … hmm, no weird rash, he's not sweating, his hair isn't falling out, he's not leaking from the nose or mouth … he isn't shaking or nothing, either. He's breathing weak, but steady, too. I don't believe he's sick at all."

"Well, go on, poke him, Chris. Get him to wake up."

"No, you poke him," chuckled Chris.

"Fine," said Joe. "I'll poke him."

"I'll cover you."

"Okay, but I want you to stand over there," Joe said, pointing to a sandy area not far from the man.

Chris stood where he was told. Joe then walked a short distance back and broke off a small branch from a nearby shade tree. He then stretched out his right arm and carefully aimed the stick at the man's ribs.

"Hey, wake up," Joe said, as he gently jabbed the man in the ribs a few times with the stick.

The man offered no response.

Joe then spoke a bit louder while repeatedly tapping the man on his head with the stick. Tap, tap, tap, tap, tap and tap, "Hey! Get up!"

The man groaned once and slowly turned his head. He faced Joe, staring hard with one eye barely cracked open. The other, black and purple, remained firmly swollen shut. He looked an inch from death.

"Why are you hitting me?" asked the stranger.

"We're asking the questions, buddy," said Chris in a stern voice as he stepped back cautiously, standing behind Joe, glancing up at the back of his friend's head while holstering the gun.

"I'm hurt," said the man.

"Are you sick, or hurt?" Joe asked.

The man simply mumbled and pointed at his upper left chest with his grimy, sandy right hand.

"What he say?" Chris nervously asked.

"I dunno," Joe replied.

"I said I'm shot." It was much clearer this time.

"Shot? Where? By who?" Joe quickly asked.

"Where I'm pointing, you idiot," the man softly replied. "I can barely breathe. Please help me. I'm not sick. I'm shot."

"Can you walk?" Chris asked.

"What's it look like?" asked the man, as he clutched the sand and softly groaned in pain.

"Let's get him to Denise. Chris, help me get him up."

"Are you sure you're not sick?" Chris asked.

"Not sick. Shot. Arrow in the back. Came out my chest. Can barely breathe. Hurts."

"Who did it?" asked Chris.

"Dunno. Upriver. Yesterday afternoon. They chased me. Shot arrows at me. Got hit by a couple. One bounced off my head. One went in my back. Pulled it out my chest. Made it to the river. Started swimming. Where am I? Who are you people?"

"This is Corbett," Chris said. "We live here. Where are the people who shot you?"

"I dunno. Upriver. By Sandy. How's Portland?"

"Portland's gone. We saw it burning from the Vista House. How many of them were there?"

"Gone?"

"Yeah, gone. How many were there?"

"Lots. Didn't count, they chased me, I ran. Portland gone? Oh, no. I used to live there. Roses, mom and dad," he mumbled as his head flopped back into the sand.

"He's losin' it, Joe," Chris said.

"Okay, we're gonna get you to a doctor," Joe said. "Right now."

Joe turned to Chris. "We'll walk him up the hill together. Leave the fishing stuff. We can get it later, but bring that salmon. We can't waste it. It'll rot in the heat."

Joe straddled the stranger. Then he put his massive hands under the man's arms and stood him up.

"I can walk," said the man. "I just can't stand up."

Joe caught him as he started to fall.

"Joe, look at your hands! Blood!"

"Whoa! We better get this guy up the hill fast. Let's go."

Chris slipped into his moccasins. He then picked up the canvas bag holding the salmon with his weaker left hand and together with Joe helped gently lift the man over a few logs. They half walked, half carried the man the rest of the way up the riverbank to the hot, smooth pavement of Southeast Gordon Creek Road. They could retrieve the poles later.

When they reached the road, the man stumbled and nearly fell on the asphalt.

"Hey, buddy. It's only a few miles. Stay awake. Talk to me," Chris said, as they helped him up.

"C'mon, man. You can make it. We're gonna make you okay again. You'll be fine soon. Denise Song Bird will fix you up good as new," Joe said.

"Hey, I'm Chris. This is Joe. What's your name?" Chris smiled and asked.

"Baccellieri. Michael. I hate 'Mike.' Don't ever call me 'Mike.' Please, don't."

"Okay. I can't pronounce your last name. How do you say your last name, again?" Chris asked, staring at the bloody-faced stranger.

"'Bah-chel-lee-air-ree.' It's easy," Michael slurred.

"'Buck-lee-airy.' Hey! That's easy to pronounce," Chris smiled, at what he thought was a small linguistic success.

"No. No. It's, 'Bah-chel-lee-air-ree.'"

"No, Chris, say it right. It's 'Back-lee-air-ee,'" Joe said.

Michael glanced up at Joe, then over at Chris. He shook his head, "Hicks. You two friggin' idiots are killing me. Just drop me. Let me die in the road. I can't take this anymore. Is Denise Song Bird, the doctor, anything like you two? Hey, you look like a Native American." Michael groaned toward Chris.

"Chris, he's about to pass out. We should just help him get to the clinic and kinda ignore what he says right now," Joe said.

"Around here we prefer the term 'Indian,' not 'Native American,' if you don't mind. And yeah, she's my wife," Chris replied, ignoring Joe's advice. "We're from different tribes. I help out in her veterinary clinic."

"C'mon, really, now. What is this place? Am I dead? Yeah … oh yeah, fer sure. Did I drown? Was it the arrow? I'm in Purgatory, aren't I? Damn it, knew I wouldn't make the first cut: must have been the crap I pulled in high school, or in the army," he slurred.

Chris spread his arms out, palms up, as if carrying an invisible bag of onions. He then looked at Joe and shrugged, not quite sure what Buck was talking about.

Joe laughed. "No. You're not dead yet. You're hurt bad, but you're gonna live. Denise is really smart. She's helped lots of us get better. For a vet, she's doing a really good job as our doctor."

"I have an arrow hole through my chest. My head's bleeding and it hurts. I can't see out one eye. My boots are gone. I ain't eat' in two days. And you morons are bringing me to a damn country veterinarian?"

Joe, dumbfounded, glanced at Chris and shrugged. "Hey, I'm sorry. It's all we got. She's our doctor now. You'll get better soon. You'll see. Hey, would it be okay if we just called you 'Buck?'"

"'Buck.' Yeah, I guess so. That's fine. Cool. I'll live with 'at. You guys jus' call me Buck." Michael slurred.

"Okay, Mike. We'll call you Buck," Chris said. "By the way, Buck, where's Purgatory?"

After Chris spoke, Buck glared at him briefly then lost consciousness, dreaming of the men with the bows.

Chapter Four

They came from the south, always hungry, walking through ghost towns and along abandoned roads in search of food. This wandering pack of feral men was thirty strong now. As they moved, they would lose a few, then pick up a few more as they travelled meal to meal. Always moving, always searching, always hungry, their craving for food was purely primal. Sometimes getting lucky, they would stumble across an overlooked hoard in a rail yard shipping container or a freeze-dried stash cleverly hidden in a basement or sometimes secreted in the dusty attic crawlspace of a long-gone survivalist's home.

Moving through what was once called California had become too dangerous, even for these savage, silently moving feral men. The once-cultivated fields had long since dried. The battles for dominance during the past two years had provided victory to none. The bloody struggles over the scraps ended when the scraps were gone. However, countless individuals and a few small groups still roamed the countryside in search of food. This no-name group from somewhere in California was one of the last, and the only one still scavenging in Oregon.

The California Central Valley heat was deadly during the summer, and getting hotter each year, so they moved north, to a cooler place, into the Willamette River Valley. They had one objective: survival.

To reach there they walked north, skirting the western Sierra foothills. They occasionally encountered farming villages, isolated heavily armed small groupings usually numbering under one hundred, although some were larger, all of them remnants of the horrifying decimation two years earlier. The members of these colonies worked hard, struggling nonstop to survive. Most defended themselves, vigilantly guarding their perimeters and brutally turning away outsiders with well-aimed rifles, especially those looking like this band of thirty-odd hard-faced men. Few let them get anywhere close.

It was becoming routine for this marauding band. Some communities made the deadly mistake of welcoming these strangers, offering them food and shelter. Those who did lost everything. The feral men would then gorge themselves and move on, packing the remains. The fortunate ones learned from their misplaced kindness and got a chance to start again, wiser and more cautious about where to direct their compassion. The others became one with the ever-present wind and dust.

As the feral pack moved north, through the eastern side of the Willamette Valley, the few survivor colonies they found were unfriendly, armed and well-guarded, allowing no one near. In April, three of their pack had been shot and killed approaching one small, but well-organized farming village south of Lebanon.

They approached the crude, makeshift gate, handguns hidden under tattered shirts. One man walked well ahead of the other two while waving a white shirt high over his head as if coming in peace. It was a clever entry tactic they had successfully used: approach with a white cloth waved high, draw close, and then kill.

They were ordered to stop twice, yet their simple plan and burning hunger drew them ever nearer to the vigilant town guards. The lead man was thirty yards away. Next, the other two moved closer. It was a tactic that had worked well before. The three kept walking closer, waving the white cloth, smiling at the guards as if they were old lost friends. Twenty yards away. Now ten. One of the sentries ordered them once again to stop yet the three kept drawing closer. The three sentries then opened fire at once, stopping them cold when they ignored the final order.

After that, the ferals avoided the well-defended towns unless their situation became truly dire, in which case they would attack a few less-defended homes on the outskirts. Instead of overpowering the armed guards, they would wait until night then attack poorly defended homes on the edges of towns under the cover of darkness, quickly taking what they could and then fleeing like rats into the night.

They had yet to move past the first level of Maslow's pyramid of hierarchical needs. They accepted no women or children into their band. "Maybe later," they kept telling themselves. Maybe when they found a place to retire, a place to stay for good. That was a distant dream, often talked about, but few believed it would happen.

The men had become desperate, hungry, as they moved north to the Sandy River, near the ghost town once called Sandy. The town was the last food stop along the Mount Hood Highway. In the days and weeks following the collapse, tens of thousands of starving people arrived, fleeing the chaos in the city. Its orchards, farms, markets and homes were stripped bare. Only a few families survived.

Scouts moved ahead of the main group in twos, searching, listening, ever on guard. They heard the distant rhythmic cracking of axes barely echoing in the silent air. They found a few sets of fresh footprints along a river beach near their camp, one set, human, another set, dog. They followed them for a time, then returned to the main pack with their walking bounty, sharing the exciting news that a town was near.

Most of their ammunition had been spent hunting deer and other game during the past winter. Their remaining bullets were divided, loaded into inaccurate rifles and rusty handguns. Bows were inspected, once again. More arrows were made ready as they cooked a scrawny mongrel over a small, carefully burning fire. Tired of eating undercooked stray dogs and raccoons, they were now excited, preparing for yet another attack.

Then, an emaciated stranger approached, a threat to their planned raid. "Kill him!" one of them muttered. Grimy hands dipped into deerskin quivers. Arrows rained on the man. The men saw one arrow strike his head. Another pierced his back. They saw him fall into the river and float away, and thought no more of him.

Chapter Five

Joe carried him the final mile and a half down the middle of what was once the Columbia River Scenic Highway, past the school buildings, past the Mount Hood Christian Church, finally reaching the town clinic midafternoon.

They turned off the highway and onto the cracked concrete walkway leading to Chris and Denise's home, which served as the community clinic. It was an off-white, classic, one-story early twentieth-century home with a wide covered porch supported by thick wooden pillars. The roof was still sound but the outside needed paint that would never get applied. It faced north, the shady side, but the two bedrooms used for patient examinations faced south. Large picture windows allowed bright sunlight to fill the patients' rooms giving Denise and her assistant, Kelly Lee, plenty of light. The third bedroom, the one Denise and Chris shared, faced east, welcoming the morning light, but in the afternoon it was shaded and cooler during the summer. People needing long-term care were treated a few days then sent home. Few remained longer than one night. She and Kelly also treated farm animals, riding their bicycles to the town's farms, but very few animals were actually brought to the clinic.

Joe shouted out loud to no one in particular as he stood near the closed screen door with Buck slung limp over his right shoulder as if he were a light jacket, "Hey! Denise! Kelly! We have a wounded man! Shot! Hurt really bad!"

"Denise, are you home?" shouted Chris.

Denise Song Bird became the town's only veterinarian when the other one, a senile seventy-nine-year-old alcoholic, died the previous summer after falling face-down and suffocating in a pile of fresh cow dung with an empty bottle of grape wine still tightly gripped in his right hand. Denise became the town's de facto doctor when it became known that, other than an eighty-four-year-old neurologist who could no longer remember his own name, not one single medical doctor lived in Corbett.

Denise and Kelly had cared for sixty-eight pregnant women, delivering fifty-six babies in the past two years. The high infant mortality rate was not unexpected. Sadly, two mothers died during labor. Without modern medical care these tragedies could not be avoided.

She opened the screen door, stared a moment at Buck, then glanced briefly at Chris and Joe. She was shoeless at home, as usual. Like Chris, she preferred to walk barefoot during the summer. She was wearing the same style of deerskin pants as Chris, along with a loose-fitting faded black t-shirt. Her single-braided raven-black hair just barely brushed the top of her pants. She was a full-blooded Native American, but, like Chris, preferred the term "Indian." Everyone simply called her Denise. She fell in love with Chris while treating his wounded arm. Chris fell in love with her at first sight months before that, but Denise didn't know Chris until he was driven to the clinic. It was his last ride in a motor vehicle. She often joked that Chris was very lucky to have been shot. Chris always nodded his head in agreement.

"What happened? Who's this?" she asked both men.

"A stranger. Found him on the Sandy, across from Oxbow. He's hurt, took an arrow clean through the back. Joe carried him here," said Chris.

"Before you bring him in, let me take a quick look, see if he's sick, first. If he's sick, we all get to live in a tent out in the woods for a few weeks." Denise went inside, grabbed a few things and returned to the porch, quickly looking Buck over, pausing a short time at the arrow wound and listening closely as he breathed. She opened one of his eyes and analyzed it a moment. Then she did the same with the other eye. She took his temperature. Then took his blood pressure and pulse.

Denise finished taking his vitals, nodded, and led them down the short dark hallway and into the small clinic's stark-white, sunlit examination room. "Bring him back here. Room one. He's ninety-eight point four. One twenty over seventy. Pulse sixty-five. Nice. I can't believe it. He's certainly not sick. But he looks like his blood pressure and pulse should both be zero. The arrow seems to have threaded between the major arteries and missed his heart and lungs. Let's get him on the table and strap him down tight. His arrow wound needs work. I can't have him waking up and squirming around."

While Denise opened the nearby five-foot gun safe and prepared the slender cleaning rod, the men carefully removed his soiled t-shirt and gently placed him face-up on the crude, wooden, waist-high planks. A short, yet thick, two-inch wide dark leather strap dangled from the middle of each side. The hole in his chest bled little, but it looked angry-red and was beginning to swell. As dirty as Buck was it was no surprise there was a bit of infection. The wound was about a day old, but the way it looked could mean bad news for Buck. Except for an impressive collection of minor cuts and scrapes, an ugly scabbed-over half-inch divot above his left ear, and a swollen-shut left eye, he appeared otherwise uninjured.

Without waking him, Denise used the two loose-hanging leather straps to firmly attach Buck's wrists to the sides of the dark, splotchy-stained, wooden table. The two-inch round, hand-drilled holes in the sides of the table secured the straps and had been used many times since the clinic opened at the start of the emergency two years earlier. They had been worn shiny and smooth from repeated hard pulling and twisting from her more seriously injured patients struggling against pain.

Due to the chest wounds, Chris buckled the thick, well-worn brown leather belt across Buck's lean waist instead, securing his hips firmly to the table. Denise and the two men thought he might awaken very soon. Electric lights no longer worked so the heavy table had been placed next to a large, south-facing picture window so patients were nicely illuminated in the warm sunlight while strapped to the table. Unconscious and suffering from pain, exhaustion, hunger and shock it was a miracle Buck was still alive. But somehow, he clung to the tiniest thread of life and Denise intended to treat and fully heal him. It was time to begin.

"Kelly, can you put the sterilized hot water on the floor? I don't want him knocking it over."

Kelly was tall, five-ten, with a cheeky, round face blessed with full lips and a delicate nose. Her athletic, twenty-three-year-old physique was maintained with daily martial arts practice and regular jogging. She was the youngest daughter of a Chinese family, one of only four in Corbett. Her degree in chemistry from the University of Oregon made her a natural for working at the clinic.

"Sure, Denise. The small, sterilized rags are soaking in it. I ground up a piece of lavender soap. Stirred it in, too. You're all set," Kelly said. "The blackberry leaves are in a bowl on the gun safe."

"Oh, this is going to really hurt him a lot. He might get lucky and stay unconscious for this. If he was awake I could give him some of that pain stuff, but he's out cold and won't wake up so I can't. First, I'll flush out his arrow wound. I'm going to try to clean it all the way through, sterilize it really well," said Denise. "Joe, could you please get ready to hold his head down? Chris, his legs. I don't wanna get kicked again."

"Okay," said Joe, as Chris moved into position.

Pain-killing drugs and anesthesia medication were a sweet memory of the past, so seconds after Denise started cleaning the arrow wound, Buck awakened in a flash, violently arching his body. He opened his one good eye wide in terror as he suddenly emerged from his peaceful empty dream. He tried his best to avoid crying out in pain, finally surrendering, screaming loudly while Denise Song Bird flushed his piercing arrow wound. She used the hot water and homemade soap to gently yet thoroughly probe through with her cloth-tipped, twenty-two-caliber rifle-cleaning rod, flushing the slender four-inch deep hole that started just below his left collarbone and ended just beyond the last place a man's right fingertips extend when reaching over his left shoulder to scratch.

With tears flowing down his cheeks, Joe, who never directed an unkind word toward anyone, cried while Buck screamed. He cried whenever he saw anyone suffer. "He's just really sensitive," Chris would sometimes say. Fighting back tears, he kept one massive, meaty hand firmly on Buck's left shoulder, inches from the wound, while keeping another pressed down just above his sternum. Buck couldn't move.

As Buck screamed, Chris helped by holding the wounded and weakened man's skinny legs firmly in place on the other end of the waist-high, solid and smooth eight-foot-long, two-by-sixteen planks that had long served as the clinic's operating table. Chris had built it last summer to allow Denise and her assistant, Kelly Lee, to hold the slow but steady flow of injured among those living in Corbett. It was strong enough to support a struggling patient, preventing Buck and those treated before him from falling off and further damaging themselves while they thrashed in pain. It also prevented Denise and Kelly from getting their teeth kicked in.

"Done," said Denise, as the screaming thankfully faded. "Now all I have to do is bandage the two holes."

First, she stacked layers of trimmed young blackberry leaves over each arrow hole. Then she placed two three-inch pre-cut squares of cloth taken from what remained of an old, yet clean, bed sheet and placed them over each wound. She secured them in place with a cut power cord wrapped several times around Buck's chest and left shoulder. The clinic had used up the last of its tape and bandaging months ago, so wounds were now bandaged with whatever makeshift supplies they could find.

"He's stronger than he looks," said Joe. "I think he has a decent chance."

"Is there anything to kill the pain, Denise?" Chris asked, listening to Buck.

"I'm trying to save it for operations, but I still have quite a bit of that stuff left from the war. Maybe I could spare a little for Buck," Denise said, referring to the bags of brown powder they found on a few bodies after the war.

After the battles, the security patrols found several pounds of drugs on the dead invaders. Denise disposed of three hundred grams of what Corey and Tweedy believed to be dangerous, chemical-laden methamphetamine. The drug find also happily included two kilograms of cocaine, which the town dentist, Dr. Stan Bohnstedt, and his assistant and wife, Karen Bohnstedt, occasionally used as a local anesthetic and, of greater use to the clinic, a roughly equal amount of what Denise believed to be fifty-percent pure heroin; a very effective pain killer, similar to morphine and pure enough to be inhaled when they ran out of syringes. Both were kept locked in her gun safe.

She walked to the far corner of the operating room and reached into her heavy black gun safe. It held several rifles and handguns as well as the remaining drugs and a few supplies. She reached in and removed a large Ziploc baggie, partially filled with a powdery brown substance. "This is all I have left for pain. It's the stuff Corey and Tweedy collected after the war. Remember? They knew exactly what it was as soon as they saw it. Anyhow, I can only use it a few times on each patient, unless they only have a short time left, then it doesn't matter. It's too addicting. I think Buck's gonna pull through, but first he needs some food, then rest. This'll give him rest. Chris, sweetheart, could you mash up a small bowl of potatoes and some blackberries, too? We just picked our first early berries. They're great! Buck'll like 'em."

Buck screamed, once again.

"Okay, be back in a jiffy."

"You gonna inject him? I'll hold his arm steady, if you want," Joe said as Buck fought through the pain, stoically glancing back and forth between the two men and Denise.

"We're all out of syringes. Used the last one on Rigo Gomez when he had that horrible ear infection last month. It was bad. Fighting his infection used the last of our antibiotics, too. All I can do now is try to get him to inhale twenty milligrams of this stuff. That should free him from the pain and give him a few hours of peace. Give us some peace, too. But my rule is two doses only. So he gets one more after this one. I don't want anyone getting addicted and attacking my gun safe with a crow bar or some dynamite."

Chris returned with the two bowls and fed Buck with a shiny spoon, just like one would a sick child. Denise held his head up a bit so he could swallow easier. She wiped away his tears. Buck, who hadn't eaten in two days, was overcome with hunger. He had both bowls empty in no time. After topping off his meal with a few pieces of dried salmon and a few ounces of water, he began to look a bit better, yet he was unable to speak clearly, still suffering with terrible pain.

Denise dipped a butter knife into the baggie and scooped up a tiny pile of the powder on its tip. She turned toward Buck while holding the knife in her right hand. "Buck. Listen to me. Buck, please listen to me. I know you're in a great deal of pain. I have a narcotic that will make the pain go away for a few hours. I know it's strange, but you gotta inhale it. Understand? Sniff quickly and deeply when I say so. Understand?"

"Quick. Deep. Okay. I'll try," Buck said as he fought the urge to cry out in pain.

"Okay, here it comes." Denise moved the tip of the knife just under Buck's right nostril. "It's on the tip of this knife, a small amount of pain-killing powder. I'm holding it just under your right nostril."

She gently touched the tip of the blade to the tip of his nose. "Ready? When I say 'now,' I want you to breathe out and then sniff in really hard through your nose. Okay? 'Now!'"

Denise briefly pulled the knife away while Buck exhaled and quickly brought it closer as he inhaled as well as he could through his nose. The small pile vanished up his nostril and soon the terror in his eyes faded. An emotionless smile then began to brighten his face just as his one good eye closed. Soon, a wonderful, healing sleep overtook him.

The room quieted.

"Okay if we untie him?" asked Chris.

"Yeah, but let's put him on those blankets on the floor. It's shady there and he won't get sunburned … don't wanna add sunburn to his long list of injuries. Anyhow, there's nothing more to do. It's up to Buck now. All I'm able to do now is monitor him, feed him, and keep his wounds clean," Denise said. "And, we can't have him roll over in his sleep and fall on the floor like Tweedy did. Remember that? Hey, could you two stay with him while I go wash up?"

"Sure," Joe said, as Denise walked into the kitchen.

"Hey, Joe, remember from last summer?" Chris said, cautiously. "Tweedy … that was too funny, guy gets a crazy-bad headache. Hadn't slept in three days. So, he comes in with his friend, Corey, to have Denise try an' fix it. He walks in crying. Holding his temples. She rubs some peppermint and lavender oil on his temples. Then she has him drink some lavender extract tea and lie down on those planks. He drinks the tea, climbs up on the planks and falls asleep. Just like that. Crazy. Denise then walks out of the room and what does Tweedy do? He rolls to one side and right off the planks. Splat! Pancakes it on the hardwood floor."

"That was hilarious. Blam! He nailed his head on the floor. Blam! Corey screamed like he just saw a monster. Then, of course, the impact wakes Tweedy up and, 'voila,' no more headache. Yeah, that was friggin' insane," Chris added, while they both giggled like school kids.

Joe couldn't tell that story often enough and went over it once more, a bit louder than Chris. "Yeah, that was funny as hell! He walks into this room and lays on the platform. Denise leaves the room to get something. He falls asleep, rolls over, falls, konks his head on the floor and his headache's all gone! It might have been Corey's scream that cured him. Denise was so embarrassed." Joe laughed again, as he unbuckled Buck's wrist straps while Chris laughed even louder as he freed Buck's body strap. "He had a huge lump on his forehead for two weeks. In like, no time at all, his usual big grin came back, still shinin' bright today."

Chris suddenly put his index finger to his lips, "Joe, shhh. Quiet. Denise is coming. She don't like that story. It really freaked her out when he fell off her table, coulda' killed him."

"What are you two laughing about? I could hear you all the way there in the kitchen. I bet Rueben could, too," Denise walked through the doorway and asked, referring to Rueben's home and workshop across the highway and a short walk to the east.

"Oh, nothing, just a joke. Hey, Denise, what about his head? Where the other arrow hit him. Is there anything you can do about that?" Joe asked, changing the subject, as he and Chris gently picked up each end of the planks and placed Buck and the heavy wooden platform on the hardwood floor. The two men gently lifted Buck, carried him over to the side a few feet and onto a bed of thick blankets where he could safely enjoy his dreams and hopefully heal.

"No. The scab looks pretty good. Solid. No more blood. It's a fairly deep wound, but it didn't penetrate or fracture his skull. So, while he sleeps, I'm going to just clean it a bit, put some blackberry leaves on it, and let it go at that. Same for the rest of his cuts. Just clean 'em, place a few leaves on each, and let 'em all heal while he sleeps. That's about all."

Chapter Six

Joe stood on the front porch looking down at the stained, dark green canvas pouch containing the salmon they caught earlier. He smiled and picked up the pouch. "Hey, Chris? I'm going to Rueben's. Get my boots adjusted and give him this salmon. I'll be back in a while. I'll wanna see how Buck's doing."

"Okay, sounds good. I'll stay here and help Denise and Kelly with Buck. We're gonna clean some more of his wounds while he sleeps."

"See you soon, unless I get a shave," Joe said, as he scratched his tangled, half-inch brown beard and limped along the narrow concrete path leading to the highway, salmon pouch in hand.

The highway, as the former Columbia River Highway was now called, had always been the main drag through town and still was. The few new businesses in town faced it, as did the now-busier-than-ever Mount Hood Christian Church, the now-closed old Country Market and the fire station, which served as an occasional gathering place for the town firefighters.

The school, which is what locals called Corbett Public School, occupied a sprawling site on the south side of the highway across from the church. Before the collapse, it taught students from kindergarten through twelfth grade. It still did, but far fewer students attended, and it only operated for a few months during spring and fall. The students learned math, English and history. Everything else they needed to know was taught hands-on. "If these kids don't learn math, there is no future!" Ralph McAfee, the school's high school math teacher, warned. During summer there was far too much work to do, and in the winter it was simply too cold in the classrooms.

If you wanted to find someone in Corbett, this was generally the road to take. Without upkeep, it was starting to age. Thin lines of grass now grew like bright green varicose veins meandering through the long fractures and fissures that were forming in its asphalt. They grew deeper each year. Soon, the lines would change to golden-brown as the grass dried in the hot summer sun. Years ago, hot tar was poured into the cracks to keep rainwater out, but no more. Now, the cracks were becoming home to grass and weeds. Soon it would be bushes and trees. Since cars and trucks no longer moved, no one bothered to pull them out, except for the hugely invasive blackberries. They had to go. Quite a few bicycles still moved goods and messages along the highway. Everyone still relied on the roads for one thing or another. Blackberry vines could tear a bike tire apart quick, so they were pulled while still young and easy to yank.

About half way to Rueben's, a dandelion pushed a bright yellow flower out of the faded centerline and toward the sky. Joe paused. He saw more growing near the highway. He walked to the bushes alongside the road, bent over, left the flowers alone, and picked a small handful of the lush green leaves. He stood back up and chewed on them as he crookedly walked the short distance to Rueben's front door. Dandelions grew everywhere. After Bryan and Shari, the owners of the Dancing Roots organic farm, gave countless talks about the wealth of vitamins and minerals found in various native plants and weeds, people began eating dandelion leaves as an anytime snack while they moved about during the day. Joe remembered his mom reminding him, "They're a great source of vitamin C. And always remember: don't eat the ones growing in the road, Joe. They've got road-oil in 'em. You might get sick."

After carrying Buck and holding him on the table, Joe was exhausted. Thankfully, he didn't have far to go to reach Rueben's. Because of his newly acquired, uneven walk, Joe was a regular visitor at the town cobbler. His good friend Rueben Moreland, who had lost the lower portion of his left leg in a severe motorcycle accident a few months prior to the collapse, could no longer move well or travel far. Wanting to be useful, he assumed the housebound role of town boot maker. He taught himself to become a master at crafting strong, comfortable boots from deer hide and used tire tread. He became damn good at it, too. Several dozen automobile and truck tires decorated his front yard in neat stacks, competing with the tall grass for airspace and light. He did the quick math and figured there were enough tires in town to last him thirty years or more as long as the tires didn't crack and fall apart sooner.

Joe saw Rueben often. He was continually wearing down the front-right edge of his right boot. He planned to visit Rueben that afternoon and have a replacement tire tread sewn onto what remained of his old, well-beaten, black Danner military boots. Rueben had become highly skilled at boot repair since taking on that task and would soon have Joe back at work, especially if he only fixed the right boot. All anyone had to do to get new moccasins or replacement soles was to bring him a few tires, a salmon or some deer meat. Interestingly, since Rueben still clung to the fantasy that precious metals were valuable, a silver coin or two really got him excited and hopping, so he accepted those, too.

Rueben's vegetable patch and dozen fruit trees offered a decent supply of vitamins and minerals, but no protein and not quite enough variety. He cared for and tended his orchard as if the trees were his children. One tree near his bedroom window was guarded more than the others because a box buried underneath it sheltered his growing silver collection.

In addition to making and repairing footwear, Rueben recently started to serve as the town's barber. Using a pair of scissors and a Heribert Wacker Anno 1890 straight razor, found in one of the late Steven Rogers' six bathrooms, he could quickly trim Joe's thick, light brown beard to a nice, trim, half-inch, then, with the sharp blade, shave his head and neck smooth in exchange for an occasional fresh salmon, like the one he brought.

Cutting hair and making shoes was much less stressful than his earlier post-crash occupation. When the bullets started flying two years earlier, someone had to process the dead. Rueben had been working as a part-time apprentice mortician in Gresham. While working odd jobs, he had been studying on the side to become a mortician, a course of study offered at nearby Mount Hood Community College.

In the months after the crash the population of Corbett fell by the hundreds. During the first winter, people were dying at the rate of twenty a week. Some died from lack of medicine, others from old age, a few, like the wealthy Steven Rogers, from sadness. A few new mothers didn't live long enough to witness their child's first day on earth.

Since the previous summer, the population had stabilized at around three thousand five hundred, which was roughly what Alison Lee, after she did her population sustainability study, believed the town could support, long-term. The dead needed to be treated properly. People generally turned to Rueben to assist Reverend Golphenee, the minister of the Mount Hood Christian Church, in this sacred duty. They still did, but it was no longer a daily task.

The door to Rueben's south facing home was wide open, allowing the air to flow through his small, yellow, one-story First World War era home. There were no screen doors, so bugs flew freely in and out. Summers were brief in Corbett, lasting about twelve weeks, so fresh air was a true luxury enjoyed by all, even with the annoying yet harmless airborne visitors.

A weathered grey four-by-eight rectangle of plywood covered what was once a large glass picture window on the north of his house. Rueben had planned to replace it two years ago, but the collapse changed his plans and he couldn't locate another window the same size. Another large picture window let the sun shine into his home and offered a full view of the highway. His home was on the north side of the highway, so during colder months, the sun shining through the large front window warmed his south-facing front living room. His shop faced south, too, and was in the former master bedroom, so it was well lit during the daytime; this made it easy to precisely punch slender holes through leather and old hard rubber.

As he approached the front door, the constant rhythmic tick, tick, tick, of Rueben's six-foot-tall, hundred-year-old wind-up grandfather clock that he inherited from his long-deceased grandmother entertained the front yard. The ornately carved and still unscratched rosewood clock hadn't moved from its perch near the fireplace since nineteen seventeen when it arrived at the then newly built house on a flatbed commercial delivery wagon pulled by two horses. His great-grandfather carried it into the house with the help of the teamster. It was believed to be the only clock in town that hadn't stopped running since the power went out two years earlier. Rueben swore it told time accurately and few doubted it. People once regularly knocked on his door to get the correct time, but as time ticked by, fewer and fewer cared.

No one except Rueben, Pete Roth and a handful of others counted minutes and hours any longer. Pete needed to know the time because his ham radio buddies around the country, a few overseas, too, connected with him for a few minutes a week on a strict schedule. Mostly they shared farming and self-defense ideas, but few personal details about themselves or their communities, Pete included. But, it was nice to stay in touch, to know others were successful in re-starting civilization. The nearest ham radio operator was in Sweet Home, Oregon.

Pete once asked him his name. "Larry Brown," he said. "My wife's name is Maggi."

"Larry Brown?" Pete asked.

"Yup," he replied.

"Well, that's certainly a common name. Mine's John Smith. My wife's name is Mary."

"No, really. It's Larry Brown."

"Okay. I'll call you that, if you like."

Pete later found out they were friends of the Lees. The Browns agreed to chat every Saturday at noon. One day, in the not-too-distant-future, they would meet.

Most now simply called it Year Three, which began the day before, on July first. Everyone still counted the days, weeks and months, but few spoke in terms of hours and minutes. Instead, they used general terms, which worked well since there was no longer a need for precise timekeeping. Time was now broken into the general segments of the day such as, "midmorning" or "late afternoon."

After the disaster cell phones and plug-in clocks no longer worked. Since few owned self-winding or solar wristwatches, or wind-up clocks for that matter, hardly anyone ever knew the exact time or even cared. So gradually, over the past two years, fewer and fewer used the ancient Egyptian system of minutes and hours. Eventually they would all stop using it. The next generation would have no idea what waking up at six in the morning meant.

"Hey Joe!" Rueben called out from his kitchen, where he was busy chopping a few of the remaining onions from last year's harvest. "I'm making an onion and fava bean soup. Want some?"

"Heck yeah!" Joe replied. He was known by all to have absolutely, positively never refused an offer of free food. Over the past year, however, an interesting new tradition had begun in Corbett. Although some did this before the collapse, it was now universal. Anyone visiting another person's home was offered food. Not making the offer or, even worse, declining the offer, was considered rude, so the offer and the acceptance had now become universal. It started during the first winter when food was in short supply and it stuck. "I didn't bring any silver, but I do have a fresh-caught summer Chinook. Plus, my boot's worn out again. And I could use a shave."

"I knew it all when I saw you walk up the highway. Well, except I didn't know about the salmon, but I did see the bag, wondered what was in it. Let me have a peek at that salmon." Rueben was glad the salmon was for him. Everyone knew Rueben couldn't walk far from home since his fancy but fragile pre-collapse prosthetic leg fell apart. He now hobbled around with the help of a wooden peg leg, which he cut and sanded from the branch of his front yard birch tree, and a sturdy cane cut and shaped from the same tree. The cut the doctors made was four inches below his left knee yet it still hurt to walk far, so he rarely did. He couldn't hunt or fish, but he could make fine footwear, so a community deal was forged. Then, when he acquired the razor from the town recreation hall, which used to be the Jeffery Rogers mansion, he became downright popular with the women for occasionally shaving coarse beards off their men. Since the disposable blades everyone used had long ago worn out, the town gossip held that a visit to Rueben's meant good news was heading someone's way, especially if the guy walked in with a good pair of boots on his feet. That, sadly, wasn't the case with Joe.

"Boot's worn out again," Joe said, as he walked inside. "But check out this Chinook! It took me and Chris a long time to get this one. In a few weeks there'll be so many you'll be able to walk across the river on 'em."

"Set it in the sink for me, Joe. I'll deal with that little rascal later."

"Hey Rueben, early this afternoon me and Chris found a guy washed up across from Oxbow. Shot with an arrow. He hasn't said much, but when he wakes up, if he wakes up, we'll have to find out who did it and why."

"I heard. Is he gonna live?"

"Denise thinks so, but he don't look too good. He looked dead when we first found him. I thought he was. It reminded me of the war. I still get nightmares from that."

"You're a warrior, Joe."

"That's what people always tell me, but I sometimes wish I had done something else for a living. Like, fix shoes or cut hair."

"No adventure in that, Joe. You saw the world. Not everyone can say that," Rueben said.

"I saw the pits of the world, mostly. Oh, I went to some nice places, Germany, Singapore, Japan ... but I pulled the trigger in the worst places."

"Well, those days are over, Joe. We have a colony, now. And, we're damn lucky!" Rueben said, pointing his right index finger at Joe's ripped chest, protruding through the openings where his t-shirt sleeves had been cut off. "Tell me more about this guy."

"He told us his name's Buck. Well, actually he said his name was Bucklary, or something like that. He said we could call him Buck, so we do. Guy got kinda sad when me and Chris garbled up his name. He's a really nice guy, from what little I saw. He sounds Italian, looks Italian, too ... something like that, maybe. Talks like he just got off the boat from Venice. Right before he passed out he said he's a Catholic. I know quite a few Catholics in town, but there's definitely no priest. He woke up when Denise was cleaning his wound, and he ate a bit, too. Then he passed out right after Denise gave him some medicine."

"The heroin? Stuff knocks a guy out cold. Sometimes too cold. Better keep a close eye on him. And don't give it to him too many times or he'll be going after Denise for more."

"Denise and Chris are. Anyhow, we may have trouble on our hands. You might wanna lock and load, at least until we figure out who shot him."

"Don't have to ask me to do that. Always ready. Let me look at that boot."

Joe took off his right boot and followed Rueben into the cobbler shop, limping even more with one boot off. Joe peeked at his left boot. The left one was fine. Lots of tread remained. "The right one's worn out already. Only been a few months."

"Lucky you. If you still weighed two hundred and fifty pounds you'd wear 'em out in two weeks. Looks like only the right one, again. Simple fix. I'll do it before the clock chimes again." The clock read two thirty-five. "Let me chisel off those face-hairs after, okay? Maybe lower your ears, too."

"Thanks, Rueben. My head's like an oversized ball-peen hammer with a collar of bristly brown string sticking out."

"Can't argue with that," said Rueben as he started skillfully tearing into Joe's right boot. Some people dropped their boots off, picking them up later. Joe liked to wait. Once Rueben started talking he couldn't stop, so Joe sat on a short wooden stool, as usual, and listened courteously. "I'm getting good at fixing these boots of yours. Good thing the uppers are Danner Acadias. They last forever. What's this? Your tenth tire tread? Easy to fix, too. I like the Fort Lewis boots even better. The tall ones. Bill Hartigan has a few pair. Dan Long has a set. He's saving his cuz he always wears moccasins. Anyhow, now that he's not patrolling every day, Bill ain't wearing 'em out like he used to. Incredible boots. Ya can't fix the junk Walmart boots people bring in. Someone brings me a pair of those I tell 'em to throw 'em out and bring me a deer so I can make ‘em some moccasins. Can’t figure out why they bought ‘em in the first place. Pure junk. People who bought those’re all wearing moccasins or going barefoot if they won’t trade somethin’ with me. Too late now, almost everyone’s athletic shoes are all worn out, too. And the women? Most of ‘em never owned decent work boots. Wasted their money on dress shoes. Fashion shoes. Completely worthless garbage. Ever see anyone wearing ‘em now? Of course not! Wore ‘em out the first few days after the crash. People paid hundreds, sometimes more. Now they’re trash. A few months walking in the woods or working on the farm kills ‘em all. Now these boots of yours, Joe, three hundred bucks and they’ll last you for decades more as long as we keep solid tread on ‘em. Anyhow, here ya go. All done.”

Rueben paused briefly and handed the boot to Joe.

“That was quick,” Joe said, as he stuffed his right foot into the size twelve boot just as the grandfather clock began to chime. “Hey, three o’clock. Don’t mean much anymore, does it?”

“Nope. But that beard of yours. Gonna take me longer to mow that than it did to fix your boot. Next time, why don’t you take a pair of scissors to it first, before you see me. Might have to start charging you two salmon instead of one,” Rueben joked.

“I just keep forgetting. Next time, I’ll have it trimmed back before I get here. It’s my problem walking. That’s all I think about anymore, Rueben, but it’s embarrassing. It’s getting crooked and I wear my boots out fast. I’m not sure what to do. Nothing Denise or Kelly can do, either.”

"Let me ponder that. Can't fix the crooked walk, but there must be a way to make your boots last longer. I'll think of something. Maybe a steel plate cut from a car door? It'd be noisy on pavement, but quiet in the woods and might last longer."

"I better get back, an' see Buck. We have to talk to him. The Chief and Reverend Golphenee should know, too. They may want to ask him some questions, too. See ya, Rueben."

"Hey, let me know what's up with Buck. And the freaks who shot him. A stranger shows up shot. I don't like this at all. I hope it isn't the start of another war. I don't wanna be the town battlefield mortician again. I hated that. I just wanna fix boots and cut hair, but if they make it this far, well, Mr. Colt will have a word or two with 'em."

Chapter Seven

When Joe returned to the clinic, the Chief was already there, waiting with Chris, Denise, Kelly, her fiancé, Eddie Cho, and two of the five town council members: Bill Hartigan, the former Oakland street cop who was in the patrol that stumbled on the invasion force two years earlier and Ed Rainier, who ran the town water supply. The two missing council members were Scott Harger, who harvested blueberries and apples on his fifty-acre farm, and Kimberly Cho, Eddie's mother, who operated a cabbage farm that for decades everyone called the cabbage patch. They were preoccupied with work but would be updated as soon as the interview was done.

The Reverend Scott Golphenee, the minister of the only church still operating in Corbett, the Mount Hood Christian Church, was the town's unofficial spiritual leader. He was the one to see if you had questions about God or needed a wedding or a funeral. Without his nod of approval, any major town issue faced a serious uphill fight, which was typical of many small towns. He needed to be in the loop and would show up soon.

Before the collapse, Corbett was a sleepy unincorporated farming area administrated by Multnomah County. It had no police department, no medical or dental clinic, no grocery stores or gas stations and a volunteer fire department with two small concrete box fire stations, each equipped with a shiny, decades-old red fire truck. Other than the dilapidated Country Store, now stripped bare, the only public place, other than a few Columbia River overlook parks, was the public school.

In the months following the disaster, after the threat of invasion had subsided, the town's first council was elected. A former Realtor, Bob Dutton, received the most votes and became chief, which is what everyone called him since he had served as the volunteer fire chief for decades.

The town had no jail and they wanted to keep it that way. When they voted on a few major issues, shortly after the council was elected, they eliminated all laws other than for murder, rape, stealing, ammunition wasting, sleeping while on patrol and child abuse.

Many other crimes were discussed at town meetings, such as food wasting and laziness, but most wanted the list kept nice and short. The only punishment possible was banishment, a shorter time for lesser offenses and a longer banishment for more serious offenses. A jury of seven citizens decided the outcome of each case and they implemented the punishment. So far, there had been only two cases. A night patrol guard was caught sleeping while on duty a few weeks after the invasion. He was banished for one year, but he was never seen again. The other case was a man who shot and killed a thief stealing gasoline from his garage. He was acquitted. Only one crime qualified for the death penalty: entering town without permission. So far, nearly three hundred people had been killed for this.

It was a monumental shift from how things were done prior to the shut down of the banks. The shift was sudden, too. The economic collapse was brought on by overpopulation, peak oil, dwindling primary resources, sovereign and bank indebtedness, unemployment, war and, most of all, unsustainable overconsumption. It hit humanity fast and hard. The first domino to fall was the violent destruction of the world's teetering and fragile financial infrastructure. It fell apart on the opening day of July, two years ago. That triggered a series of destabilizing events leading to the rapid destruction of nearly everything humans had created during the brief yet wondrous and glittering Age of Oil.

Within twenty-four hours the rest of the dominos toppled. They fell, one after another, in a relentless march, circling the globe, smashing every fragile, just-in-time delivered, card swiped, greed filled, human designed institution one after another, leaving none standing. Every single social, economic and political human construct, forged in lakes of blood since the beginning of time itself, disintegrated as the day wore on.

The citizens of Corbett, much like thousands of similar bands of survivors, cautiously clung together, salvaging what they could. Outsiders trying to enter were treated harshly, often brutally. Warning signs went up. The gates to Corbett had slammed shut for good.

In time, bands of outsiders smaller than the ones who attacked Corbett formed across North America. Most were rejected by the many tightly knit colonies. Some established their own towns in unoccupied valleys and along rivers. Others established towns for themselves by a violent take-over. Finally, a few became raiders, attacking anyone in their path. Their numbers had diminished over the past two years. Corbett was about to be attacked by one of the last of these groups, the same one that had attacked Buck.

Chapter Eight

Buck would soon wake up. It was midafternoon and as the pain returned to life, so would he. The next and final twenty milligrams of sweet dreams would have to wait until after the interview, no matter how much his wounds hurt. The townspeople all knew how important it was to learn what had happened on the outside, and to Buck. So whether it hurt or not, he was going to be asked to share his story.

"He just blinked and moved his arm," Kelly excitedly announced.

Within moments the small crowd in the clinic was gathered elbow to elbow near the blankets where Buck was resting. The small examination room was packed.

"My chest hurts," Buck groaned.

"Son of a gun, he's still alive," Chris said.

"Yup. Wanna lift him up on the platform so everyone can see him better?" Joe asked the crowd.

"We better leave him on the ground. Each time he takes a breath his wound lights up. Moving him to the platform would be cruel," Denise replied.

Bill and Ed each gave Joe an admonishing glare for even suggesting such a thing.

Joe simply shrugged back.

Bill Hartigan then sat on the shaded floor next to Buck, on his right. Ed Rainier sat next to him. Joe sat on the floor on the other side of Buck, on his wounded side, with his three-quarter-inch thick, Goodyear BFG truck tire boot soles facing the others as they sat waiting for Bill to start the interview. Bill, with his crew cut, thinning white hair, was dressed in a pair of Levi jeans and a clean, once black, now grey, t-shirt. About seventy-five percent of his shiny black Danner Fort Lewis boots were buried under his faded black denim jeans, but he still somehow managed to sit cross-legged on the examination room's hardwood floor. He was fifty-four, a vegetarian for many years, but at five-eleven and a hundred and seventy pounds, he had the physique of a star high school quarterback. He could keep up with almost anyone. When the disaster struck, he was several hundred thousand dollars in debt from poor investments and a financially devastating failed marriage. He now lived alone in a tiny, two-hundred-square-foot home he built from scratch from a plan he bought from the Tumbleweed Tiny House Company. Two years of farm work, weekly winter hiking and regular year-round biking, along with hundreds of shoulder-damage-restricted morning push-ups does that to a body. If not for the many wrinkles forming on his sun-worn face and his close-cut, receding white hair he could pass for much younger. As a former Oakland police officer, he was good at interviewing people and had a knack for coaxing valuable information out of the most recalcitrant street punks.

Kelly walked into the room with Eddie Cho and they sat on the floor next to Joe, Kelly between the two. She glanced into Joe's eyes and smiled. Eddie missed it when Joe returned the smile, staring a moment longer than necessary back into Kelly's eyes. They then nonchalantly joined the others in the room, looking straight ahead at Buck.

Kelly met Eddie not long after the disaster. He, like Kelly, was a chemistry major graduating from the University of Oregon three years before her. They never met on campus, which was not unusual for students separated by that many years. Coincidentally, they were the same height and weight. Eddie wore his hair in a long, straight ponytail, just like Kelly. From a distance it was tough to tell them apart until they started walking. Then, it became apparent which one was Kelly. Like many in Corbett, Eddie now wore patched blue denim jeans, the same pair day after day, and a dark t-shirt, rarely the same one two days in a row, but usually a black one, partially camouflaging his eighteen-inch-long hair.

He wasn't the type to serve in the militia. He spent most of his time working on the family farm. Firearms frightened him, but he understood the need for them, and encouraged Kelly with her participation on the response team. He performed his town defense duty, too, generally at the clinic or, more often, at the Vista House, the Columbia River overlook offering a panoramic view up and down the river and far to the north. There, along with two or three others, he often performed a lonely, boring static patrol which not only provided a breathtaking view of the Columbia River, but more importantly guarded one of the two access roads into Corbett on the north side of town.

His family was well known in Corbett and grew one crop: cabbage. Eighty acres of it once grew in long straight rows. Petroleum-based chemicals killed the pests and fertilized the soil. For six decades they poured and sprayed a wide variety of poisons and soil-enhancers onto their land until it was as dead and useless as an old dried sponge.

Area supermarkets and restaurants once snapped up their cabbage, and combined with tens of thousands of dollars earned through Asian exports, it generated a six-figure net income for the Cho family. Occupying one of the three spaces in their garage sat a new BMW sedan. In another, a low-miles red Ducati Streetfighter S leaned against its kickstand. A four-door GMC long-bed pickup truck sat without tires, slowly rusting in their driveway. The bed was missing. It was removed long ago and converted into the cargo bed of a horse-drawn wagon.

Their nutrient-depleted land needed help. With petro-chemicals no longer available, they sought help from Deborah Lee and the owners of the Dancing Roots organic farm, who advised them to allow the land to lie fallow one full year before growing more cabbage. "Just let the weeds grow. Let a few goats roam around on it. Some horses, chickens and sheep, too," Shari suggested.

It needed feeding and recovery. JP Lenet, Corbett's former physical education teacher, organized a brigade of two dozen teenagers to carry decomposing material from along roadsides to the farm. They labored hard mixing it into the Cho's dead land. As native grasses and weeds started growing, the horses were brought in to graze. Humanure was carried over and mixed into their soil. Chickens roamed within their small mobile enclosures. Apple trees were planted along the property perimeter. Eventually they would help slow the fierce Corbett winds from clawing at the topsoil of the Cho family farm. After two years, their land was showing signs of life, once again. Bryan, constantly bemoaning the lack of beer, was eager to get some hops and barley planted. The Dancing Roots Farm seed collection was extensive. He thought the Cho farm would be an ideal location to test out those seeds, so early last spring an acre of each was planted and it was coming along better than expected.

Kelly told Eddie everything about her relationship with Joe, except she didn't say a word about his unfortunate medical condition. Like an apple tree at full blossom, the romance Kelly and Joe shared two years earlier quickly bloomed brightly, then it withered just as fast. After three months it faded away without acrimony, leaving behind the buds of a wonderful, tight friendship, which they treasured ever since. The devastating news that shattered Kelly's hopes for a life long bond was delivered to her on a cool, October morning as they sat together on the dried grass of the school soccer field.

The romance hadn't quite developed to the point that Joe's condition may have been obvious to Kelly, but it didn't take long before she suspected there might have been a problem. A few days before he broke the news,

Kelly shared with Joe her deep desire to have a child, only one, and to do so before she got much older. The subject hadn't yet been touched since other, more pressing concerns faced the town in the months following the disaster.

After hearing this, Joe went home to his room and started crying, as he often did when emotions overtook him. He cried long and hard. It was much more difficult on him when something sad impacted another. He felt sadness inside, but worse, he felt terrible for Kelly.

He now knew his growing fondness for Kelly had to change into one of friendship only. He decided to call off their relationship, but it took him a few days to gather up the courage.

Joe, tears flowing down his face, told her the harsh news: he was sterile, unable to father children. It was a war wound, the details of which he refused to reveal to Kelly. Not even his mother and father knew. No one outside his SEAL team knew and they didn't care. As long as he could complete his missions, he was one of them. He could still perform in battle, but after three tours in Afghanistan, one completed after his injury, he felt he'd had enough and ended his military service with an honorable discharge.

The message from Joe wasn't a surprise. It wasn't hard for Kelly to put the pieces together. She had long suspected, but now knew, and would keep the secret to herself. Their bond would remain intact, but without the romance, without the affection they both craved. For that, they would each have to wait. For Kelly, the wait was short, only a few months. For Joe, the wait hadn't ended. His affection for Kelly would continue.

"Hey Bill, he's ready to talk," Kelly said, interrupting Bill and Joe while they discussed the merits and deficiencies of some long-forgotten professional basketball teams. Harger had meanwhile arrived and he jumped right in, loudly voicing his opinion about some basketball team from Los Angeles.

"Hey, guys," Eddie said. "It's time."

"Hi, Buck. I'm Bill. You know Denise, Chris and Joe. By the window, that's Kimberly, she's on the town council along with Ed and Harger over there. Over there, by Joe, that's Kelly and Eddie." Bill glanced briefly at each of them as his right index finger skipped around the room, finally aiming straight at Buck. "Right now I need to ask you some questions."

"A debriefing. Just like old times. Hi, Bill. I'm Michael Baccellieri. Just call me Buck. How long was I sleeping?"

"Since around noon. Not long," Bill said.

"I could use some water," Buck said.

"Could someone bring Buck some water?" Bill asked no one in particular.

Denise had some ready and handed a short dark blue plastic cup to Bill.

"Here, Buck. Water," Bill said, as he gently raised Buck's head a few inches and brought the cup to his lips. Buck drank it all.

"Could I have another cup? Maybe some more of that salmon, too?"

"Sure. Water now, maybe salmon later. We talk first." Bill turned and handed the cup to Denise, who filled it from a large plastic pitcher. Bill drained the second cup of water past Buck's parched lips.

"Better?" asked Bill.

"Yup. Chest hurts. Hurts bad. Hey, what was that stinky powder?"

"Medicine," Bill said.

"Funny, the things people remember," Denise said. "I hope he never remembers the cleaning."

"We'll tell you all about the medicine later. I need to ask you a few questions. First, who shot you?"

"I don't know. I was heading north, just past Sandy. I saw a group of men. It was late afternoon. I walked closer to them and asked for food. I hadn't eaten in two days. The river had only a few salmon …"

"We'll discuss the salmon later. Tell us about these men," Bill said.

"Okay. I was about fifty, maybe seventy-five feet away from them. They all saw me. They said nothing. Skinny guys, long hair, scruffy-looking. When I got closer I saw they had a dog head on the ground next to a cooking fire and a guy tied to a tree, maybe the dog owner, I dunno. I stopped, then started backing away. Seen this before, desperate small groups. Killers. They were all over the country at first, not so many, now. Anyhow, one of 'em drew an arrow from a pouch and placed it on his bow. Then others did the same. I ran fast. He shot the arrow. Guy was fast. It glanced off my head. They all ran after me. Arrows flew past me. I made it to the river and as I was about to dive in, another arrow hit my back. I felt it, but it didn't hurt. I dove, swam hard, downriver. Swam 'til dark. Climbed on a log … floated. I remember I lost my boots. They were worn out so it's no loss. Anyhow, next thing I know some big bald guy is hitting me on the head with a stick."

Chris looked at Joe. Then Buck did, too, while Joe shrunk back a bit.

"Hey! It was you! Why'd you hit me?" Buck asked, pointing a wobbly, unsteady finger at Joe.

Everyone else looked at Joe, some shook their heads without a word, making Joe turn red and shrink back even more.

"You hit him in the head with a stick?" asked the Chief.

"Well, yeah," Joe said, a bit sheepishly. "Not very hard. Only, like, maybe, five or ten times."

"You hit a wounded man, an unconscious man, in the head with a stick five or ten times? Did you get into your dad's blueberry wine?"

"Well, I, uh ..."

"JOE!" Kelly blurted out, glaring at him.

Chris sat motionless, not saying a word.

Eddie and Bill turned to Joe and shook their heads.

"Well, I guess so, but let me explain," Joe replied, sneaking a quick glance at Kelly, then at Bill, a bit embarrassed about having his actions scrutinized this way. "We wanted to wake him up without getting too close. We wanted to know if he was sick. So I tapped him to wake him up. Not too hard. He wouldn't move, wouldn't wake up at first, so I hit him a little harder. Tapped him on the head a few times. Just little taps to wake him up. Then he woke up and I asked him if he was sick. He told us he was shot. Not sick. We checked him out and he didn't look sick, so I carried him here."

"Okay. I understand. You guys did the right thing, Joe, Chris. It looks like we might have trouble nearby, trouble of the worst kind possible."

"How many were there, Buck?"

"I don't know, exactly. Twenty, thirty, maybe more. It was a big group. They had a fire and were cooking something. Meat. Probably the dog. Don't know what kind. Looked like a mongrel, maybe. Smelled funny, but I ain't eaten cooked meat in months so I went to the smell."

"Any of 'em carry guns?"

"Yeah, quite a few carried them, rifles and handguns. Some had 'em strapped to their backs, the rifles. But they just shot me with the bow. I don't know how many had bows. Probably saving ammunition. When I saw the dog's head, and the guy tied to the tree, then the ugly freak aiming the bow at me, I ran. I didn't see much of their stuff, so I really don't know what they had … or have."

"Did they have a set camp, buildings, or did they appear to be on the move?"

Buck spoke through shallow breaths. "They were in a clearing. Just them. It was north of Sandy. Next to the same river. A mile or two downstream from that town. Saw no women or children. Saw no boats. That's all I know about them. Oh, man, they were desperate, hard, hungry, like they were on the move."

"Were you part of their group? Don't lie to me."

"No, no. I'm all alone, on my way to Portland. I've been walking for two years, off and on. Started in Georgia, right after the country died. Left Fort Benning. I'm in the army. Was. Just trying to get home now. That's all."

"We'll talk about your walk later. Right now, I'm more interested in this group of men. When you walked through Sandy, did you see anyone else?"

"No. I didn't exactly walk through Sandy. Just outside. I saw a road sign, that's all. I was trying to follow the river. I knew it would hit the Columbia eventually. I've been trying to follow rivers, you know, they got steady drinking water. Plus food. I learned to eat fish raw, but they're hard to catch now. I've been eating small animals, slugs, grubs, roots, anything I could find. Hey, got any more of that pain powder? My chest is starting to hurt bad. I'm warm, too."

"I took his temperature just before he woke up. It was over a hundred. When he got here it was a few degrees under that. He might be getting some infection. I'll check carefully," Denise said to Bill.

"Oh, we want this man Buck to make it. I wanna find out what he saw walking across America, the whole story," said Scott.

Bill asked Buck. "Hey, what happened to the arrow that nailed you?"

"It was really skinny. Hand made. Had a tiny steel tip, like cut sheet metal. Sharp. Made for killing small game. I saw it poking out after I dove into the water. Cut my hand on the tip, see?" Buck raised his hand, looked at it briefly, then showed the gathered group where Denise had made two neat stitches in the palm of his right hand. "You stitched it! Thanks. I pulled it the rest of the way through after I started swimming. My other arm kept hitting it. The hole bled awhile, not too bad. Then I saw that log floating by and draped myself over it. Floated. That's all I remember."

Chapter Nine

The Chief spoke calmly and slowly to Bill. "Let's get a crew together. I wanna find these guys before they find us. Bill, you activate the response teams and get ready to move immediately, okay?"

"Yup. I was thinking the same thing. We should make it official, though. Take a quick vote," Bill said.

"Fine. We have four out of five town councilors here right now. All in favor of sending out a war party, say aye," said the Chief.

"Aye," said Ed.

Scott looked down at Bill briefly. "I don't want 'em raiding our farms. Our homes. I say we send 'em packing. Let 'em know they've made a wrong turn. Do it now. Do it hard. No repeats of last time. Let's bring the fight, if there is one, to them this time."

Bill stood up and replied to Scott, "I agree."

"That makes four. It's official, now," said the Chief. "Kimberly, she'll agree, too. This is what we were elected for: protect the town. I'll explain to her we didn't have time to arrange a formal, special town meeting."

Bill glanced around the room briefly. The townspeople had gone over this situation dozens of times in practice drills, but this was no drill. He wasted no time, blasting out a list of instructions as if he'd been thinking about them for days. "Chief, let's get JP Lenet. Have him and Ed's wife, Mary Lou, activate the security patrols. Have 'em set up perimeter guards along the Sandy and along the south. I'll head out now. We've gotta get the volunteers of the two response teams ready to intercept this group. The first response team'll meet at Harger's farm as soon as possible. The second response team meets at the school. We got lots of sunlight left, but let's not waste it. I'll put together the full crews. JP and his crew will wait at the school in reserve. I want all of the first response team ready right now. All twelve, with Kelly and Pat. Arm the first team up with AKs. Team two needs to get their ARs. A few hundred rounds for each member, plus a small backpack for a few overnights. I'll spread the word on my way home to pack."

Each of the two response teams consisted of a dozen well-trained men and women who regularly practiced attack response and combat scenarios. They often took overnight missions, but never more than a few miles from town. It was all dry-fire since they didn't want to waste ammunition, so they hadn't fired their weapons in two years, but their assault rifles were cleaned and ready, all in perfect condition. Pat O'Malley, a gunsmith, had regularly inspected all of them, certifying the weapons as combat-ready.

"Good, let's get the response moving, like right now," said the Chief.

"Ed, you're heading up Larch Mountain, right? Find Corey, send him to Harger's farm immediately. Get Tweedy, too. When you find one of them, you've got both. They're like twins."

"On my way," Ed replied, as he headed out the door. "I'll get Dan Long, too. He's in charge of the first team now and he'll wanna be in on this one. He's probably out at Pete Roth's place. I'll remind Pete to stay put. He'll wanna go out on patrol and that's not okay with me. We can't risk our number one inventor getting shot at. Maybe he can pull static patrol at the Vista House with Eddie Cho and his buddies, but that's about all."

"Harger, get Kyle. He lives near you in that house overlooking Oxbow Park. And Kevin Sakai, Dan's cousin. He's always on his farm. That's where to find him. Remind him to pack food. He never does when the team practices, but if this lasts longer, I don't wanna worry about anyone starving."

"On my way," replied Harger, as he raced out the door. Scott Harger was always called, "Harger," not "Scott." The name "Scott" was reserved for Reverend Scott Golphenee, who was called either "Scott," or "Reverend," or, "Reverend Golphenee," but rarely "Reverend Scott Golphenee." That took too long to say. Therefore, Scott Harger became "Harger," and to avoid confusion, that's just what everyone called him.

"Have 'em all stop by the fire station for ammo, if they need any. Tell 'em all to drop what they're doing and get ready right now," Bill said, to those remaining.

"Joe, you stay here. Help organize the patrols. Send 'em out patrolling in groups of six. Start 'em at the Troutdale bridge, or what's left of it, and as more show up cover the river south to Oxbow, no, a mile south of that. Then, after that, send the rest east, all around the southern perimeter. Chief, you able to drum up a few solar or wind-up wristwatches? It'd help for dividing up watch duty and in case we gotta split up. I don't care what time they say, just so they're all showing the same."

"I'll ask around. Mine quit running a long time ago."

"Kelly, you're on the first team. You ready? We could use you, too. We'll need a medic who can shoot. You okay with that?" Bill said.

"I'll get a medical kit ready now. Then I'll ride home, get my dad's AK. Me and Alison'll meet you guys at Scott's."

"Alison? No way. We shouldn't risk that. I don't wanna take that chance. We've been through this before. We all know why," the Chief replied.

"Hello, Chief. I second that," said Scott, as he walked in the door.

"Hey, Reverend. You're just in time. That's Buck, an outsider ... the guy on the floor in the examination room. He was shot with an arrow. Floated down the Sandy. Chris and Joe were fishing and found him near Oxbow. Carried him here. He told us what happened. We might have trouble soon. We're sending the first response team out to intercept the men who did this. They may be heading our way and we can't have them enter town. It's safer to find them before they get here. We don't need another Hoffman incident," Bill said, referring to the lone farmer,

Brad Hoffman, who was brutally tortured a few weeks after the collapse. His fingers, toes, hands, feet, ears, all of his body cut apart piece by piece and tossed on his front porch by a group of freed inmates.

"Smart plan. Oh, I know Alison's been practicing with the second response team, but I'm not too crazy about her heading out to intercept unknown, dangerous men. I suggest we keep her with the second team, the back-up team. Have JP get 'em all together at the school, team two, that is. Brief 'em. Drill 'em. Have 'em ready to move immediately, just in case. Tell JP to not send Alison out unless he absolutely has to," the Chief said.

Weeks before the disaster, Alison had been hired to serve her nation as a nuclear physicist at the national lab in Los Alamos, New Mexico. She earned her PhD in physics at age twenty-three, and it was to be her first job. The collapse cancelled her plans and she never made it.

Since arriving in Corbett with her sister and parents, her ability to study and solve tough, complicated, long-term dilemmas made her valuable to the community. She conducted several sustainability studies. One was to determine how much game could be hunted to avoid depleting the wildlife such as the deer and wild cats. Another studied what crops would be best to grow to keep the proper nutritional requirements. Her skill in creating these studies meant she was off the first response team. It was too dangerous, too risky, to allow her to get into situations where she could be hurt or killed. Plus, she had been shot in the chest during the battles at Oxbow and, although the Kevlar vest she was wearing saved her life, once was enough for her parents, who didn't want her facing grave danger again. Alison had other thoughts, however. She had the skills and wanted to do her part, so she and her parents compromised and she became a member of the back-up response team, team two. It was considered the last line in the sand, a line everyone in town was expected to defend regardless.

A few months after the disaster, she had written a population study, the toughest issue of them all. No one wanted to touch that one, but she stepped up and tackled it anyhow. She calculated how many people Corbett could support. The answer scared everyone: three thousand.

At the time of the disaster, the population was around five thousand, a bit less, maybe, with people out of town on vacation. The current population was around three thousand, five hundred, which meant limiting the number of children people could have, which, in turn, led to the town adopting a voluntary three-child limit, a limit no families had successfully tested, yet.

She had also become Pete Roth's assistant, meeting with him regularly to repair things and invent ingenious devices to make life easier for all, such as the solar-powered still, used for making corn whiskey, and the small water-powered generator made from pulled-down power lines. She and Pete also invented an airless bicycle tire, made from strips of used car tires, which allowed people to ride bicycles long after their original tires wore out, but just not quite as fast.

Bill smiled. "Scott, could you ride your bike around town, tell everyone to arm themselves? Draft the security volunteers, too. Oh, get O'Malley. He's getting up there, a bit, but he's still the energizer bunny of security patrols.

Still can't believe he lost seventy-five pounds. Have you seen him lately? Dan will need him on the first response team, him and that old Soviet rifle of his. Tell 'em all we may have an attack coming our way. The response teams need to pack food for a few days, but pack light. It's warm outside, so no sleeping bags. We'll sleep on the ground in our clothes. No cooking either. Can't have any smoke from fires. We can't have anyone else getting ripped apart by invaders like Hoffman was. Let's do this right. Let's do it just like JP and Dan trained us."

"Here we go again," said Scott, as he jumped on his bicycle and took off east toward Larch Mountain.

Kelly grabbed a small canvas bag and started packing it with clinic supplies.

The examination room emptied out as Bill and Kelly headed toward the door.

Denise spoke quietly to Kelly so Buck couldn't hear her. "Kelly, I didn't want to mention this in front of the others, but take a few hundred milligrams of this stuff, in case someone gets badly hurt. It might damage morale if they know you have it. It's in this small paper envelope, folded like an origami. I've placed it inside another one so none spills. And don't get it wet," she reminded her.

Denise always dismissively called the heroin, "stuff," as if it didn't rate highly enough to be called its medical name. However, when someone was seriously ill or badly hurt, it became a wonder drug.

"Hey, what about me? I can shoot. I wanna pay those bastards back," said Buck, as he eavesdropped and struggled up onto his elbows, trying to get into a sitting position, fighting desperately to not grimace in pain.

"Have you seen yourself in a mirror lately, Buck?" said Denise. "You look nearly dead. It's time for you to eat something, then rest a few days."

"Screw that. I'll be ready to fight those bastards tomorrow. You watch me." The words "crap" and "bastard," that he occasionally used, was about as close as Buck, a devout Catholic, ever got to swearing.

"Oh, sure you will. I can see it now," Denise said.

"You watch me. I'll be better after a good, solid sleep."

"We'll see how you are tomorrow."

"I'm ready right now!"

"You're ready to fight. Ha! You can't even walk. Plus, you want pain medicine?"

"Well, maybe just once more. Then I'll sleep a long time and be ready."

"Oh, sure you will, Buck. Once more is all you were gonna get anyhow. Let's get you washed, fed, then I'll give you just a little bit to help you sleep. When you wake up, we'll get you some decent clothes. I cleaned your shirt. It's drying now, and it still stinks, but it'll be okay. The pants you're wearing now are another story. Chris has some spare deerskin pants. They'll be big on you at first, but in a few weeks of decent eatin' you'll grow into 'em. We'll have you switch pants when you wake up, get you a warm shower, too, right from a sun-warmed garden hose."

"A warm shower? You have running water, too? It's been a long time."

"We have running tap water, just like in the old times. It flows off Larch Mountain, east of us. The warm shower's primitive. You stand on a stone platform out back. Then, you hold the garden hose over your head 'til the warm water's gone. It's only good for a quick one. Sorry, no soap. We've made a little from vegetable oil and lye leached from wood ashes, but that's mostly for the clinic. We ran out of the good soap, like, two years ago. Warm water and quick scrubbing is what we mostly do. You'll look forward to it when you wake up tomorrow."

Chapter Ten

Kelly and her sister, Alison, both lived with their parents, Jimmy and Deborah Lee, in a small three-bedroom home. It was about twelve hundred square feet, one story, and sat on the north side of Southeast Smith Road. It had been painted white the year prior to the collapse and was well maintained. It had a fireplace and two large windows faced south, allowing sunlight to warm the well insulated home even during the winter. Roses grew along the sunny side of the house. It sat on four acres, large enough to grow fruit trees and a decent garden, but not too large for a sixty-something man and a fifty-something woman to maintain. Dozens of assorted fruit trees grew on the land and a moveable chicken coop was parked near the road alongside the driveway in the shade of a mature Fuji apple tree. The original owners were on vacation in Uruguay when the disaster struck and never returned. The Lees moved into it nine months after they fled their suburban home in Troutdale.

The disaster hit Multnomah County hard. Street gangs controlled most East County cities. The gas and electricity stopped and food ran out. The water stopped flowing. Police and fire services no longer functioned. During the second week Troutdale was torn apart by an army of freed jail inmates numbering in the hundreds. Most homes were looted and burned. Bodies were strewn about. Few survived. The same group that attacked Troutdale attacked Corbett a week later. They called themselves the Inverness Army, named after the county jail.

Jimmy, Alison and Kelly were on one of the two patrol groups that stumbled upon and fought off the attackers. They became town heroes, their names chiseled into a stone marker commemorating the heroes of the victorious battle. It was placed in front of the fire station, alongside the no-longer-used driveway. The stone marker contained twelve names. Three of them were Lees. Another marker was placed in the parking lot at Lewis and Clark Park, near the blown up railroad bridge. It commemorated the heroes of that battle. It also included Charlie and his buddy, Tim, the two recluses who used their explosives to destroy that bridge plus the Troutdale and Stark Street bridges one morning a few days after the collapse.

The Lee family spent their first nine months in Corbett living with the Hancocks and working on their berry farm. Joe, his dad, Joseph, and his wife, Mary Kay, invited them to stay in their home when the collapse occurred. As the population of Corbett declined, and those out of town when the disaster hit failed to return, dozens of solid houses became available and when the first spring arrived, they moved into one.

Deborah, Kelly's mother, was a Chinese American, too. Unlike Kelly's father, she was born in China in 1965 during the Cultural Revolution of the 1960s. For her, hardship was a part of life. While growing up, she saw people starve to death in her hometown. Her parents often told her that a period of starvation comes every second generation and they taught her to be thankful for and to treasure what she had. And she did, very much so.

Her life in Corbett was rich compared to the life she knew as a child. Growing up, she owned one dress and a pair of shoes. Another dress or a second pair of shoes was considered bourgeoisie. No one wanted that label.

The economic collapse seemed to have little effect on her. She constantly worked on the lush family garden with Jimmy. Both were vegetarians and, with fish and meat scarce following the disaster, their daughters had followed the same diet. Deer again freely roamed throughout Corbett, the chicken population had multiplied and fish were once again becoming plentiful in the Sandy River, but it just wasn't enough to provide a daily meal of meat, fish or poultry for everyone in town.

With a population of around three thousand five hundred, offering one daily meat or fish serving for all would require a million non-vegetarian meals each year. Even if they stripped the river of its fish, and the hills of wildlife, and the farms of all their animals it simply wasn't possible. Therefore, many adopted a vegetarian diet, or nearly so, and none suffered from the change. In fact, the people of Corbett had become much healthier and, with the daily exercise, strong and fit, too.

An author of three organic gardening books, Deborah was considered an expert in chemical-free vegetable growing. She, along with Bryan and Shari, the owners of the nearby Dancing Roots organic farm, shared organic farming methods with everyone. Neighboring farmers often dropped by seeking her advice.

Today, she was dressed in her usual faded blue denim pants and a long-sleeved tan button down shirt. Soiled black sandals made by Rueben from used car tires guarded the bottoms of her feet. She stood next to her husband as Kelly approached on her prized silver Trek model 7200 bicycle.

Kelly pedaled down their gravel driveway and put her bicycle on its kickstand near the chickens. "Hi, mom! Hi, dad!"

"Hi, Kelly!" they both said.

"I heard there's a stranger at the clinic," said her dad.

Kelly's father, Jimmy Lee, was sixty-four years old. With excellent posture, he was a slender, five-foot-seven, third generation Chinese American with thinning black hair, only a narrow ring of which was visible under his homemade straw coolie hat. Deborah wore a coolie hat, too. They were becoming more and more popular during the summer months. Coolie hats were simple to make and, as cheap, factory made baseball hats wore out, everyone still needed protection from the sun since all the sunscreen was long gone.

He wore the same patched, denim pants each day topped by a faded old blue t-shirt. His revolver was stuffed into a brown leather holster, which hung low and loose off his right hip. He stood alongside Deborah in their front yard vegetable garden. His posture was ramrod straight, two inches taller than she, but three inches shorter than Kelly, something never mentioned in his presence.

He was the seventh of eleven children. The family was raised in severe, food stamp poverty by his parents in Oakland, California. He saw his oldest brother get gunned down over a bad drug deal. Two others died by their own hand. Another died on the streets at age forty-eight, toothless and wasted away after years of methamphetamine abuse. By age eighteen he knew he had to get away from Oakland. He escaped the run-down city's too-common cycle of poverty by fleeing town and working his way through college at the University of Washington as a steelworker.

He retired early, at fifty-six, after spending his working career with the State Department. Fluent in Cantonese and Mandarin, something not unusual with Chinese Americans, he spent the last six years assigned as an intelligence analyst in Dublin, Ireland, where he developed a fondness for Irish culture. He never discussed the nature of his work, but a few times he mentioned that it involved gathering information from Chinese immigrants in Europe. A few years before he retired, Kelly noticed that his thick US passport, accidentally left on the kitchen counter, was filled with entry and exit stamps from throughout South America and Asia. She never asked about them and he had yet to tell her about his government travel.

"Yeah, guy's name is Buck. Did you two hear the story yet?" Kelly asked.

"Yup," her dad replied. Word flashed around town fast, even without electronic assistance. Maybe even faster. The story of Buck's arrival was common knowledge throughout Corbett not long after Joe carried him into the clinic. The frightening tale he told travelled through town and back, growing in scale a bit each time it bounced from one side of town to the other like an echo that grew rather than faded.

People dug through their closets and under their beds searching for family firearms. Garages and attics were rummaged through. Long forgotten ammunition was finally found. Thousands of bullets were soon getting stuffed into handgun and rifle magazines, one at a time. Neighbors hooked up with each other. Doors left unlocked for months were once again secured. Farmers strapped pistols to their work belts, and moms toted shotguns while they pulled weeds in their gardens.

"I heard he was shot with an arrow, not far from here. Some are saying we might be under attack soon," said Jimmy, as he glanced down and brushed his right hand against his holstered Smith and Wesson model sixty-six revolver.

Often in Corbett, as elsewhere, stories had a tendency to evolve somewhat as they were shared from person to person. They generally grew into something bigger, something more exciting as each person salted the story.

This was no exception. Rather than getting shot just north of Sandy, the story had morphed somewhat. Now, people who heard it third, fourth or fifth hand mistakenly believed a farmer had been shot and that an organized and well-armed band of raiders was near, and now moving in. They heard one of the raiders had been shot with a rifle while escaping.

The Chief, Scott, Kimberly and a few others were travelling around town on bikes, activating the community militia, and calming everyone by letting them know the real story about Buck. But it would take until evening before they finished. The threat was near, it was real, but it wasn't going to be a war like last time.

"No. They're probably still far from here, just outside Sandy. A day's walk, maybe less. They may be from far away. Maybe they've not heard of us. We've been laying low for two years. I doubt if anyone even knows we're here, and those that do know we're here, know to stay away. Anyhow, he was shot with a skinny arrow. It missed the good parts. He'll live," Kelly said, as she then shared the rest of the details, a somewhat different story than the one Jimmy's neighbor excitedly told.

"Kelly, I don't want you to go. Can't you stay at the clinic with Denise? Why can't one of the men be the medic?" asked her mother.

"The council just voted to activate the response teams. Bill Hartigan asked me to go along, serve as medic. I told him I would. It'll be safe. We have the best in town on my team." Kelly quickly rattled off the members of her team, counting them one-by-one on her fingers plus two toes. "Mom, I'm on the first team. We're leaving soon, from Harger's farm. The back-up team is meeting at the school with JP. The militia's been activated, too. This is real. We're actually heading out of town for the first time. Overnight. Maybe two. Patrols are starting this afternoon. We're going to stay out until we figure out who these people are and where they're headed. I'll be safe, mom," Kelly said.

"What about Alison. Where is she?" asked her mom.

"She's at the school. Remember, she's on team two."

Deborah and Jimmy were aware of their daughters' training exercises, but didn't believe they would actually be activated to fight.

"Wear the vest, Kelly. I insist," Deborah said.

"I'll go get it. It may have a dent, but it's all we have," said Jimmy.

"I'll wear it all the time. I promise. I gotta pack now. We're heading out immediately."

Chapter Eleven

Like the Hancocks, Scott Harger and his wife, Katie, grew primarily apples, blueberries and raspberries. Their fifty-acre farm was on a rolling section of Corbett on the south side of town at the east end of SE Rickert Road. It was about as far south as one could get and still be in Corbett. It was unremarkable with its straight rows of apple trees on the east side and berries on the west interrupted near the road by the white two-story, nicely restored Harger family home. The broad front porch had thick, thirty-inch tall railings and the ceiling supported a two-person dark green swing chair. Their three sons were out of town when the disaster hit and, sadly, hadn't been seen since. Few who were outside of town on the day of the disaster ever made it back, but the Hargers still held out hope.

He was five-nine, slim, and still farm-worker strong after losing fifty pounds of fat in the past two years. His fifty-five-year-old round, a-bit-too-large face still held its pre-disaster chubbiness, which surrounded his sharp

German nose and his baggy, deep-set blue eyes. His teenage hair was still all there and everyone quietly wondered how he managed to keep it pitch black these past two years.

His once-black, faded Ben Davis work pants still held up, although, like many in town, they hung loose. Baggy clothes were the very height of Year Two, Corbett fashion. Year Three had just started the day before and the town fashion would probably remain unchanged for another year. He wore his youngest son's t-shirt, which fit him just right. It was dark blue and read "Seattle Seahawks" across the front in crisp, silver letters.

He stood alongside his petite, green-eyed wife of thirty years. Dressed in a full-length plain yellow dress, her straight, short brown hair barely reached her collar. She stood the same height as Harger yet had an air about her suggesting she set the house rules. She was known as the farm planner and it still ran like a Swiss watch, providing the town with twice as many berries as the more well-known berry farms.

"I expect this to be your first stop when you all get back," Harger said as he and Katie waved and said goodbye to the team.

"We'll crack out the last of our blueberry wine to celebrate when you get back," Katie shouted from the front porch. "I have two gallons set aside, plus a case! If Scott touches it I'll hide his last bottle of black you-know-what."

The team members laughed and cheerfully waved goodbye as they started moving out.

"Let's roll, people," Dan calmly said, as the twelve members of the first response team started walking south from the Harger farm. "When we get to the river, spread out, ten yards apart. No more talking after that. Hand signals only. Let's work this like professionals. All twelve of us'll walk back to town when this is over. All of us. None carried. That's an order."

Dan Long, dressed in dark green military ripstop, led the response team. He was a half-Japanese, half-European, knife-fighting expert and at fifty, he still moved like a twenty-year-old. With his eighteen-inch, dark brown ponytail he looked like one too. His eyes retained his Japanese mother's almond shape, but he inherited his father's sharp nose. Like others in Corbett, he biked everywhere, managing to keep his weight at a steady one-fifty. He was one of few in town whose weight hadn't changed since the disaster.

Dan was a retired Eugene, Oregon, police sergeant and he set the pace. Dan had that special rare quality that made others confidently follow him anywhere. The response team he led was made up of twelve, mostly experienced fighters: Dan and his younger Japanese American cousin, Kevin Sakai, each of whom was patrolling near the interstate highway two years earlier and luckily avoided the deadly combat; second-in-command, Bill Hartigan; Afghanistan War combat veteran Kyle Howard; sharpshooter Pat O'Malley; "invisible" Rigo Gomez, who rumor had it could sneak up on a deer in broad daylight; easygoing, baby-faced, but tough as a rock Don Mershon; the two eighteen-year-olds, Blake Raymond and Conner Skiles, each of whom could perform one hundred pushups and outrun anyone in town; Kelly Lee, serving as team medic; and lastly, the inseparable buddies, Joe Tweedy and Corey Anderson.

All carried a light daypack containing fruit, vegetables, four liters of water and a tightly rolled ground blanket. Those eating meat carried dried salmon or venison wrapped in a cloth. They didn't have radio communication.

Bill, Kyle, Tweedy and Corey each carried their DPMS AR-15s on matching shoulder slings. Everyone else carried other assorted variants of the Colt AR-15 in order to keep all members using the same cartridges and magazines. Each rifle was fully loaded, a round in the chamber and safeties set. Pat was the only exception. He carried his Dragunov SVDS over his shoulder with the stock folded out. Each team member except Pat carried an additional six, thirty-round magazines either in pouches secured to their outer clothing or in their packs. Each high-capacity rifle magazine was loaded with twenty-seven, not thirty, rounds, in order to not over-compress the magazine springs. Pat carried only four magazines: one in the rifle and three in a belt pouch. Each member also carried a fully loaded semi-automatic handgun with additional magazines on their belts and in their packs. The packs were small, but heavy.

Although reloading was possible, primers were in short supply, so ammunition conservation was imperative. They knew they would never acquire any additional ammo so no one had fired a weapon in nearly two years.

Dan and Bill also carried wristwatches. The Chief could only drum up two on short notice. Each read exactly six o'clock when they departed from Harger's, but that was inaccurate because the Chief forgot to check with Rueben's grandfather clock first.

The group moved west on Rickert Road, then hiked south along Southeast Evans Road. It eventually became Southeast Gordon Creek Road and they took it to the Sandy River. They saw the beach where Buck washed up, marked by the two fishing poles Joe and Chris left behind. Although they walked on pavement, they moved silently. Someone fifty yards away wouldn't hear them marching. Soon, the road moved away from the riverbank and they were zigzagging back up to the bluff along the Corbett side of the river. The road followed the river for about a mile, then turned east.

They planned to reach the heavily wooded area just east of Camp Namanu before dark, and they did. That would get them to a point about a mile east of Dodge Park. It was located at the convergence of the Sandy River and the Bull Run River and had been a popular place for fishing before that day the world's financial system stopped working. It was where they believed Buck had been shot. It was also where they planned to start searching for those who shot him.

To get there they took Southeast Gordon Creek Road east until reaching the one hundred yard wide treeless space that cut north and south through the forest, clearing a path for the Bonneville Power Administration power lines. They followed it south. When they reached Eisner Road they turned west, hiked a few hundred yards through the thick forest, and found a place to settle in. Although their watches read ten-fifteen, it was still daylight. Shortly after sunset, a full moon rose. Dan and Bill reset their watches to nine.

Night watch duty would be divided into three, three-hour shifts starting at nine o'clock. Four members remained awake and on guard each shift, silently listening and scanning through their quadrant of the trees. They all remained quiet, believing they were within a mile of where Buck was shot and possibly within voice range of those who shot him.

They were right on both counts.

Chapter Twelve

It was still warm, nearly seventy, as darkness fell. The clearing they chose was small, snuggled into a tight group of thick, tall, secondary growth evergreen trees. The response team prepared to fold themselves into their light bedrolls and try their best to fall sleep. The full moon peeked between the distant trees carpeting the hills to the east in soft yellow light. A few beams reached through nearby trees and grazed the team. Birds fell quiet. A family of coyotes cried crazily along the hill near the moon, not far away.

"Shortest blade of dry grass gets first watch. Longest gets second watch. Draw, everyone," Dan announced to the gathered group in his deep whisper.

Rigo, Kyle, Corey and Tweedy drew the short blade of grass. They got the first watch and would remain awake until midnight. At midnight, they would awaken Bill, Kelly, Pat and Don, who drew the longest blade. After, they planned to rest six hours until awakened before sunrise by the third shift.

"Kyle, you and Rigo take the two wristwatches. Give 'em to Bill when you wake him and the others up at midnight. And all of you, remember, keep your safeties on. We can't have any accidental discharges. Whisper quietly if you need to communicate with words. We gotta maintain absolute silence. You all know why," Dan quietly said to the gathered foursome. "Plus, just a reminder, no whistling, no sound signaling. Only the full alert: a fired weapon. Pair-up. One pair very quietly walks the perimeter every now and then during the shift, two hundred yards out, just like we trained. No farther. Be invisible as you move, just like we practiced in training. Like Rigo does. Allow the forest to report to you, listen for the messages. Do not send any out."

Moments after the ones resting grew still, the absolute silence of the small, tight camp was suddenly broken by a loud snore, a nasty ugly growl that originated from deep inside Pat O'Malley's chest.

While the others slept though it, Dan was jolted awake. He tossed his blanket aside, stood up, then moved a few feet to where Pat, lying flat on his back, was sleeping. Just as Pat drew in another tremendous breath, preparing to fire off another snore, Dan nudged him gently in the shoulder with his tan moccasin then kneeled, moving his face closer to Pat's. "Pat. Get up. Anyone within two miles'll know we're here with your snoring. Pat, get up. Pat, up … up, get up."

Pat, a very sound sleeper, finally opened his eyes, rattled awake from a forgotten dream. He reached under his blanket for his long Soviet sniper rifle and whispered to Dan. "What's going on. We got bad guys?"

Dan put a calming hand on Pat's shoulder. "It's okay, Pat. We don't need the rifles right now. But your snoring can't happen. Gotta stop. Too loud. Can you sleep without doing that?"

"I was snoring?"

"Yup. Loud."

"Damn it. I didn't know I still snored," replied Pat, who lived alone. He had been mightily and unknowingly snoring away to his heart's content for nearly seven years, ever since his wife ran off to Santiago, Chile, with a man she met on Facebook. The new man promised he didn't snore and held true to that promise, but few of his others. "I thought I quit snoring when I quit drinking."

"How about you lay on your tummy. Can you try that?"

"Yeah, okay. Man, I'm sorry. I had no idea I still snored that loud."

"Hey, no problem. But even quiet snoring can't happen here. If you keep it up, I'm gonna have you airlifted outta here, like quick. Seriously."

"Oh, man, I totally get it. I'm so sorry. Won't happen again," Pat said, repeating his apology as he flipped over onto his tummy and solved the problem.

Pat had been widely known as a hotheaded drinker, a fist fighting bad drunk, downing a half-liter bottle of Irish whiskey each weekend. His Irish ancestry and his predilection for whiskey were, it was commonly believed, responsible for his short-fused temper. Since quitting the booze, running out, actually, he'd had only one fight. It was in self-defense against a man he severely pounded years ago in the Springdale saloon. The man wanted another chance to even the score and he failed. Pat didn't hurt him the second time, just knocked him down with a sharp jab to the nose, no blood this time, then begged the man not to fight him again. He'd become the politest man you'd ever meet.

Rigo and Kyle moved out while Corey and Tweedy, inseparable for reasons few asked and fewer told, remained together at the camp, awake and alert, listening and searching into the forest. The truth of the matter was that they were simply long time best friends, but their actions and behaviors did little to dispel what Tweedy simply laughed at and Corey called "that stupid rumor."

Rays of moonlight reached out and still touched the forest floor and the sleepers as it shifted its position in the sky. The coyotes had calmed down and the air was still. The forest became quiet, too quiet. They knew dozens of desperate men were somewhere nearby. If not for the simmering anxiety, it was a perfect summer night.

Rigo, who could silently walk unseen down a path of dried twigs in broad daylight, proved his well-known invisibility and stealth by vanishing into the forest, ten yards ahead of Kyle. Kyle knew he was still moving because that was the plan: walk fifty paces straight south, wait a short time, turn left and complete a counterclockwise circle returning to the same point where the circle started.

When Kyle counted off step number fifty to himself, he saw the grinning Rigo standing alongside a tree between shards of moonlight three feet away.

"What took you so long, homes? I've been waiting here forever," he said, in his thick Spanish accent.

Rigo was born in Zacatecas, Mexico, thirty-six years earlier. He arrived in the United States on a warm June evening, at midnight, on a direct TAESA flight to Oakland, California, when he was eighteen. The sleepy government officials at the airport hardly looked at him and didn't ask him a single question while stamping his passport and papers admitting him into the United States for a six-month vacation. The officials may have quizzed him if they had paid more attention and noticed the unique, black, Zetas gang tattoos on his hands, arms and neck.

The tattoos were common among poor teenage boys in that part of Mexico. The drug gangs in Zacatecas had overwhelming power and influence, more than the law, more than family or school. For a brief time he was a part of that cash-rich, deadly scene. Rigo never mentioned a word to anyone about that brief period in his life or the tattoos. People who knew him didn't ask about them because after a time, they didn't notice them. They, too, had become invisible.

His solo journey was never intended to be a vacation. He was planning to stay in the United States for the rest of his life and never return to Mexico, not even for a visit. He made his way quite by accident to Corbett, a safe, isolated farming community far from any city. The day after he arrived in America, he found himself in the Greyhound bus station in Portland, Oregon. He had seven dollars in his pocket and a change of clothes folded neatly into a small, blue backpack.

At the bus station he overheard two young Mexican men talking about taking a bus to Troutdale, then walking to Corbett where they could get work picking blueberries. He followed them and found work that afternoon, not at the farm the two men chose, but at a distant, more remote farm: the Harger farm.

He learned English, worked hard and saved his money. His goal was to buy a small farm, like the one his family owned in Mexico. For years he worked on Harger's farm, earning minimum wage, plus overtime. Unlike most farm workers who commuted daily, working only during the harvest season, Rigo lived on the Harger farm year-round, sleeping in a small, rusty trailer rent-free. Harger liked and trusted Rigo. He wanted someone he could trust on the property at all times, and Rigo never went anywhere.

The third summer in America he married a girl from Mexico. She was twenty-one at the time, the same age he was, and worked on a nearby cabbage farm. He had already saved thirty thousand dollars and she was impressed by his common sense frugality and hard work ethic. They struggled together, saving and enjoying the safety of the cozy trailer, soon sharing it with their first child.

Three years before the disaster they bought a foreclosed, ten-acre lavender farm on a sunny, south-facing slope not far from Harger's berry farm. It was accessible by a half-mile-long two-track dirt road. The home was advertised as a one-story fixer-upper. The thousand square-foot home turned out to be a nightmare of endless repair projects, but it was all theirs and they wouldn't have it any other way. They paid nearly all their money, one hundred and fifty thousand dollars, which they used as a fifty percent down payment on the remote lavender farm.

During the year prior to the collapse the farm earned over eighty thousand dollars, mostly in tax-free, roadside sales. His goal was to pay off the bank loan in ten years, but the economic collapse changed that plan. He had found the American dream, but fearing deportation he refused to leave town or drive. He wisely stayed under the radar. The farm was in his wife's name because she had United States permanent residency, a green card, allowing her entry into America's legal and economic system. His two teenage daughters had his wife's last name. No police officer or federal agent had approached within a mile of Rigo since his Mexican passport had been stamped. There was no record of his presence in the United States other than that entry. No one knew he was an illegal alien and after the disaster, no one cared. He felt safe. He had become invisible.

When the disaster hit, he joined the town militia, patrolling the southern flank of town every day until the threat had subsided. He still grew four acres of lavender that he used for medicine, soap and perfume, but converted his other acres to vegetables, berries and fruit trees. He had become part of Corbett. The collapse had provided him with full citizenship.

"Dude, you were gone. We should stick together," Kyle said.

"We were together. I could hear you behind me, like maybe five yards back."

"Okay, I've got fifty paces. You?" Kyle asked.

"Yeah. Same here."

They stood quietly for a short time, reading the message from the forest. Again, the message was the same: silence, too much silence.

"Okay, let's move out, get that circle walked. This forest spooks me tonight," Kyle said. "It's too quiet. I have a feeling we're being watched."

Kyle, five-foot-eleven and a hundred sixty pounds, was a twenty-eight-year-old Afghanistan War combat veteran with two purple hearts. His light brown hair was tied into a tight ponytail with the remnant of a long, brown leather bootlace. The ends hung half way down his back, swinging loose. Like many others, he wore faded blue jeans and a black t-shirt. His light skin required an extra layer of ash to quiet the shine. His blue eyes stared out from his ash-darkened, angular face. He rarely spoke and almost never smiled. When he spoke, people listened. When he smiled, it was an odd, asymmetrical facial expression resulting from one of his two war wounds. People said his smile looked like someone was about to get hurt.

While riding in an armored vehicle through an unpronounceable, God-forsaken neighborhood near the outskirts of Khost, in eastern Afghanistan, an RPG struck. The explosion caused a horrific blast that failed to penetrate the vehicle. However, the tremendous shock wave slammed him, leaving him deaf in his left ear, which trickled blood over his shoulder and down his arm, staining his camouflage shirt with cruel red splotches.

He was otherwise uninjured by the blast, but while returning to base for medical treatment that very afternoon, an Afghan child, a warrior-in-training, a true patriot among his peers, shot a steel toy arrow at his vehicle. It passed through the open passenger side window piercing Kyle's face, causing nerve damage to his check and knocking out two molars, including a painful upper wisdom tooth scheduled for extraction later that week.

The driver saw the arrow sticking out of Kyle's face and the blood running down his neck. One side of his shirt was splotchy with drying blood from the RPG attack, while the other was getting decorated with lines of fresh blood. With the short metal arrow sticking out of his bloody face, Kyle aimed his rifle at the boy, brought his index finger inside the trigger guard, but couldn't bring himself to pull the trigger. The higher ranking driver screamed at Kyle, "Waste him! Do it! What are you waiting for?" The shooting might have been justifiable. As the military vehicle passed, the boy smiled at Kyle with his empty bow in his hand and waved with the other. He was about ten years old. He thought about that child defending his homeland as he walked through the forest with Rigo.

"There's nothing here. Quiet. No smells, nothing," Rigo said, peering deep into the forest with his big, round, fully dilated eyes. "Let's roll."

Heading east initially, then gradually turning north, they crept through the woods. They had completed just over three-quarters of the circle, just reaching the outskirts of Camp Namanu when Rigo suddenly froze. They were only a few hundred yards east of the Sandy River. The sound of the water didn't reach that far. Kyle, trailing close behind, almost bumped into him. The moon was bright, so bright they easily saw the warm, but no longer smoldering remains of the campfire as they approached it. If it were darker they would have stepped in it. Kyle squatted down, sticking his bare fingers into the ashes. He slowly stood, turned, placed his lips a half-inch from Rigo's left ear and whispered. "It was just put out. Ashes are still wet. Footprints everywhere. A huge group. We've got trouble, Rigo. Big trouble. Let's head straight back. They could be watching us right now."

In fact, they were, and had been since long before sunset.

Chapter Thirteen

"Once more! We've practiced this a hundred times over the last two years. Let's get it right this time! Move quietly!" JP shouted. "We're lucky the moon's out so we can practice tonight with some light."

JP, wearing his off-white, heavily stained Corbett Cardinals hoodie and a faded pair of blue denim short jeans, shouted out loud repeatedly to the second response team as they practiced basic stealth movement drills in the woods near the school. He barked out orders as he paced back and forth between the trees and blackberry bushes with his toes sticking out of the solid Michelin tire treaded sandals Rueben crafted for him last Christmas.

JP was delighted at the performance of this team. They were performing brilliantly, moving about almost unseen in near total silence. JP was proud of them, but he demanded perfection so he kept hammering away at them.

"Down means down! It means your chins touch the dirt, not your elbows! Vladimir, your forehead's too shiny. When you stick your head up to peek the whole world knows about it. It's like a flashlight. Remember those? Use more ash on your face when we practice. And if we move out for real cover your face completely black, understand?"

"Got it," replied Vladimir.

"Alison, your glasses reflect off the moonlight. Someone'll mistake you for a raccoon an' put an arrow in your hair. Pack 'em away when we practice. You still have one decent eye, use it, girl!"

"What glasses?" Alison jokingly responded as she quickly slipped them into their case and stuffed the case into her shirt pocket. She had nearly perfect vision in her right eye, her shooting eye, but was unable to tell a cow from a fence post at one hundred yards with the other.

"Alright, that's enough for today. Get rested. You're the back-up team, but remember: as soon as you're called, you're no longer the back-up team Remember, you're equal in every way to team one." They gathered and slept in three clumps of bedrolls in the middle of the football field and would remain together until the threat ended.

Their unloaded rifles were all AK-47 variants. Some had been traded with the other team in order to maintain ammunition and magazine uniformity. The rifles remained by their sides. Each of them packed six thirty-round magazines as well as their personal or loaned handguns. Alison carried her Walther PPS, which her family friend Chris McClanahan had taught her to shoot. Vladimir had his CZ-75 nine-millimeter. Others carried whatever they could drum up. None had fired a weapon in nearly two years, but all of them had experience. The weapons were kept clean and had been inspected numerous times. They were believed to be in good working order.

The ammunition they had was all they would ever get. For a short time after the disaster, limited hunting was done with rifles, but after a few months it stopped. It soon became apparent, even to the most libertarian and individualistic outdoorsmen of the small Corbett colony, that not only was running out of ammunition unthinkable, but the survival of Corbett depended on everyone pulling together as a group, especially in its defense. As a result, tens of thousands of rounds of common defense ammunition was stored at the fire station. Plus, firing a weapon sent a signal to people miles away and could attract outsiders. Therefore, JP's training was always done without a weapon fired. And, with the exception of wood chopping and the occasional banging of hammers on metal, Corbett was always silent.

Chapter Fourteen

Kyle followed closely behind Rigo, step for step, silently moving fast, back to the others. Tweedy and Corey were sitting apart, at opposite ends of the encampment, listening and staring into the moonlit trees and saw them as they neared the camp.

"Found 'em," Rigo said to both, as soon as he reached the camp.

"Found who?" Tweedy replied, his mind momentarily elsewhere.

"Probably the guys who shot Buck," said Kyle. "Well, not them, but their camp."

"Better wake up Dan," Corey said. And he did.

The commotion awakened Dan. He rose up on one elbow.

"Tell me what you found," he asked, glancing back and forth at Kyle and Rigo.

They quietly explained the warm, damp fire pit and the unusual eerie silence of the forest.

"Everyone up now," Dan said, as he stood rolling his blanket. He wasn't about to allow this team to get ambushed. At sunrise they would return and find the men who shot Buck. "Everyone up. Let's move. Straight east until we find a clearing, we gotta get away from the river. Move!"

Kyle, already packed, glanced at his left wrist. His borrowed watch read nine-forty.

By the time Kyle's watch read ten, or, twenty-two hundred hours, they had moved a mile east into a forest clearing about three hundred yards square. They paused alongside a thick patch of not-yet-ripened blackberries growing under the intersection of two sets of high power lines. One line cut a wide path through the forest roughly west and east, and another set of orange legged towers marched from the west and turned north, disappearing up the path they walked earlier that evening. The moon was high. Only Jupiter and the brightest stars shone.

The full moon gave them a clear view in all directions. They could rest safely, keeping the same watch shifts. It was still warm, cloudless, calm, a beautiful summer evening.

Dan sat low and signaled with both hands, drawing the group near. They sat in a tight circle. "Listen up. Get some rest everyone. Tomorrow, just after sunup, we'll find these guys. Nice and early. We'll move out before sunup and surprise 'em. They probably think we split, scared. But it's them who need to be scared, not us. If they shot Buck in cold blood, they'll do the same to any one of us, or our families. We're true warriors now. The best there is. We shoot first, ask questions later. Tomorrow we'll make our town safe again. That's what we're here for," he said, as he smiled into the windless, silent air, offering his calming full confidence in the team.

Dan pointed his finger at Tweedy, Corey, Kyle then Rigo. "No perimeter walks. No standing. Keep your butts on the ground. We're safe. No one can see us here. Let's get some sleep."

At just before three, two members of the second night watch, Kelly and Don, were startled by the horrible sound of a man screaming in the distance. It was so faint that Pat and Bill, each with bullet-deadened hearing, couldn't hear it. The others slept through it, but Kelly and Don told no one that their hearts raced wildly and they couldn't sleep for the rest of the night. The sound, barely audible, wailed from deep within the woods, from somewhere near the far off coyotes. It lasted only a few moments. It was a scream that sounded like it came from within a horrible dream. It arrived from the northeast, the cry of a madman, a scream that carried far in the quiet, dry summer air, announcing to everyone for miles around that terror was near.

Chapter Fifteen

"Rise and shine, people," Blake said, smiling as he moved quietly about the small camp shaking a shoulder here, pulling a foot there. He was one of the four on the final watch and it was his duty to awaken everyone. There was a joke hidden in almost everything he said. Blake lifted the team's spirit each time he spoke, even if it was just a whisper. "Everyone up. Pack it up. Let's all get up and roll. Let's go out and get some psychos."

"Blake, at least try to make it rhyme," Conner said.

Only eighteen, Blake was considered by some to be not old enough for this assignment. Although he could run from one end of Corbett to the other faster than anyone, he was too young to perform guard duty in the months following the disaster. His desire to become a soldier was well known among his family and friends and after endless pestering, JP, who made the final decision, relented and allowed him to practice with the response teams. His drive and relentless efforts earned him a slot on team one with his former classmate, Conner Skiles.

He was the only team member who hadn't fired a weapon. JP's instructions were simple. "You line up the front sight, that's the thingy on the end of the barrel, with the back sight, that's the thingy at the front. Then, when both are lined up with whomever you want to kill, you gently squeeze the trigger. That's all there is to it. Is that clear?"

At six-seven and a hundred-ninety pounds Blake was the classic beanpole. His green eyes gazed happily from each side of his long, narrow beak. His elongated, ever-smiling face was topped by his large, flat Celtic forehead never touched by his precisely crew cut, light-brown hair. He was one of the very few young men in Corbett who shunned the popular, easy to arrange ponytail.

The team was moving almost immediately after they stood.

"Five yards apart, that's five paces. Stagger your positions. From now on it's hand signals only unless we're firing. Everyone good?" Dan said.

Everyone responded with a quick, silent thumb-up, except Conner, who replied, "I'm good."

Conner was five-eleven and one-fifty. Slender, like everyone else, he was lean and could run as fast as Blake, which was part of the reason he was on this response team. He wore his Viking-yellow hair in a foot-long ponytail, keeping pace with current, post-disaster fashion. He was blessed with an early, wispy beard, keeping it clipped to about a half-inch, maybe a bit shorter. He wore faded blue Kirkland brand denim jeans, which were still as good as new after two years of daily wear. He didn't even pack a shirt. If it was over sixty degrees he was always shirtless, showing off his new tattoo.

He had an AR-15 and an AK-47 tattooed to his back in a criss-cross fashion. The tattoo appeared last winter over the course of three weeks just after he was selected for team one. His parents found out days after his eighteenth birthday and were not quite as thrilled as he was. He explained to them that it reflected his desire to offer his life guarding the community, a patriotic desire expressed by uncounted millions of brave young men since the beginning of time.

Dan moved close and stood nose to nose with Conner. He stared at him for a few uncomfortable, unkind morning breaths and finally raised his right index finger to his lips and smiled. His finger nearly touched Conner's lips, too, and would have if Dan were two inches taller.

Conner responded with an embarrassed, quick, triple nod of his head.

The team moved out with Rigo in the lead, ten yards ahead; Dan behind and the others scattered back, five yards apart; and Conner sixty yards behind Rigo in the tail position. They left the clearing and entered the woods, where they walked out late last evening.

The moon had just set. The sun had yet to rise. The air was already sixty-seven degrees. Birds were singing the songs nature granted them. A small herd of deer silently moved into the clearing they just vacated. They began grazing just east of where the group slept. They, too, felt safe directly under the drooping, forever empty power lines the orange power cable support towers securely grasped.

Chapter Sixteen

While the team was entering the forest, Buck woke up. He was lying on the hardwood floor, flat on his back. His head rested on a stained, uncovered, blue-striped pillow, and a rough, prickly brown blanket was wrapped around his body. His filthy, scraggly hair was tied back, flopped over a corner of the pillow, keeping it away from his bandages.

The pre-dawn light seeped through the large picture window and into the examination room. It found his face and tickled his right retina. He had slept since midday. It was time to wake up.

He felt alert. He also felt helpless and that had to change fast. His body sent a cascade of signals to his brain telling him he was sore, hungry and thirsty. He needed a bathroom, too.

He managed to prop his body up on one elbow, grimacing slightly as his upper body bent. The door to his room was straight ahead about twelve feet away, near the far corner. A tall, black gun safe stood near the other corner against the wall. The large window was behind him. He propped his body on the other elbow.

Flushed with the small success, he moved into a seated position, legs splayed out, both hands on the floor behind him supporting his upper body weight. Yes, another victory! He wanted to test his chest wound before he tried to stand. He inhaled. Not too bad as long as he breathed shallow. Time to stand.

He pulled his feet inward, into a partial lotus position and raised his body perpendicular with the floor, back straight. Again, he inhaled. The pain was mild, manageable. He maneuvered into a kneeling position, balancing his body with his right hand braced flat against the wall, the wall that his pillow had rested against for so many hours. He held his left hand out as far as he could for balance. His final goal was the door through which he could find water, food, and most importantly, a bathroom. But first, he had to find out how badly he was hurt. He hadn't urinated since the day before. He realized he needed a bathroom immediately.

In the kneeling position he slowly turned ninety degrees to his right and faced the cool, white painted wall. He leaned forward slightly and allowed his hands to land flat on the wall, just under the wooden windowsill. The bottom of the wide window was just below his eyes. A few birds sang. Trees, their east sides softly illuminated by the soon-coming morning sun, gently appeared.

He paused, drew in a few deep breaths and rose. One hand after the other he grasped the windowsill, pulling while his feet and legs, one after another, shifted position until he was finally standing, legs unsteady. The palms of his hands gently pressed flat on the waist-high windowsill, and he gazed outside, southeast, toward the thousands of miles he had walked over the past two years. The sun had just risen on his first day at his destination, the Columbia River. It flowed just a mile north. Close enough. He smiled through the cuts on his face, one eye swollen closed, barely believing he had made it.

Chapter Seventeen

"Here they come!" said the lookout. He had been clinging halfway up the distant transmission tower watching for the scouts to return. The two men arrived just as the man in the tower jumped the last five feet, landing in the grass at the tower's base.

"They're all asleep, except the lookouts, four of 'em," one of the just-arrived men reported.

"Okay, then. Let's get moving," said another, their alpha, for now.

This band of thirty feral men had no intention of facing the well-armed dozen in combat. That would be suicidal. Their goal was food and, if they got lucky, more ammunition for their few rifles and handguns. They gathered their meager possessions into nearly empty backpacks and moved out, jogging north. Their carefully organized plan was to silently raid some of the outlying, less protected farmhouses. Their targets were the three isolated homes their scouts had been observing since yesterday.

Afterwards, they would all retreat east, hiding deep in the forest, then feast, rest, and wait a few nights before making another raid.

Experience had taught them the hard way that directly confronting a colony was costly in men and munitions. During their time on the move they had learned that quiet, simultaneous night raids on a few close-together farms provided the best prizes and the lowest risk.

When they drew near, less then a half-mile away, they paused to observe the farmhouses one final time before they attacked. They saw the foot patrol pass through the tidy rows of blueberries and had to pause a bit longer, melting low into the forest floor, waiting for the four-member patrol to pass. Most of the established communities they encountered were well patrolled, so this was not a surprise, nor was the earlier sighting of the well-armed dozen who were patrolling far from their community. They hid as the four-man patrol moved west, toward the river, dropped down a steep narrow footpath through a wooded slope, over a few fallen trees, and to the shore.

The pack alpha stood, smiled, and signaled with a raised hand, his index finger aiming forward, then jabbing three times in the direction of each of the farmhouses with the awaited signal, "Attack!"

It was not quite midnight when the thirty men rose at once and moved fast. They ran toward the homes, eager men, all of them excited knowing their hunger would soon be satisfied. They drew near like a tornado. All three farmhouses were in view, well lit under the rising full moon. Without a word they drew their bladed weapons, split into three groups: ten for each farmhouse, and moved in for the kill. No firearms would be used. As usual, it would be only silent knives.

They were now experts. The plan was to nail all three homes at once. Ten men would smash into each one at the same time, attacking each room, looting what could be quickly packed and carried. First, they had to find all the occupants and kill them before they could defend themselves. Next, load their packs with ammunition, knives, food, matches and anything useful they could find. In and out within a hundred breaths of air. Grab all the clothes and food they could easily carry. Load up all the knives and weapons, if any. Then disappear miles to the east. The three farms they chose were within a thousand feet of each other at the end of Rickert Road. One belonged to Scott Harger and his wife.

Their plan worked flawlessly. Two of the homes they attacked, including the Harger residence, were unoccupied. One had been vacant since the disaster and offered no bounty. The ten men raiding this home left empty handed, but split in half, running to help the other members of their pack raiding the other two homes.

Harger and his wife, Katie, had wisely decided to stay closer to the center of town at the home of their good friend, Vicki Luttrell, until they felt safer. The men swept through their home clearing out everything useful to them. They packed out most of their food, all of their kitchen knives, the case of blueberry wine, two gallons of blueberry wine, and a twenty-two-caliber revolver with five hundred rounds of ammunition. All of his work clothing was stuffed into pillowcases and carried away. Some in this feral pack were very skinny and undernourished, so a few pairs of her jeans, size five, were taken, too. Harger was left with the clothing and boots he was wearing, but Katie's clothing was otherwise untouched as was his last remaining bottle of precious black hair dye, which was the first thing he checked when he returned home the following morning.

The third farmhouse was occupied. Fred and Julia Ebi were sound asleep when the ferals silently swarmed through their unlocked back door. The family black farm cat sat in a nearby tree during the attack, watching from a safe distance.

Throats slit while they slept, they had no chance to offer resistance. The food in their home was stuffed into backpacks and taken. Fred's indestructible Carhartt work clothing was stuffed into a large duffle bag and pillaged. Although several hundred rounds of nine-millimeter were stolen, no firearms were found in the Ebi home. Their guns were in use, carried by their two sons, Andy and Rocky, both of whom were out on night patrol. They wouldn't return home until midmorning.

Chapter Eighteen

"They were here," Dan said. "But they didn't leave anything."

"Yup, I bet they don't have much to carry either," Bill replied. He had a worried expression on his face as he and the others surveyed the abandoned camp. "Just weapons."

"Look! Footprints. Heading north. Look at all of 'em. Through there," Corey said, as he pointed into the forest, in the direction of Corbett. "We missed 'em."

"I wonder how many there are … or were," Rigo said, squatting low near the many shallow indentations in the soft earth. "I bet there were at least twenty. Maybe twenty-five. All men, too. None of these footprints are small. Like, size eight and up. No kids either. This is one strange group. Warriors. Peligroso. On the move. I don't like this at all."

"Look. In the ashes. They left bones. These don't all look like dog bones," Kyle said, as he dug once more through the remains of their fire, this time using a short stick. "If Buck saw a dog being cooked, fine, I believe him, but there's more bones ... like a really big dog. Maybe a deer."

"This is no doubt the group we want, the ones who shot Buck. Eating dog. They're desperate," Bill said.

"Deer bones aren't like that. Their ribs aren't curved that much. I don't know. If they weren't busted up so much we could tell better. They went at the marrow inside, too. These people are really hungry. And there's lots of 'em. Anyhow, let's see where they went, let's follow their tracks," Dan replied to Bill.

"Yeah, you're right, let's find out where they went," Bill said.

"I bet they saw us, hid, waited until we left, then moved out. I bet they're migrating, like caribou," Corey said.

"If they saw us they know not to mess with us," Conner replied.

"Well, they know how to make bows and arrows – fire, too, and that's never a good sign," Blake joked.

"Okay, let's head back to town. Whoever these people are, we missed 'em. They're probably long gone by now. We should be able to get back in time to put in a few hours working," Dan said.

Chapter Nineteen

"Buck, what're you doing up at sunrise?" Chris Saunders smiled and asked, as he walked into the kitchen and filled a cold glass of water from the faucet.

Corbett was fortunate in one major respect. As long as the pipes didn't break or leak too much, water wasn't going to be a problem for them. The town's water supply was gravity fed, flowing off Larch Mountain to the east, and pumps weren't needed to keep it flowing. Toilets flushed. People could take cold showers, too. Or, they could turn on the faucet and get a glass of water any time they wanted.

"You have running water!"

"Yup, sure do. Just like the old days."

"May I have some water, please? I'm really thirsty. I think I slept nearly a full day."

"You sure slept a long time," replied Chris, as he filled a glass for Buck and handed it to him. "How long have you been standing here, in the kitchen? How long have you been up?"

Buck drank the water and placed the empty glass on the counter. "Just got up. Wasn't sure if I could even stand, took me awhile to get up, but I did. Went outside, had to whiz. Came back. I suppose I could have used your bathroom instead," Buck said, "but I didn't realize the water still worked. In fact, this is the first faucet with water I've seen since the big crash."

"Yeah, we're really lucky. Without the water, we couldn't live here ... well, at least most of us couldn't. We can irrigate crops, water vegetable gardens – we do it all because of the free water. Oh! If you want a warm shower, the hose is always full. The sun warms the hose and when you pour it on your head it's a warm shower. We all do it that way. A Chinese guy, Jimmy Lee, he lives not far from here. He showed us how."

"A warm shower? Man, I haven't had a warm shower in two years. Maybe I could wash these holes, maybe clean all the other cuts, too."

"Sure, the water warms fast in the sun, and the sun's rising right now. I'll set you up, show you how. It's easy."

"Hey, guys. How's the patient? And, why are you letting him walk around, Chris?" Denise said, as she poked her head in to find out who was talking in her kitchen.

"He lives," Chris said. "Good morning, dear."

"Yes, Good morning, Chris. Good morning, Buck."

"Buck, you really should be resting. At least for another week or so," Denise said.

"It really doesn't hurt too much. I was thinking of taking a warm hose shower in a while."

"It might be a good idea to rinse the wounds, then I'll wash the bandages and re-apply them. They're tied to your chest because we have no more tape, so don't remove them. Let me do it. In fact, let me wash the wounds so I can see how they're healing. But first, breakfast. You won't recover unless you're eating well," Denise said, as she surveyed Buck's body, head to toe. "From the way you look, I bet you haven't eaten well lately."

"Some. Lots of berries. I hid out in orchards a while, eating squirrels and fruit, some nuts, too. Plus, I had fresh fish, and I mean fresh. I would catch 'em barehanded, or jab 'em with a sharp stick, and eat it uncooked. I haven't had cooked fish or meat in a long time."

Buck didn't mention the countless buildings and vacant homes he had searched, room after room, cupboard by cupboard, rooting around, scrounging for a can of food, a package of seasonings, anything edible, as he made his way alone and on foot across the continent.

"Has anyone seen the guys who shot me?"

"A small group went out to find 'em last night. If anyone could find 'em, they will," Chris said, leaving out the important details, not yet fully trusting the outsider. "In fact, they should be back later today."

"I sure would like to talk to 'em. Just to get the facts, first hand, find out why they are like that. Anyhow, that was the very first time I was ever attacked. Well, I was attacked a few times, but I always either got away without getting hurt, or I won the fight. This is the first time I was shot and I don't like it. I wanna see the guys who shot me, find out why."

"You have no idea why they shot you, why they chased after you?" Denise asked.

"No. All I wanted was a small piece of cooked meat. Man, what they had cooking sure smelled good. Funny, their fire didn't smoke much. The only reason I found 'em was the smell. I was walking along the riverbank and there they were. I hadn't seen anyone in a long time and thought it might be interesting to talk to them, too."

"We haven't had anyone drop by in a long time. Right after the crash we were attacked by a few hundred. We killed 'em all, well, most of 'em. Since then we've had a few walk in now and then, but not for over a year," Denise replied.

"Ya don't see too many bands of men, well, long ago there were lots and lots of 'em. For the past year, well, I haven't seen a group since before winter. And a group this big! Man, was I ever happy to see 'em! People! I wanted to share stories with 'em, let 'em know how far I walked. See how Portland was. Wow. I really screwed up. I thought they were friendly. I should've known when I didn't see any women or children with 'em," Buck said.

"Listen, Buck. If you don't mind a shower with lukewarm water, we can get to it right now. It's almost seventy degrees already. Another hot one's comin', I'm sure. I really would like to see how you're healing up," Denise said.

"C'mon, Buck, let's get you ready. Let's get you cleaned up," Chris said, smiling, gesturing toward the back door.

"Okay, if you insist. I'll wring out my clothes at the same time. That'll be good enough. Ya know, my wounds are healing. It only hurts bad when I breathe."

"Your shirt's clean and dry," Denise said.

"Thanks!"

"Well, you're one lucky guy. The arrow was thin, and it missed all your good parts. Plus you slept a really long time. When Big Joe carried you here we thought you might die."

"I don't remember much. I do remember a dream, though. Or, more like a nightmare. Oh man, it's like it just happened moments ago. It was so real. Wanna hear about it?"

"Sure," Chris replied.

"We're in no hurry. Tell us about your dream. The messages they hold are very important," Denise said.

"Okay. Some pretty Indian lady with long hair was stabbing me in the chest with a rifle-cleaning rod, smiling the whole time. Then she poured hot water in the holes. I remember she said, "Everything will be just fine." She was drilling me in the chest, over and over again. In, out, in, out. Grinning at me. Pouring hot water. I remember she was grinning, smiling like crazy as she poured the hot water into the stab holes. I tried to scream, but couldn't. Then, there was this guy. Some monster of a guy, a big galoot, baldheaded, like some skinhead, sorta like the guy who carried me here, he was crushing me down, solid, like a ton of concrete. I couldn't move. Couldn't hardly breathe. It was crazy. Then, the big guy started crying. The more he crushed me, the harder he cried. Then, she stabbed me some more, then poured more hot water down the stab holes. Then, the more he cried, the more she stabbed and grinned. Then, the more she stabbed me the more he cried and the two of them kept the circle going:

crush, cry, stab, hot water, crush, cry, stab, hot water, over and over and over ... can you imagine people that sick in the head? It was a nightmare! Man, I hope I never see anyone like that insane bald guy in my dream. I'll run for my life. Anyhow, the Indian lady, she tried to stab me in the nose with a butter knife. Thankfully it ended just then, all of a sudden, like. Then I dreamed about horse riding. A pretty girl handed me the reins to a horse. It was nice. She told me to get on it and ride away. Then the horse turned into a dragon and I rode the dragon into the sky. Then I woke up. I can't remember any other dreams from last night."

"What a terrible, terrible dream, but at least it had a nice ending: a dragon ride! What fun." Denise said. "Anyhow, there are no mean, sick-in-the-head people like that bald man or the Indian lady here in Corbett, I promise you."

"Nope. No one like that here. We're all decent people here," Chris said, just as someone banged out a swift triple-tap knock on the front door. "I'll see who it is."

Chris went into the lobby, also known as the living room, and opened the front door.

"Hey, Chris, what's up?" Joe said, standing at the door in short jeans and a black tank-top t-shirt. "How's Buck doing?"

"Fine. C'mon in and see for yourself."

Chapter Twenty

By midmorning the response team had made its way to the edge of the Harger farm, the most outlying one in Corbett. They followed the ferals' footprints for a time, then they disappeared when they reached paved road. The team picked up the footprints again about two miles south of the Harger farm, then followed them straight to the farm.

"Hey! The Ebi boys are in a hurry, running like that. Like they're in a panic," Bill said to Don.

"Who knows? Maybe they're late for breakfast," Dan replied.

As they drew nearer, they saw the boys step out of the Harger house, walk across his wide front porch and pause at the top, near the edge of the front steps. They took two steps down and sat together on the top step, projecting an empty downward stare as the group approached.

"Hey, how did patrol go last night?" Dan asked as he approached the natural stained wooden steps.

"Mom and dad 'r dead. In bed. Been dead all night. Cut up. Our house is cleaned out. So's Harger's house. They hit both last night. We gotta find whoever did this," Rocky said, holding back tears more successfully than his younger brother Andy was.

"Blake, Conner, Kyle, Rigo, go now. Split into twos. Check all the nearby farms; see if any others got attacked last night. Run!" Dan said. "I want you guys to report back to Ebi's as soon as you can. Move!"

"Did the Hargers get away?" Dan asked.

"We just checked. No one's home," Rocky said. "They might've stayed at Vicki Luttrell's. They were nervous 'cause their house was on the edge of town. We were too, but for two years there's been nothing, nothing at all, no threats, now this. Everything's gone. The Harger's black lab's gone, too. She probably went with them."

Dan didn't even pause. "Rocky, you and your brother come with us. We better check out your farm, then plan a response. Tweedy, you and Corey check the perimeter, find their footprints and see where they went. What direction. Kevin, could you and Don get back to town? We better let the others know what we're planning. We're heading out to get them as soon as we can. Pat, you and Bill and Kelly, come with me. Let's give the Ebis a proper burial. Then we move out."

When the small group reached the Ebi home, they walked right up the steps and went inside. Rocky and his brother waited in the walkway, a few yards from the door.

"Wow!" Bill said. "Tore 'em to shreds."

"I feel like an idiot. While we slept under the power lines, these animals came right up here and did this," Dan said.

Corey and Tweedy arrived, winded somewhat from sprinting. They huffed a bit as they walked into the house. "Hey Dan, we got 'em," Corey said, breathing heavily. "Dozens of footprints heading east, clearer prints this time, like they were carrying heavy stuff."

"Good work, guys," Dan said.

"We can't let the Ebis stay in the house," Kelly said to Dan and Bill. "I suggest we bury 'em right now. It'll get hot soon and, I know it's tough, especially for their sons, but it's gotta be done now."

"I agree," said Dan.

"Me, too," said Bill.

"Everyone agree?" Bill asked.

Pat nodded his head. After a pause Dan said, "Okay. That's it, then. Kelly, could you and Pat break the news to the boys? And Bill, maybe you could find us a few shovels once the boys are onboard. It might take a moment or two. They'll need awhile to think, then to pick the place."

"Sounds like a plan. The others'll be returning soon so we better get a move on."

After sharing the plan with the Ebi sons and securing their approval, a common gravesite was selected and dirt was shoveled. Their cat was nowhere to be seen. Blake and Conner soon returned and reported no other attacks. The two of them went to Harger's, borrowed a few of his shovels, and helped with the digging. Soon, the hole was dug and it was time to lower the bodies.

Generally, Reverend Golphenee or one of a small handful of other local religious figures would officiate during a funeral but none of them were available for the Ebi's burial. Invitations weren't needed since word of mouth spread news throughout town with 4G speed. Among those present was Nanette Phelps, a well-respected member of the Mount Hood Christian Church. She officiated, reading a few appropriate Bible passages and sharing a brief summary of their lives.

A few kind words of remembrance, shared memories or notable achievements of the deceased would bring comfort and a sense of community to the family and friends of the deceased. It was important to the townspeople. A bonding of the survivors, a sense of oneness and purpose delivered through a short ceremony was now the norm and had grown into a town tradition since the disaster. In this, they were united.

Since the disaster, they had developed a sense of divine purpose, a common understanding that they were somehow selected for survival and that they must carry the torch of humanity, protect the message of good, so-to-speak, handing it to future generations. Corbett wasn't transforming into a religious colony, not even close. However, the message of the Ten Commandments, or that of the Five Precepts, as shared by the few Buddhist families in town, was taken seriously for the first time, for many. The understanding that everyone must live with nature, rather than take from nature, and to work for the benefit of all was becoming universal.

But today, there simply wasn't time for ceremony. The danger level was too great. A memorial service would come later, but the burial would be immediate. Only a handful of town defenders and dozens of people living nearby would be present.

The rest of the response team had by now arrived, too, bringing with them six more armed men and women. It was time to move out, but first they had to take care of the Ebis.

Word spread fast. Nearby friends and neighbors started arriving. Fifty-seven townspeople had gathered, including the dozen members of the first response team as well as the Ebi boys.

The service was brief. The sheets were removed, saved for later like everything else, and the bodies were lowered into their grave without coffins. The townspeople shared the chore of filling the grave and visited among themselves awhile, eventually drifting back to work. The militia members and a handful of townspeople remained behind, consoling the Ebi brothers and planning what to do next.

Chapter Twenty-One

"We can't just run after them, charging into the woods like a bunch of friggin' idiots. We have to somehow plan it right," Bill said in a low tone of voice as he stood away from the others, quietly talking to Dan.

"Yup," Dan replied, staring off to the east with his hands in his front pockets.

"We're dealing with pure evil, here, Dan. It scares the hell out of me."

"Yup."

"They could keep this up."

"Yup."

"One house at a time."

"Yup."

"One-by-one-by-one they could eat our whole town."

"Yup."

"People are moving out of the outlying farmhouses, staying with friends closer-in. Their homes are vacant. Easy pickin's for the maniacs."

"Yup."

"The whole town is countin' on us, me and you, to come up with a plan. Not the Chief, not the Reverend, not the town council, us. Quite a few are lookin' our way right now, watchin' us. This is something new for all of us, but it's our job to have a plan, like right now."

"Yup."

"Any ideas?"

"Nope."

"Me neither."

"What do we tell the others?"

"I dunno," Dan said, as he kicked a small rock across the field. It skittered about. Then he kicked another one.

Chapter Twenty-Two

Kevin Sakai and Don Mershon ran the entire three miles to the fire station where the Chief had his office. "They attacked a few farms last night. They killed the Ebis, too," Kevin said, hands on his knees, trying to catch his breath.

"Who did? Slow down. Tell me what you know," the Chief replied.

"We don't know who, exactly. It was the group that shot Buck, most likely. Took everything they could carry from Harger's and Ebi's house. The Ebis were home, sleeping. They were cut up really bad. Sliced apart. Killed. Probably went fast. We found their camp, where they had a fire near Camp Namanu. Probably the fire Buck saw. We stayed the night just east of there, under the transmission cables. We had lookouts up all night. No one saw anything. At around three in the morning the night watch thought they heard a man scream, a short, loud scream. It ended quick. But it came from far away, northeast of where we were. Maybe west of Larch Mountain, hard to tell. It might have been one of them."

"Where're Dan and the rest of his team now?"

"At Ebi's."

"Okay, you and Don take the bikes, head over, tell JP. Send him up here to the fire station. Get Golphenee too. We need to have a meeting, decide what to do next."

"JP knows. We stopped at the school and let him know. He's getting the other team ready, extra ammo, food, blankets, all that stuff," Don said.

"Good. On your way back get Harger. He may still be at Luttrell's. Get Kimberley, too. Ask 'em all to get here as soon as they can. Tell 'em an executive session town council meeting is starting as soon as they get here.

"We're on our way," Kevin said, as he and Don pushed the bikes into the driveway.

"Oh, one more thing, drop by the clinic. You might wanna let Denise and Chris know they should get the clinic ready to take in wounded. They'll need help. Tell 'em I'll ask Kimberley to send Eddie over."

Chapter Twenty-Three

Kevin and Don rode onto the clinic walkway and set the two bikes on their kickstands near the steps. They knocked on the closed screen door and Kevin shouted, "Denise! Hey Chris and Joe! It's us, Kevin Sakai and Don Mershon. Anyone here?"

"Hi, Kevin, Don, what's up?" Joe asked.

"Trouble. The guys who shot Buck killed the Ebis last night. Robbed their house and Harger's, too."

"I thought the first response team went out to get 'em yesterday. What happened?" Chris asked.

Kevin and Don told the story.

"What are you guys gonna do?" Chris asked, a bit out of the loop. He wanted to be on a response team. He asked JP several times, in fact, but couldn't make the teams because of his arm injury. His left arm still functioned, but caused him severe pain, at times. Plus, it couldn't carry much weight, and JP demanded the town's best for the teams. Since there were hundreds of men and women interested, he had the luxury of being a bit selective. That meant, because of the arm injury, Chris was out.

"I dunno yet," Kevin replied.

"You don't know?" Chris replied.

"Well, we're not gonna sit around and do nothing, that's for sure," Don said.

"Anyhow, we just stopped at the fire station and saw the Chief, filled him in on things. He said for us to tell you to get ready to take on wounded. Eddie Cho's gonna drop by and help. Oh, how's Buck doing?" Kevin asked.

"Showered up. All I need's a haircut and a shave!" Buck said, sticking his head out of the kitchen with a piece of deer jerky in his hand. "Maybe a dentist, too. Chewing this jerky isn't as easy as it used to be."

"We'll have Stan Bohnstedt take a peek at your teeth later," Denise said. "He's our town dentist."

Stan and Karen Bohnstedt arrived at the remains of the Stark Street Bridge a few weeks after the world fell apart two years earlier. They had survived the disaster locked in their well-hidden, partially underground home safe room, hidden from the carnage occurring on the streets in Gresham. Realizing it would be impossible to survive for long in what remained of their home, they packed his field dental kit and headed east to Corbett where they hoped to find safety. Corbett didn't have a dentist so they accepted him and his wife into their community with open arms.

"Is his clinic close by?" Buck asked.

"Yes, it is. It's just a few houses from the fire station, maybe a hundred yards from here. This is the main drag. They originally set up the dental clinic in a classroom at the school. For eight months they lived in it, too, but after the first winter lots of houses became available. So now, they work on teeth right from their home. He's cut out a few tonsils, too. The dentist and I work together on a lot of patients. We make do the best we can. So far, we've been very lucky," Denise said.

"Hi, you must be Buck. I'm Kevin, and that's Don."

"Nice to meet ya!"

"Oh man, we've heard parts of your story, second hand, of course. It'll be nice to hear it from you directly, but I bet you'll soon get tired of repeating it all the time," Don said.

"Oh, it's okay. I'll be telling it a bit differently each time I tell it," Buck jokingly replied.

"Heck, someone ought to run him over to see Rueben. Rueben will love the story of Buck's walk across the United States," Kevin said.

"You mean what was the United States. The ol' country is all gone," Buck corrected Kevin between bites. "What I walked across was the continent, or whatever it'll be called some day in the future."

"Yeah, it'll be hard not calling this land America anymore. We still call it that, here," Kevin said, as he and Don headed for the door. "Sometimes we call it the United States, too. Hey, nice to meet ya. We gotta get going."

"It'll be a tough habit to break, that's for sure. See you guys. Be careful," Denise said, as she poked her head in the living room. She had been working on a new recipe for converting birch bark into a pain reducer. She was boiling water on the outdoor oven, a few yards from the back door. Denise knew birch bark could be made into a traditional pain medication, but her ancestors' way of making it, as stated in one of her herbal medicine guides, wasn't working for her. She couldn't quite get it right, but eventually she would if she kept trying.

"I have a hunch you didn't talk to very many people on your walk. I bet you mostly avoided people, if they're anything like the ones who shot you and killed the Ebis," Joe said.

"Few. Anyhow, who's Rueben?" Buck asked no one in particular.

"He's our town barber, boot maker, sandal maker, face shaver, time keeper, salmon smoker, bow maker and story teller. His place isn't far, a short walk," Joe said.

"I could use a haircut," Buck said.

"Maybe he could set Buck up with some shoes in exchange for hearin' his story," Chris said to Denise, who just walked in from out back. Rueben always wanted something in exchange for his services and Buck had nothing to offer except his story. If Rueben could be first, that might be payment enough and he'd be mighty happy.

Buck stood there in his disgusting t-shirt and borrowed pants, unable to take a deep breath. "That'd be great! I haven't had a haircut in two years. Not since the one on base a few days before the crash. Guy could cut hair perfectly. Took him only three minutes, too."

"I'll walk him over right now," Joe said. "Man needs shoes. And that hair, like a Rastafarian. If Rueben isn't too busy, I'll see if I can talk him into stitching Buck up some moccasins. That salmon I brought him yesterday was good for two boot repairs, so maybe this'll count as the second repair."

"I'm going to ride back down to the Sandy while you're out and get our poles. I won't be gone long," Chris said.

"Thanks, Chris," Joe said.

"I wish I had some way to pay you all for your generosity," Buck said to everyone.

"Oh it's nothing," Joe said. "C'mon, let's go to Rueben's before he gets busy."

They walked outside, down the walkway, and turned right on the highway. "Joe, see all the grass and weeds growing in the road?"

"Yeah. We pull the trees and blackberries, but let the grass and weeds grow. There's no way to pull it all."

"Well, it's like that all across America. Some roads have small trees, like three feet tall already, growing out of them. In northern Arizona, ya can't see the road for miles 'cuz of the sand. Nature's taking it all back, fast," Buck said.

"I once heard nature always bats last," Joe said.

"Looks like she's winning."

"She won."

"Yeah. Quite a victory. Wanna hear something strange?"

"Sure," Joe replied, not quite certain what this skinny, scraggly-looking man had on his mind.

"I had a dream last night. It was vivid this morning, early, but now I can't remember much about it, but in the dream a guy just like you was trying to crush me. He was crying, too. Crazy, huh?"

"Yup, sounds crazy. Must've been the pain killer powder Denise gave you."

"Yeah. I have lots of stuff to ask you, you mind?" Buck asked.

"Sure, ask away."

"Well. When I was on the beach, I heard one of you say outsiders aren't allowed in. I'm an outsider. Why did you allow me into town?"

"Well, it's been a long time since any outsiders have shown up. At first we had lots of 'em. Thousands of 'em. They were swarming in here; we even had to blow up the bridges into town. Some were starving, some sick, some hurt, some were crazy, insane. All of 'em were turned away. Some were dangerous. A bunch of really dangerous men showed up a few weeks after the disaster. They attacked a man's farm. Then, they attacked the town. They didn't get far. We fought 'em. Killed nearly all of 'em on the beach where you washed up. I guess you could call that beach a special place, for us."

"Wow. The same beach. That's quite a coincidence."

"Maybe not too much. The river's wide there, shallow, moves slow. It was the best place for 'em to cross the river 'cuz the road's close by, too. Plus, it's a stretch of river-bank logs and all kinds of stuff wash up on, just like you did!" Joe joked.

"Okay, I get it. But here's the big question: You guys ever let anyone stay? I like everyone I've met here. This is a great town. If Portland's gone, then I gotta stay somewhere."

"Well, no. No one's been allowed in. See, we know only three thousand people can live here. If everyone was allowed in, there would have been tens of thousands, even more would have heard about it and swarmed in. Then everything we have, all our crops, all the farm animals, they all would have been eaten, used up in weeks. Then what? Then everyone starves to death. So we made the hard decision and closed the town to all outsiders. But after a month or two, hardly anyone tried to get in. That's when we figured out there must have been a huge die-off. Oh, a dentist wandered in. We let the dentist and his wife stay. We didn't have a dentist and we were damn glad they showed up."

"No dentist? I heard there's no doctor either. Why's that?"

"Well, we were unincorporated in the old days, Buck. No cops, no city government, nothing. No grocery stores, no malls, no doctors and no dentists. We're a rural farming community. That's all. Any time one of us needed a doctor or dentist he had to go to the city. We didn't even have a gas station or a store, 'cept for the little market and its one pump gas island. My dad liked the owners, for some reason, but most people around here didn't. They were a bit unsociable. They didn't survive long, by the way."

"What did they die from?"

"They couldn't adapt. Couldn't get along with people very well. All they knew was counting money and that's a skill we don't need. They died the first winter from malnutrition or starvation, like a bunch of others."

"Anyhow, it was mostly just tourists who stopped in there on their way to the gorge."

"Wow. This really is out in the sticks. No one was allowed in. Well, I gotta tell ya, that's the way it is everywhere."

"Oh, one family was let in. The Lees. They came in right before we stopped allowing anyone in. They have two daughters ..."

"Married?" Buck interrupted.

"One's engaged. One's single. Both pretty, too. Anyhow, they both fought like Spartan warriors. Brought their own rifles. You shudda seen 'em! One was shot, a Kevlar vest saved her. Chris, you've met him, he took a bullet in the arm. He's the one who told Alison she was shot, pointed out the tear in her shirt. His arm's still jacked up. Well, Alison, that's the older sister's name, the younger one's Kelly, anyhow, the bullet nailed her in the center of her chest, and she didn't miss a beat. She ran down a hill, bandaged Chris's arm, told him - ordered him, more like it - to keep fighting. Just like that. Pulled him to his feet and said, "Let's go! You can enjoy your pain later! Right now you gotta fight!" She flung his rifle on her back, then put Chris's Glock in his hand, and off they went chasing the bad guys. Oh yeah, Kelly, she works at the clinic. She's the engaged one, draggin' her feet about it, too. I don't think she'll go through with it. She's been hooked up with that Korean guy, Eddie Cho. Guy's kinda frail, not exactly a fighter. But, he's smart, hardworking and loyal. Maybe that's enough. Anyhow, right now she's out hunting the guys who shot you."

"I saw one Asian chick looking at you," Buck said, as his face brightened a notch. "Been a long time since a woman's looked at me like that."

"Whoa! You definitely don't wanna call 'em that. It'll get 'em mad. They'll kick your ass, both karate black belts. They practice all the time with a few others in town. One of the classrooms at the school is where they train. You don't wanna get them mad," Joe warned, with a smile.

"Oh, sorry about that. It's been awhile. I should work on my manners a bit," Buck said.

Joe laughed. "Oh, it's not that big of a deal if you say it friendly, like that. They're cool. We treat each of 'em like they're one of the guys, but they earned some respect and we give it to 'em."

"I'll remember that."

"You probably don't need it, but I'll give you some friendly advice. We don't insult women. A few years ago a teenage boy teased a girl on our farm. He called her fat and smacked her on the ass with a shovel. Hit her hard. She hit him in the back of his head with her shovel and they went at it on each other. The poor girl lost an eye. He took a shovel in the throat and died. We called it self defense, but no one ever teased her again."

"She stood up for herself! Sounds like my kind of woman!" Buck said.

While Buck and Joe headed over to Rueben's, Chris and Denise stayed home, boiling water, sterilizing old sheets, t-shirts and rags to be used as bandages. Wounded men and women could arrive at any time.

Chapter Twenty-Four

"Hey Rueben. You here?" Joe shouted, as they walked down the narrow concrete walkway toward the already wide-open front door.

"Be there in a second," Rueben called out from within his house.

"This is his shop? It's a house."

"It's both. You'll see. He does it all here. Guy's incredible. He can't get around too well, though. You'll see."

Rueben hobbled over to the door, sending a sharp rhythm of clunking sounds outside. "Hey, Joe." He paused a moment, tipped his head sideways and squinted, checking out the scraggly haired, skinny barefoot stranger in the stained grey t-shirt and deerskin pants standing alongside Joe. "I bet you're Buck."

"How'd you guess?" Joe said, laughing at Rueben's quizzical facial expression as much as his remark.

"C'mon in. Water, anyone?"

"Sure. Water would be fine," Buck answered. "I still can't get over the fact you guys have running water here."

"Thank gravity for that," Rueben said. "Oh, and Ed Rainier and his crew, they run the water district. Have forever. They do whatever it is they do to keep the big pipes maintained. They got a horse and a wagon, a few shovels, I suppose, too, and they keep at it."

"You're all pretty lucky," Buck said.

"Yup," Joe replied, while Rueben poured Buck a glass of water. Reuben tossed a scrap of something fleshy to a nondescript mongrel dog making him or herself comfortable on the kitchen floor. The dog snapped it up.

"Your water," Rueben said.

"Thanks."

"Dude, you ain't got any shoes. I'll fix that problem, if you like."

"Thanks!" Buck excitedly replied, then drank half the water in the glass.

"It's gonna cost you."

"Huh?" Buck said.

"Not you. You're a guest. I'm talkin' to Joe."

"Name your price."

"Help me out. You could do me a favor, speed things up. Could you take my scissors, see 'em on the table, by the television?"

"You mean these scissors?"

"Those."

"Cut that rat nest of his down to about one inch all over. Hack at that scraggly beard of his. Make it as short as you can, too. We're gonna turn him back into a human being, right now."

Buck's good eye bugged out, and his bad one cracked slightly open. "A shave, too?"

"Yup, just whack the hair all down to an inch all over. I'll trim it the rest of the way when his shoes are finished. Then a shave. Oh, let me measure his feet, first. And, Joe, could you cut his hair out in the street? No offense, Buck, but I don't want that hair of yours in my house," Rueben said as he pointed at Buck's hair while contorting his face into an expression of disgust.

"Can you make it two inches?" Buck asked.

"Okay, two," Joe replied.

"Oh man, I must look like a wreck."

"You ain't seen yourself yet?"

"No, haven't looked in a mirror in a long time."

"Seriously?"

"Seriously."

Rueben coughed out a barely audible sinister laugh. "C'mon over here with me. Let me show ya somethin' crazy: you."

Buck walked into the bathroom and faced the mirror. "WHAT THE ..."

"That's you, Buck. How old are you, anyhow?" Rueben asked.

"Twenty-eight. But I look fifty."

"Maybe closer to sixty. Okay, 'nuf of that. C'mon, let's knock a few decades off your age. Change you from a man-skank into a chick magnet in no time. First, let me look at your feet."

Buck stood still a moment staring at the one-eyed stranger in the mirror while Rueben studied his feet.

"Size ten, regular?"

"Yes."

"Okay, that's it. Go outside with Joe for a few minutes. I'll have something for you soon."

Rueben had pre-made around twenty pairs of deerskin moccasins in common sizes. He had them lined up in a neat row along the floor of his workshop. He reached over carefully with his cane and pierced a pair, one shoe at a time, flipping them each onto his workbench as he'd done hundreds of times before. "After a few minor fixes, these'll fit 'im perfectly," he said to himself. "Then we'll see about his hair, and a quick shave, too. Then, I wanna hear his story."

Chapter Twenty-Five

Rigo saw Dan and Bill talking and noticed the way Dan kicked the rock. The frustration and anger were clear. He walked over to them. "May I offer a suggestion?"

"Sure, Rigo. I'm ready to listen to anything at this point." Dan said.

"We might have more success against these men if we bring the fight to them with just a few of us. Too many of us are impossible to hide, no matter how quietly we walk."

"What exactly do you have in mind?"

"Just me and Kyle. I already talked about it with him. He's ready. You see, I bet we could sneak up on 'em, I mean get really close, like, smellin' their stink close, without them knowing. Then light 'em up."

"Tell us more," Bill said.

"Well, they were obviously nearby. They knew we were there the whole time."

"I agree," Dan said.

"My guess is they're now hiding out, not too far away, less than ten miles, maybe, enjoying some of the stuff they took," Rigo said.

"That scream the guards heard. That was them," Bill said.

"Yup. It was party time. Someone screamed, a few others probably shut him up quick," Rigo said.

"If we had known about the raids we could have gone after them. In hindsight, we should have anyhow. But we need to plan for the future, not kick ourselves for the past," Dan said, slowly moving out of his funk.

"I believe a smaller, well-armed group could do better," Rigo replied.

"But they're nomads, always on the move, so they might be moving on already," Bill suggested.

"Nope. They're feeding, getting their strength back. Remember they were eating dogs and who-knows-what-else," Dan said.

"I agree. They'll be back for more, at least once more for enough food to get 'em to the next place, wherever that might be," Bill said. "They might even keep hitting us if they think they can get away with it. I would if I was them."

Kyle walked up to the three men. He knew what they were discussing. It's all anyone was talking about at the moment. Interrupting, he blurted out his advice. "Guys, at a minimum, they're planning a few more hits, then they'll leave for good when it's too dangerous to stay. I suggest we make it too dangerous for 'em before they get another chance. I say we hit 'em right now. I say we leave immediately, follow those footprints. We're rested, ready, and they're expecting a large force."

"Yeah, let's give 'em a large force: me and Kyle," Rigo said.

"Are you crazy?" Bill asked.

"Maybe, just a little," Rigo replied, smiling slightly. "We, just the two of us, can sneak up on 'em. Really, check it out. If we get close, like fifteen, twenty yards away, and I know we can, we could light 'em all up, once and for all."

"Yeah, whack 'em all quick," Kyle said, getting a little excited, rising up on his toes. "It'll just take a few seconds. It'll work, too. We sneak up, pour a few hundred well-placed rounds into their camp, then walk through, check 'em close, one-by-one, slice, slice, slice, make sure they're all out. Then, we go home and tuck our loved ones into bed, safe and sound at last."

"Exactly. Then everyone sleeps good tonight," Rigo said.

"Bada-bing, bada-boom," Kyle replied with a big grin, as proud as a new papa.

"It's brilliant," Dan said. "But I suggest three go, Rigo."

"Three go, Rigo. Hey, that rhymes," Bill said, cracking a rare joke to break the tension.

"Cute, Bill. Anyhow, not two, three. That way two can carry one wounded, or maybe drag back a prisoner," Dan said.

"No prisoners," Bill said, then he repeated himself, in a soft voice. "No prisoners."

"Who's the third man?" Rigo asked.

"Me," Dan said.

Just then, a short, stocky old man with an untrimmed bush of white hair sticking into the sky as if he just received a fifty-thousand-volt jolt and a beard Santa would be jealous of walked up, carrying two packages snuggled close to his body as if they were newborn babies. The middle, ring and pinky fingers on his left hand were missing. He shuffled along with a decidedly rickety limp, placing his body weight on the outer sides of his feet like he'd been riding a mule for fifty years straight.

One of the two packages he clutched was wrapped in plain brown paper, about twice the size of an AK-47 thirty-round magazine. The other was wrapped in an old towel, but it was much larger. "Hey there fellers, I have a little somethin' you might be able to use against those animals."

"Hey Charlie, whaddya got there?" Dan asked.

Charlie was among a surprisingly large number of town oddballs, weirdoes and recluses. His particular claim to local fame was a beautiful collection of illegal military weapons and explosives, a collection that in the old days would have earned him a lifetime in federal prison if the authorities had discovered it.

Over the years an explosion would occasionally rock the western slope of Larch Mountain, sending its echo rumbling across the sleepy farm town and toward the Sandy River. People would shake their heads and say, "There goes ol' Charlie. He's at it again. Someday he'll blow the rest of his fingers off, or maybe his head." But no one ever notified the authorities. Snitching to the law on ol' Charlie was unthinkable. Doing that would have earned the tattler a lifetime of shunning or worse.

"Huh?" Charlie replied.

"He can talk, but he's stone deaf. Ya gotta write, or use hand signs when ya talk to him," Bill replied.

"Oh, that's right, I forgot," Dan said. He squatted and carved a one-foot-tall question mark in the dirt. Then he stood and pointed at the plain, paper-wrapped package.

"C-4." When Charlie said it, he was loud and spittle sprayed out.

Dan stepped a bit to the side, wiped off his shirt and pants, and pointed at the larger package, the one wrapped in the ancient stained towel.

"Dynamite." When Charlie blasted out the one word, saliva once again rained out. This time Dan dodged left, and it missed his pants and shirt.

"That's what I'm talkin' about!" Kyle excitedly said, as he actually jumped into the air like a cheerleader, flapping his arms in jumping-jack style, "I know how to use that stuff. We practiced with it in the Army all the time. I got awarded a nice certificate for not killing myself learning."

"Just keep what you don't use," Charlie said. "You guys should have your own supply. I won't be around forever, you know."

"Gee, I wonder why." Rigo jokingly asked.

"Huh?" Charlie relied.

"Nothing," Rigo said, much louder this time.

Rigo had never been close to high explosives in his entire life and warily moved back, unsure of Kyle's out of character excitement, and this wild-looking old man with his two crudely wrapped packages.

Kyle laughed at Rigo. "It's easy to use, bro, safe, too, unless ya screw up just once."

"I can imagine, homes. I saw the man's hand: lots of missing fingers. Some missing brains, too."

"Oh, stop. Leave it all to me. This'll really come in handy, make our job way easier. You'll see."

"Yup, way easier," replied Dan, as his stern, unhappy face slowly transformed, now sporting an excited grin matching the one on Kyle's face, but not quite as bright as the one Charlie was sporting.

"Response team! Get over here!" Dan shouted toward the crowd.

Bill smiled. The team members gathered around.

"May I?" Dan gently took the two packages from Charlie, held them high.

"Huh?"

"It's time to fight back!"

Chapter Twenty-Six

"Wow!" Denise said, as Joe and Buck walked up the path and onto the front porch of the clinic. "C'mon in, guys. Chris! Get over here! Check this out! You won't recognize Buck!"

They gathered. "Rueben did that to Buck? I hardly recognize him," Chris said, as he walked into the room circling Buck a few times, examining him from top to bottom. "And your eye, it isn't swollen shut anymore. It's just swollen. Purple, maybe a bluish purple. But your eye, I can see it."

"Yup, it works, too. It opened a crack while Rueben was shaving my neck with that blade of his."

"You let Rueben shave your neck?" Chris said, comically checking Buck's neck for cuts. "Do you have any idea how he sharpens that wicked blade of his?"

"No, didn't ask."

"He has this river rock, you see ..."

"New shoes, too," Buck said, nervously trying to change the subject away from the wicked-looking straight blade that made his swollen eye pop open. "And, he gave me a clean, black t-shirt. He said the one I was wearing stunk. He said he was going to burn it. I liked that shirt. Wore it for six months."

"Ha! He won't burn it. He has some secret ancient Roman way of bleaching clothes. He won't tell anyone what it is, but it sure works," Joe said.

"The Romans had bleach?" Buck asked.

I dunno. Anyhow, he took the payment out of our salmon, Chris," Joe said, through his big country smile. "The shoes, shirt, shave and the haircut."

"Figures. Rueben always gets his cut," Denise said with a smile.

"Yeah, no leg, and he'll be the last one standing," Joe said, and they all laughed, as footsteps clunked on the porch.

"Hey, Chief. Hey, Reverend Golphenee. Good morning!" Denise said. "Any news?"

"Still waiting for more news. Wow! It's hard to believe it's really him!" Scott said, walking around Buck, staring at his hair and face.

"Holy Toledo. What happened?" the Chief asked.

"Rueben went at him," Joe said. "Nice, huh?"

"Hardly recognize him. Your eye is better, too. Can you actually see out of it?" Scott asked.

"Yup, ain't blurry either. My eyes are twenty-twenty, or at least they were last time I had 'em checked," Buck replied, as he munched on dried salmon. He'd been drinking tons of water and munching on salmon, vegetables, berries and dandelion leaves since he got up.

"Well, nice to see you're healing up so fast. Appetite's back, too, I see," Scott said.

"Well, we dropped by to see you, Buck, maybe ask you a few questions, if you don't mind," Scott said.

"Ask away," Buck said.

"Okay, well, I'm not sure where to start," Scott said, "so, I'll try to explain. You see, I'm the minister of the church across the highway, the Mount Hood Christian Church. Well, um, lots of people come to me in times like these. They're frightened. Some are sayin' the ones who attacked you, the ones who tore through those three farmhouses, are demons."

"Demons? Those scumbags?" Buck replied, as his swollen eye opened a few more millimeters.

"Well, let me explain further. You see, there's a sense in this town that, for whatever reason, the survivors believe they've made it this far due to some kind of divine, holy plan, as if they've been chosen by Him. There might be a grain of truth to it, too. I don't believe it's a coincidence, either."

"Him?"

"Yes, Him."

"I understand that, for sure. Millions of dead, billions, probably, and we have a few nice friendly colonies here and there scattered around the world. Y'all've kept this town running almost like before. I've seen a few places, but there aren't that many, let me tell ya, and few I saw are as nice as this," Buck said.

"Well, yeah. But we've lost about a thousand people over the past two years. Some old age, some ran out of medicine, a few let their sadness take over. We also had a couple of dozen go psycho on us, didn't hurt anyone, fortunately. About a quarter of the babies born don't make it, a few moms, too, which is something we're not used to. None of it is. It hasn't been easy. Anyhow, to get back on track, I need to ask you about the ones who attacked you since you're the only one who's seen 'em."

"Okay, but I can't say anything special about 'em, 'cept they're skinny, ratty-lookin' pukes. If the enemy of Him was gonna send a crew out to nail this town, he'd do better than that bunch. They're chicken-crap murdering scumbags. These half-dead pieces of ... pardon my swearing, Reverend. I usually don't cuss."

"It's fine, son. I've had worse words than that briefly cross my mind since this latest episode started. Anyhow, so what you're sayin' is I can tell my congregation that you didn't see anything about them that would lead anyone to think ..."

"They ain't demons, Reverend," Buck interrupted. "No way. I remember reading that 'thief in the night' stuff, too. The 'thief in the night' in Revelations ain't the kind that'll die from an AK bullet. These filthy pieces of garbage are. No, these men are evil, through and through, no doubt about it, but they're not demons."

"I appreciate hearing your opinion, Buck," Scott said. "Thank you. I'll share it with those who come to me for comfort."

"Hey, I understand you asking. It can make anyone nervous."

"We're all nervous, Buck."

"Well now, there's still room for optimism. For example, you certainly look much better than you did yesterday," the Chief said, looking at Buck with a sincere smile.

"I slept from the time I got here yesterday 'til this morning, before sun up. I'm feelin' healthier all the time. Denise and Chris keep stuffing dried fish and fruit juice down my throat. My arrow holes are healing, no infection so far. Plus, new pants from Chris, and this is what Rueben got me!" Buck said, pointing proudly at his new shoes and t-shirt. "But it's still tough to breathe hard."

"Not quite ready to go jogging?" Joe asked.

"Not today, I don't think so, but I did plenty of running in the past, moving fast at night through some parts of the country. But, yeah, if I bumped into these guys today, I couldn't run away the way I feel right now. Just give me a few days, you'll see."

"Well, you're in good hands here. Thanks again, Buck," the Chief said. "We're gonna get 'em. The town'll be safe again soon."

"I'd like to get a piece of 'em myself, if it's okay with the town," Buck said. "I can shoot. I was in the army for years. I've learned to get really close to people without them knowin' it, too."

"You didn't get too close to them," Scott said.

"That was different. I walked right up to 'em all and said hello. That was a mistake. Only done that a few times, only when I was really hungry. This's the first time I was shot at with arrows, first time I was chased out at all like that."

"Well, if you're healthy enough to walk, maybe you can help out. Everyone here contributes."

"That'd be great! Thanks!"

"Joe, since Buck's walking, maybe you could take him to the school. Ask JP. See if he can find something for him to do, unless he's left already."

"Okay, we'll go over there right now. I heard from Rueben he's still practicing with the second team," Joe said.

"Okay, we've got work to do. We've gotta head over to the Ebi farm, meet with Dan and Bill, and the Ebi boys," Scott said, still hesitant to mention the response teams in the presence of the outsider. "I'm going to try to make it to the burial, but I'm probably gonna be late. In times like these, especially in the summer, we bury the dead without delay."

The Chief and Scott didn't know it, but the funeral would be over and the first response team would be long gone by the time they made it to the Ebis. Only their two sons would be there.

Chapter Twenty-Seven

Don and Kevin rode to the Ebi farm on their borrowed bikes, arriving just as Dan started outlining the plan to the response team.

"Okay, then, it's all set. Each group understands what they're gonna do, right?" Dan said.

Rigo and Kyle nodded.

Kelly, Kevin and Bill nodded.

Tweedy, Corey and Don nodded.

Pat, Blake and Conner nodded.

Charlie smiled, too, and before he started walking home, he said to the group, "See y'all later! If ya don't wanna keep the leftover explosives, bring what's left back to my house. I don't have that much left."

"What'd you say?" Kyle asked.

"Huh?" Charlie said.

"We'll just bring you back whatever's left," Dan shouted.

Dan, Rigo and Kyle moved out, travelling light, following the footsteps made by the feral men, or simply "the ferals," as they were now called. The footprints of the thirty ferals were easy for them to follow.

In addition to their handguns, with spare magazines for each, they carried eight thirty-round magazines for their AR-15s. Kyle and Rigo each carried a solid self-defense knife and Dan, as usual, carried four knives stashed here and there, in and on his clothing. Rigo wore a daypack filled with the explosives so Kyle could quickly access the C-4, the dynamite and the assorted items needed to make them explode.

Each of them, except Rigo, who was overloaded with explosives, weapons and related paraphernalia, also carried two old and yellowed one-liter water bottles, each topped off. These precious plastic bottles were never crunched or tossed. People kept them in the shade, too, so they'd last longer. Plus, most carried a replenished pocketful of deer jerky and a string-tied deerskin pouch filled with dried nuts and berries, each of which Alison Lee estimated contained over two thousand calories.

The others followed behind in groups of three. Bill's group was to follow a parallel line a few hundred yards north of Dan's group. Tweedy's group would follow the footprints, but a quarter mile behind Dan's group, a two-minute run, at most. Pat's group would also follow a straight line, but a few hundred yards to the south. The idea was for the groups to form a quarter-mile-wide triangle, sweeping east through the forest following the footprints. The groups to the north and south would keep in constant sight of Dan's group, moving closer together if the woods thickened. At least that was the plan, until the south group got disoriented after stumbling into an impenetrable field of thick blackberry bushes and, later, slowed by a steep cliff.

The primary assignment for the other groups was simple: move in fast and hard in case the ferals slipped past the leading group or be prepared to kill them all in the unfortunate event that the first group of three entered Valhalla after earning the sacred silver medal.

The trailing three groups expected hundreds of gunshots and a series of explosions. Then silence for a time followed by an occasional gunshot as the few fleeing survivors were hunted down one by one. The signal they had agreed upon to let the others know they had found their prey was simple: lots of gunfire and explosions.

Tweedy, Corey and Don stood a short distance apart from the others, checking their gear one more time. "Corey, whadda we do if we never hear any shooting?" Tweedy asked.

"Listen, bro. It's impossible to make a perfect plan. We all know that. But we can't just sit here and mope," Corey replied.

"I mean, look, everyone in town expects us to do something. Plus, they're right. We gotta stop 'em. It's up to us."

"Yeah, you're right buddy, but still, we'll be right behind 'em, Dan, Kyle and Rigo. If we walk all night long and hear nothing …"

"If we all walk together, all twelve of us in a mob, we'll create a wake, like a boat through the forest, no matter how quiet we try to walk. We'll awaken the woods like we were tossing firecrackers while we walk. No, this is the only way. Small, quiet groups. Far enough apart to keep the noise down, but close enough to join the fight," Corey said, as he gave his American Lawman knife a few close, loving caresses.

That knife saved his life two years earlier when he was grabbed from behind and choked by an attacker. Corey had grabbed his knife, stabbed the man in the leg, dropped low, twisted his body around and driven the knife into the attacker's throat.

"Well, we need some kind of signal, something to alert us in case of trouble," Don said.

"HA! The signal will be a thousand bullets flyin'," Tweedy replied.

"Oh, yes, but of course," Don said, raising his forefinger in front of his face like a university professor emphasizing an obscure point.

"And if we never hear it?" Tweedy asked.

"Simple, my man," Corey said, immediately wishing he had used a different term of endearment.

Don looked at him, then over at Tweedy, then back to Corey offering each a strange expression as he tilted his head a bit sideways. "My man?"

"C'mon, Don. Be nice," Tweedy said.

"Ahem, well, what I mean is, if we don't hear nothin', then either we ain't found 'em or Dan and Kyle and Rigo are down in the dirt filled with arrows. I hope it's okay with you two, cuz that's all the plan we got."

By midafternoon they were a mile into the forest, heading east toward the previous night's scream.

Chapter Twenty-Eight

"Buck, nice to meet you. What's your real name?" JP asked.

"Michael Baccellieri."

"What?" JP replied.

"Bah-chel-lee-air-ree."

"I can't pronounce that."

"I know, I know. No one can. Just call me Buck. It's way easier."

"Okay, Buck. So, what brings you to see me?"

"I wanna join your crew. I would like to do my part, help nail the guys who killed the Ebis."

"They're saying you've been shot by 'em, too."

"Yup. An arrow. Two days ago. It's healing fast, though."

"I heard you got shot in the head, too. Can you think straight?" JP said, joking with Buck.

"Yeah, my eye was swollen shut, but it's open now and Denise says there's no sign of concussion."

"Outstanding. Can you do many push-ups?"

"I don't know. Haven't tried lately."

"Ya gotta do fifty to be on a response team. Run ten kilometers in full gear, too. Lookin' at ya, I doubt you're ready. I can assign you to a patrol, maybe a static patrol. If you wanna try that until you're all better, we could use more eyes out on the town perimeter. It's easy duty. All ya do is stay at one place. If you see or hear anything, send someone back to report it to me."

"I don't care. Anything I can do. I was in the army for six years and I can handle pretty much any weapon. And I'm pretty decent at hiding in the woods for a long time, too."

"Okay, no patrolling for you. A fixed post would be better until you're healed all the way."

"I'm healing fast with this great food you guys have here. It's the best I've eaten in ages. Everyone's been great to me. I wanna do whatever I can."

"Okay, go to the church. Joe'll walk you there. Tell Mary Lou that I said it's okay with me if you help on a static patrol. We're gettin' as many as we can doin' this. You'll probably be night shift, somewhere on the east side of town. The west side's all covered, that's late afternoon to sun up, but we don't tell time here anymore. Just stay out 'til your relief shows up. Joe'll tell ya what happens if ya fall asleep on duty. We don't shoot ya. To save ammo we drown ya instead, okay?"

"Just like in the army. I get it."

"What about you, Joe? You wanna try a static patrol? I know you aren't much for running these days, but we sure could use you on the east side, someone who knows the area well, like you. Maybe you could team up with Buck since you know him. It'll be easier. That way someone else don't have to get acquainted with him."

"Sure, I'll take Buck out at dinnertime. We'll let Mary Lou know right now."

"Hey, Joe, come here. Excuse us, Buck. I need to ask Joe something."

JP walked with Joe, about twenty yards from Buck and shot the big question at him. "Can we trust this new guy, this outsider? He's kinda strange."

"Well, I heard his story twice. Says he's from Portland, knows the area. I heard him tell his story just after he was brought in and once more at Rueben's. It was the same each time and sounded believable. My opinion is he's telling us the truth. I know, I know, at first we thought he might be one of that pack, the ferals. But after hanging out with him, no way. The guy's really not strange at all, just a normal, good, honorable guy. He's hurting more than he's letting on. That arrow went right through him and he's walking around like it's nothin' at all. Yeah, I believe we can trust him."

"What about Chris? Will he be okay with Denise? I mean, if we start getting wounded, she'll need help." JP said, as he glanced over at Buck's face twisting in agony as he tried doing a few partial push-ups in the tall grass while waiting. "Joe, look at that knucklehead."

Joe looked toward Buck and smiled. "Eddie's gonna help. He'll have a problem shooting at people and would rather work at the clinic anyhow, be closer to Kelly."

"Okay, no problem with that. It happened last time, too, with a few. We'll always find something else for them to do. But when we get a threat like this, everyone drops what they're doing and helps out somehow. Corbett does have a draft, and it's universal."

"Yup, good thing, too. Makes everyone feel like they're doing their part," Joe said, glancing at Buck as he stood up and began slowly jogging around the old soccer field. "After talkin' to Mary Lou, I'm gonna go drop by the Lees, see how they're doing. Let 'em know we're on full alert, too."

"Sounds good. But Jimmy's over sixty. Sixty-four, if I remember correctly. Patrol is optional for him, 'specially since his name is chiseled next to yours on that monument. But let him know he can do whatever he wants. Deborah, too, but it might be best if they stay out of the fun, just supervise the kids on their farm or at the berry farm, if that's where they're working now," JP said.

"People are gonna get tired, patrolling all day or all night, then working on farms all morning or afternoon."

"Just like last time, two years ago. Tough. It's damn fortunate for all of us we kept the watch going like we did back then. We all patrolled twelve hours each day, day and night for two weeks before the big attack and no one died from lack of sleep. No, Joe, if there ever was a time to sacrifice some sleep for a little while, this is it. If you hear anyone whining, light 'em up good for me, okay? Remind 'em of the Ebis, Nelson, Houston and Pritchard, the three who were killed that day. And if that don't work, just give 'em a bit of that mean glare of yours."

Joe smiled. "Be happy to. It's mean and ugly, but not as ugly as that grey Cardinals hoodie you've been wearing since I was ten."

"I bet you'd be happy to scare someone with that glare of yours. And, what's wrong with this sweatshirt, anyhow? Why do people keep askin' me about it?"

Joe's smile disappeared and his serious face took over, "Your sweatshirt is nasty-lookin', JP, an' stained. Look at it in the mirror," Joe said, as JP's face started to frown, playfully.

"I'm just screwin' with ya. When people come lookin' for you, they look through the fog and rain for that beautiful hoodie. That old grey hoodie is a part of you. Never lose it."

"I don't intend to."

"Hey, JP, do we have enough people out on patrol?"

"No, Joe. We're spread pretty thin. As much as I'd prefer you stay at the clinic, we need everyone out. We have something over four hundred armed men and women scheduled on patrol. That's two hundred at a time on duty. We have thirty of 'em here in town, including the second team and they're out of shape, a bit. Some can't run ten kilometers. A few can't even do the fifty push-ups. I'm trying to hammer 'em into shape, like right now."

"You gonna send the second response team out?"

"No. They're gonna be held back, just in case. It'll give me time to whip 'em into shape in case they're needed to protect the clinic and the town armory," JP said, as Buck jogged by. JP gazed across the field at him from beneath his fresh grey crew cut.

"He's running," Joe said.

"Yup. Anyhow," JP continued, "with static patrols at the Vista House, and along the bluff, and more patrolling the Sandy, plus armed groups at a few outlying farmhouses, that leaves us only around one hundred and fifty patrolling the perimeter at any given time. Most patrol groups are six or more. We have sixteen miles of east, west and south borders. It's heavily wooded. Understand? There are constantly huge sections left wide open. These guys could slither through anywhere and do it easily. Go home after you see Mary Lou. Get you an' Buck each a decent rifle. Borrow one from the Lees if you prefer an AK. And get him a good knife, in case things get close and personal. In the woods, expect the very worst, Joe. Be careful. Stash your bikes somewhere safe. Go get help if things get ugly. There's no need to be the hero. You already did that once. Your main mission with Buck is observe and report. Not killing. There are thirty or more of them. Only two of you, and you two aren't in the best shape."

"Okay, sure, no heroics."

"Joe?"

"Yeah?"

"This town needs you. You're one of the solid rocks of this town. Don't get hurt."

Joe started to tear up, as usual. "Sure, JP. We won't take 'em on alone. Don't worry."

Chapter Twenty-Nine

"Hey, Mary Lou!" Joe said, as he and Buck walked into the church lobby.

Starting yesterday afternoon, Mary Lou was in charge of the draft. The subject of town defense came up at every monthly town meeting. The townspeople rarely agreed on anything, but on this one single issue everyone was in agreement: when there's an attack, everyone in town either fights or helps the fighters. Period.

She kept count on who patrolled where and what shifts they worked. Right after the disaster, she and JP were responsible for assigning people to farms where they could tend crops in exchange for three meals. Sometimes two, when food was scarce. Switching from television to farming was a tough transition for many, but with her kind mannerisms and infectious mile-away smile that brightened Corbett's darkest days, everyone knew and trusted her. For many years she was the secretary at the school, which made her the very center of the small farming community. The principal thought he ran the school. He was wrong: she did. The people of Corbett were used to doing whatever she said, and she never steered anyone wrong.

"So this is Buck?" Mary Lou asked.

"Yup, I'm Buck. JP sent me over here to sign up for a static patrol."

"Well, we can certainly use all the help we can get. Joe, you going with him?"

"Well, JP suggested it. Buck says he's good in the woods, and I'll stick close in case his wounds act up."

"Okay. You two be at the end of Donahue Road late this afternoon. It's paved now, but a long ways out, so leave early. No one lives out there, so all you'll do is observe and report. There's only two of you so don't lose a war out in the middle of nowhere, guys, Understand?"

"I understand. No fighting. Just observe and report."

"You're the first ones doing an overnight shift. Right now, go see Mr. Ng. He's out back. Take two of the town bikes. We have four men out there now, but when you get there, if you find them, they'll leave and head over to some farmhouses. You two replace them. It's six miles from here, so you'll need to take bikes, especially with the way you're walking these days. And you, Buck. That eye. Well, I'll be out shortly to see which ones you guys took, and make a note of it."

"Okay, thanks," Joe said. He and Buck then walked out the front door and around the church worship hall.

The church was across the highway from the school, on the north side of the highway. It served as a sort of command post, city hall and, because it had a sprawling paved parking lot, a general assembly site. It also had dozens of bicycles available for anyone to borrow, bicycles acquired after the collapse from the garages and back yards of those who never made it back after the collapse or who passed away soon after. Mary Lou helped Mr. Ng monitor who had taken what bicycle when and heaven help anyone who didn't return the bike on time.

A long-retired church member, Ng Ling Cheow, squatted on his heels, greasy fingers busily wrenching away at the rear wheel hub of a red Trek 7000 hybrid bicycle partially disassembled alongside the shady north side of the main building. With the exception of Mary Lou and a few others, everyone called him by his full name. He took it upon himself to serve as the town bicycle repairman. An ever-smiling Chinese immigrant who came to the United States from Shantou, after a brief stay in Singapore, his calm and peaceful demeanor was contagious. Although he could repair a bicycle in moments, people would extend their visits simply to be near him longer. Some would even drop by to have their brakes adjusted, when they really worked just fine. They would tell their family, "I'm gonna get my brakes adjusted." That meant they wanted to visit awhile with Ng Ling Cheow.

With a pocketful of small tools he could repair or adjust anything short of a cracked frame. Although that problem had yet to occur, between Alison, Pete Roth and Ng Ling Cheow, they could probably figure out a simple fix for that, too. In no time at all Ng Ling Cheow could precisely fit and install the recycled, reheated and reformed automobile tire strips that Alison Lee and Pete Roth developed as bicycle tire replacements. This ingenious tire replacement invention extended the life expectancy of the town's fleet of bicycles by decades, though the ride would never be as swift or as comfortable as it had been.

"Ni hao ma, Ng Ling Cheow," Joe said, offering a respectful greeting to the elderly man in one of the few simple Mandarin phrases he knew while Buck stared at him incredulously.

"Han how, han how," Ng Ling Cheow replied in his usual contemplative manner, letting Joe know with his eyes as well as with his words that he was doing well. He slowly shifted his gaze from Joe over to Buck. "Is this Mr. Buck?"

"Yes, this is Buck. His real name is ..."

"Pleased to meet you, sir. My name is Buck. How do you pronounce your name, sir?" Buck interrupted Joe, kindly saving him the embarrassment of mispronouncing his name.

"Ng, Ling Cheow," replied the man, as he stood, the top of his head level with Buck's chin.

Buck repeated his name. "Ng Ling Cheow, Ng Ling Cheow. That's easy to remember."

"Hey, you have a problem getting air. Your breathing's not very good. It's too shallow. You're not healed properly. You need rest."

"It's getting better fast. My eyes are better now and I can jog slow. As long as I don't breathe hard I'm fine."

"Drink blackberry leaf tea and lots of water. Go see the Lees, they always have some. Drink a liter."

"We're heading there next," Joe said. "I'll make sure he drinks plenty of their blackberry tea. It cures everything!"

"Blackberry tea? Never heard of it," Buck said.

"Oh man, it's like a magic drink. Cures anything, especially wet wounds."

"Yes, we had this in China, too. If you're hurt, drink this tea. We put the leaves right on a clean open wound, too."

"I'll make sure he does. Anyhow, Mary Lou said you might have a couple bikes we could borrow until tomorrow afternoon. We're heading out to patrol east, way out east at the end of Donahue Road," Joe said.

"Can do," replied Ng Ling Cheow, "I have many. Pick two. Please, you're soldiers now, pick any one you like. No, wait. Buck, you can't ride and carry a rifle. Take this bike. It has a deerskin rifle rack. Just made it. You can ride one handed without the rifle touching your back."

"Thank you, sir," Buck said, and he sat on it, gripping the right handlebar.

Joe walked between the two rows of bikes neatly lined up on their kickstands. He tried out a few, finally sitting on one. He leaned forward, feet flat on the pavement. Buck did the same with his, following Joe's lead.

"I like this one. Buck, you okay with that one?"

"Yup. This one's fine."

They grinned at each other, making silly vroom, vroom, vrooms, then busted out laughing. Ng Ling Cheow joined in making the same vroom, but with a decidedly Chinese accent, the "r" oddly emphasized. Joe looked over at Ng Ling Cheow and laughed so hard he slipped off his bike, landing on his rear end, knocking over a few of the bikes next to him.

"We'll borrow these, if it's okay," Joe said, still giggling like a schoolgirl while looking up at Ng Ling Cheow.

"Sure, no problem. Just come back after your patrol. If you need these bikes longer, you gotta let Mary Lou know. Go see her now, let her know."

"Nice meeting you, sir," Buck said.

Mary Lou walked outside and stood near the three men with her shining, straight yellow hair blowing across her smiling face in the early morning breeze.

"What's so funny?" Mary Lou asked. "Joe, why are you on the ground, laughing? Mr. Ng, did you tell these two men one of your crazy Chinese jokes?"

"No, not me," Ng Ling Cheow said, shaking his head side-to-side with his palms crossed over his chest, wearing an innocent expression as he faced toward the ground near her feet. Then he smiled, pointing accusatorily down at Joe as he struggled to get back on his feet. "It was Joe. He's to blame."

"Who, me?" Joe playfully asked.

"Yeah, you. Every time you visit I get blamed for making you laugh so hard you get a headache or your stomach hurts," Ng Ling Cheow said, smiling at his buddy.

"Well, Joe always gets blamed," Mary Lou said, looking at Joe as one would stare down a misbehaving kindergartener, shaking her head with her fists positioned squarely on her hips. "And there's a good reason for that! You're always there when things get out of hand! Anyhow, you two guys be careful."

"Yeah, you and Joe don't get hurt. That would make me very sad, make everyone very sad," Ng Ling Cheow said, as he resumed his squatting position next to the partially disassembled wheel.

"Okay, Ng Ling Cheow, nice to see you!" Joe said.

"Nice to see you, too, as always."

"Nice to meet you, Ng Ling Cheow," Buck said.

Buck smiled at Ng Ling Cheow, then turned to Mary Lou. "Nice to meet you, too, Mary Lou," Buck said, as he and Joe prepared to ride away on the bikes.

"Well, I must say you don't appear quite as badly hurt as everyone's saying," Mary Lou said.

"Wanna see his arrow holes?" Joe said, offering her his trademark, extra-wide country smile.

"No, no thank you. You two just be careful with the bikes. If you wreck 'em or don't have 'em back by tomorrow afternoon Ed'll shut your water off. And don't get yourselves hurt out there. If you see anyone, just ride back here and tell JP right away."

"Okay, we will. Thanks! See ya!" Joe said as he and Buck headed away from the front of the church waving back.

"I'm really wobbly on this bike, haven't ridden since forever. Hey, will she really shut your water off if I wreck this bike?" Buck said to Joe, as they were part way through the parking lot.

"You bet I will!" Mary Lou shouted, once again demonstrating her uncanny ability to stay in the loop on everything by listening in on far away conversations.

Buck and Joe smiled, waving back at her.

"Her husband, Ed, he keeps the water on. If she says she can do something, she can. That's why she's in charge of all the important stuff," Joe said as they slowly pedaled down the highway.

Chapter Thirty

The two men peddled the borrowed bikes down the Lee family driveway and set the kickstands near the front porch.

"They're probably in the garden, well, it's actually more like a small farm. They waste nothing, and I do mean nothing. Remember the stories about night soil?" Joe asked.

"Uh, yeah. I remember reading about it in high school. People in ancient times would recycle human waste in the fields to get close to a natural balance. The nutrients from the crops they took from the ground would almost equal what was put back in and all that. This was before chemical fertilizers. It was so nutrients wouldn't be lost. The ultimate recycling, one could say."

"Well, the ultimate recycling is the way we bury the dead: in the orchards, near the edge of the farthest branches. No more six feet down, either. Now, it's closer to three feet, and no casket. No clothes, either, 'cept a little, uh, something to make 'em decent, respectful. Can't buy any more clothes so we don't waste anything."

"Damn, you guys think of everything, don't ya?"

"Not everything, we're learning more all the time."

"It's like living in medieval times, again, right?"

"Well, we're permanently back in those times again. No more fertilizer. But we had some help. There's an organic farm up river on the northwest side of town called Dancing Roots. Bryan and Shari, they're the owners, they never used chemical fertilizers even before the crash. They taught us how to do it that way everywhere. Actually it was Deborah Lee, you'll meet her shortly. Anyhow, she and her daughter, Alison, calculated that the soil was still being depleted and we had to find a way to keep potassium and other nutrients in the soil or the crops would eventually fail. Guess what that would mean for us?"

"No food?"

"Yup. But, we couldn't let that happen so we found a source of rich free fertilizer," Joe said.

"Night soil?"

"Yup."

"Yikes."

"Ya get used to it. Get used to almost anything if ya have to. What was the alternative?" Joe asked, rhetorically.

"I bet it was tough getting everyone on board with that plan."

"Still is, but in time pretty much everyone will do it that way. Ed, the water guy, thank goodness he's on board. A long time ago we had a town meeting to discuss it all. The meeting almost broke into a brawl when someone wanted to make using night soil a law with a banishment penalty. It was crazy, but the vote, we follow the majority around here, was no more flushing it all away, but it's voluntary. The better vegetables from those who do will send 'em a strong enough message. We still got running water, so the septic tanks are still there for sanitation and those who don't want to participate. The human fertilizer is mostly saved now, mixed into compost then into the soil. I've been studying this lately. Did you know urine is eighteen percent nitrogen, two percent phosphorous and five percent potassium? Plants can't grow without them and we can't afford to flush it away. Some people just put it into the soil directly. If you want, maybe later I'll try to explain it all."

"No thanks. I get the drift. I'll take your word for it, Joe."

"Okay, let's walk out back, see if they're around."

"They won't mind us walking around on their farm?"

"Ha, no way. None of us do, well, almost none of us. Everyone's always cutting across each other's farms going places. People here aren't uptight about property lines like they were before the crash. Since it's mostly all getting around on foot, everyone understands the most direct path sometimes isn't the road. Only a few idiots get uptight about it, and none of them are in the middle of town, just a few on the north, along the bluff, and I almost never go out there anyhow so screw 'em."

"That's nice, nearly everyone getting along."

"Well, I wouldn't go that far. You should come to the next town meeting. It's like, no one agrees on anything. People are shouting, sometimes soundin' like they're gonna fight. But there's one thing everyone agrees on:

getting together to fight outsiders, especially when they attack. So, Buck, what you're seein's the united side of things. Yeah, it is kinda nice in that regard. But after these ferals get nailed, well, you'll see. The bickering over stupid small stuff'll start all over again," Joe said, suddenly realizing that whether Buck could stay or not would be on the next agenda. Joe knew it'd eventually come down to a vote, a yes or no raised hands vote, by everyone over fifteen who showed up at the meeting. With the paper supply dwindling, secret ballots were a luxury of the past. Whatever way it went, everyone'll have to follow the majority, including Buck.

The Lee farm was only four acres, but for them, it was just right. Their small cozy home was easy to clean and heat. The home was located near the road and had dozens of assorted fruit trees growing on their side yards. Young, recently planted nut trees struggled skyward out front where the lawn once grew. The backyard was long and narrow, about two hundred feet wide, with neat rows of vegetables and blueberries extending all the way back to a wooded area, which offered plenty of wood for heating.

"There they are," Joe said.

"Nice farm," Buck replied.

"Yup, sure is. There are lots of nice farms around here. Everyone's spending their time gardening during the summer. That and chopping wood. Lots of that goin' on this time of year, so it'll dry by winter. In a few weeks we'll have berries and firewood drying on the hot roads, right smack on top of the pavement. It sure looked weird, at first. The roads get really hot and things dry faster that way. This place gets really busy when the sun's out," Joe said, as they got near to where Jimmy and Deborah were working.

"Hi, Joe," Jimmy said. "Is that our new friend, Buck?"

"Yup, this is Buck. Buck, these are the Lees, Jimmy and Deborah."

"Nice to meet you, Jimmy, Deborah," Buck said, courteously not offering to shake hands. He saw their soil-calloused hands and also noticed the old, but very deadly, stainless steel revolver stuffed into a weathered tan holster strapped to Jimmy's black leather belt.

"We've heard all about you. You're the biggest news to hit our town since the ancient spillway at Bonneville Dam finally fell apart last April, causing that big flood," Deborah said, her pretty almond eyes peering up at Buck from under her straw coolie hat while holding a wooden handled garden rake in her right hand and a green, quart-size Stanley thermos in her left.

"Flood?" Buck asked.

"Yeah, we had a huge flood. Water went way up the Sandy, but not as far as where we found you," Deborah said.

"Then, those two sixteen-year-old boys sailed twenty miles up the river to take a close look. It was brave of 'em, crazy brave, but it was good to know what caused the river to rise all of a sudden. Some said they got into their dad's blueberry wine then had a little boat ride. Boy, did they catch hell when they got back that evening," Joe said as he shared the story.

"Remember, their dad made 'em pick moss off roofs for a week ... barehanded ... in the rain," Jimmy said, laughing at their misfortune.

"Well, it wasn't really funny at all. It was reckless and dangerous for them to go upriver by themselves," Deborah said, as she glared a moment at Jimmy much like a judge would at a petty criminal.

Jimmy's smile suddenly disappeared and he submissively bowed his head and stared at his sandals.

"Yeah, they came back all excited telling everyone what they saw. Water was gushing out the north side. I imagine it started with a small leak. Then, it got worse and worse as the spring snowmelt really got moving, finally cutting a new path for the river. I'm interested in going up there myself after this mess is over. Anyhow, apparently it wasn't the first time they'd sailed upriver, too, and that's what lit their dad up," Joe continued. "The kids found the sailboat in an abandoned garage along the Sandy. Clever kids, they taught themselves how to sail."

"Kids are sure growing up fast these days," Deborah said.

"Hey, Deborah, what's that?" Buck asked, pointing at a contraption with a large wooden wheel in the center and a flat, wrap-around bench half way up. Two thick wooden arms stuck out behind the wheel, protruding from the bench.

"That's a Chinese wheelbarrow. It's more efficient. It holds ten times the weight of an American one. It's easier to push, too. We used them in China. I drew a picture for Jimmy and he made one. The other farmers saw it, tried it out, and a few copied it, making their own. Now, they're used all over town," Deborah explained.

"That's cool. When we get back, I'd like to try it out," Buck said.

"Oh, of course, but they're all over town. I'm sure you won't have to ask anyone twice to help haul stuff," Deborah said.

"Anyhow, the reason we're here is to ask if we can borrow a few rifles. Mary Lou assigned us to the end of Donahue Road. Our rifles are out on patrol, with my dad and a few others. Kelly has one and my dad has one, plus a few guys dropped by and took the rest," Joe said.

"Well, Alison has one. I just happen to have two AKs left. You and Buck may borrow them. You'll need magazines and ammo, too."

"That would be great. We probably won't use any ammo and we'll keep the rifles safe," Joe said, as Deborah set her rake down and gripped her thermos in both of her ungloved hands.

"Buck, you're hurt. You need to drink this," Deborah said, unscrewing the top of the thermos and pouring an odd-looking, light orangish, yellowish, liquid into it as Buck's swollen eye opened the rest of the way. "Drink all of it. It's fresh, still warm."

Buck's eyes pleaded, silently asking for Joe's help.

"Don't worry, Buck. We all drink it here in Corbett," Joe said. "It's the healthiest drink ever. Denise even put some on your arrow holes."

Buck crossed his arms over his chest and gazed across the fields and far away toward the horizon with a terrified look on his face, searching for escape. "Uh, I dunno if I can," he said, absent-mindedly kicking at a nearby dirt clod with his tire tread toe.

"It's ours. We all do it around here. Here, drink it up, drink the rest. This'll cure just about anything. Jimmy and I just filled the thermos. It's fresh from this morning," Deborah said, as she stepped toward Buck, holding the three-quarter-filled cup out all the way toward Buck, inches away from his face.

"Oh, I don't know, Deborah, thanks anyhow," Buck said, as he held his breath, turned his head to the side and stepped back.

"Why not?"

"I'm, uh, I'm just not used to it, that's all. Thanks, anyhow."

"Oh don't be silly. It's the best blackberry tea in town. Jimmy makes it right here on our farm. It even has freshly cut peppermint leaves in it. It's delicious!"

"Oh! Blackberry tea? Mint leaves? I'd love some, thanks!" Buck said, feeling warm relief settle over his body as he drank the soothing tea in one long gulp. "May I have some more, please?"

"Of course. We can always make more. Blackberries are growing everywhere. You'll notice it's sweet. We put some honey in it."

"You have honey?" Buck asked.

"Yes, we do. Carrie Sherrill, she lives not far from here with her husband Peter Coonradt and their two sons, Everett and Easton. Her husband doesn't mess with her bees. He's a handyman. We have quite a few of them. They fix things. Stuff keeps falling into disrepair. He even made Carrie a loom. We now have quite a few looms in town. Two years ago there weren't any. He's making me one, too. He got the plan from a kindle book, which Pete Roth, another friend of ours, can charge at his house. Anyhow, she's having the best year ever with her bees.

She's the town beekeeper around here. Well, one of two. The other one's smaller, on the other side of town. I'll probably never make it that far. It's six miles from here. Maybe some day I'll make the trip. Anyhow, the bees are doing well because we're no longer using chemical fertilizers and pesticides. Her bees are thriving this year!" Deborah said.

Chapter Thirty-One

While Buck was enjoying his first cups of freshly made blackberry tea, Dan, Rigo and Kyle had started moving east, toward the southern slopes of Larch Mountain.

Avoiding trails and roads, they moved quietly between standing trees and over or around fallen ones. The forest felt alive as they hiked, which meant they were still far from their targets. It also meant they could, for now, communicate in softly spoken whispers as they walked.

"Hey Dan, what time is it?" Kyle asked. Dan still carried one of the team's watches. Bill, walking far behind, carried the other.

"Almost four."

"So, how far you think we've gone?" Kyle asked.

"Maybe four or five miles."

"Their prints are still clear, we're still on 'em," Rigo said. "We should be ready to party soon."

"We could move faster if we weren't worried about noise," Kyle said.

"Well, we should see something soon. As soon as the forest gets quiet, we'll know we're close," Rigo said.

"Let's stop for a final check. Kyle, could you check on the explosives once more? Make sure they're all ready so you don't have to do anything but toss 'em. Everyone drink some water, too. And have some of that high-energy berry mix Alison made for us. Might be our last chance."

Rigo stopped and stood, nervously turning his back toward the two.

Kyle unstrapped Rigo's pack and started rooting around up to his elbows inside the pack while Dan watched. Kyle was shoving small packages this way and that, making the backpack shift back and forth while Rigo closed his eyes and prayed, "Our Father, who art in heaven . . . "

"Looks good," Kyle said.

The mysteries of high explosives were fully understood by a club of very few members, and they had a tendency to keep the knowledge to themselves. Kyle and Charlie were the only members of the small club left in Corbett and no one expressed an interest in learning the trade, especially after taking a look at Charlie's mangled hand, or trying to have a conversation with him. This meant that when the last of the explosives were gone, so would the club.

"Okay, let's make sure all the safeties are off," Dan reminded the others, as all three made yet another final inspection of their already thrice inspected weapons and gear.

"Good," Rigo said.

"Good," Kyle said.

"I'm good, too," Dan said, and he gave the universal arm-wave, finger point signal letting the other two know it was time to start walking.

Chapter Thirty-Two

Since most of their ride was uphill, and since neither of them were in the best of shape, Joe and Buck pedaled slowly, dodging hundreds of assorted evergreen seedlings sprouting in the countless cracks splitting through the long, freshly paved, dead-end roadway.

They pushed the bicycles over the last mile of Donahue Road to better survey the terrain. Brilliant lines of tall green grass and yellow-flowered weeds welcomed them into this wonderland of nature. It gave the road a surreal, fairyland appearance, especially with the late day sunrays cutting between the ever-encroaching trees and illuminating the marching rows of fantasy.

"Corbett is absolutely beautiful, Joe," Buck said as they coasted through a narrow canyon of trees along a short downhill.

"Yup," Joe smiled and said.

"It's like paradise."

"Can be," Joe said.

"I feel like I'm dreaming," Buck said.

"Yup, we've worked hard, and fought hard, to keep this place nice," Joe said, thinking of the short, bloody war.

"Is it like this most of the year?" Buck asked.

"Just in the summer. You might have a different opinion if you're still here in the winter."

"Lots of snow?"

"Not really. My grandparents said it used to snow all the time, but now it's just the cold, wet wind," Joe answered.

"The wind? What's so bad about that?" Buck asked.

"It gets nasty."

"I'm sure I've seen worse. But I'll do fine no matter where I end up. Plus, I'll always remember how kind the people of Corbett were to me … and I'll tell no one," Buck said, suspecting his days in the closed community of Corbett were drawing to a close.

The sun was getting low when they finally arrived and the trees offered shade to the tired men, and to the hot, decaying road. They didn't find the men they were supposed to meet, so they decided to set up their position. There was still some sunlight left in the day, but soon it would be night. The moon was two days past full, so it would rise just after dusk. Once the sun went down, there would be just barely enough light to see for a short time. They had to find a well-hidden place to set up their static patrol. It had to be away from the road, but not too far away. They wanted to be able to see the road while safely hidden.

Joe, who had lived in Corbett nearly all his life, didn't need a map. He knew exactly where to go. There was a large logging clear cut just north of the end of Donahue Road. It had been gouged out of a hillside a few years before the collapse, but new trees were now waking up, ready to take their parents' and grandparents' place in nature's endless life cycle. It was about a half-mile wide and a mile long and somewhat visible from the top of a short hill a few hundred yards north of the road. From that vantage point, they could silently observe the large clearing and Donahue Road at the same time. While unseen. Perfect.

They stashed their bikes, laying them flat, partially hidden in the grass and weeds, ten paces into the woods behind a thick tree near a big yellow caution sign. The perimeter of the sign was brightly festooned with orange fist-sized reflectors. In large black letters, the sign shouted, "END COUNTY MAINTAINED ROAD."

Chapter Thirty-Three

They had walked east for hours, following the mass of footprints through the woods just south of Southeast Louden Road, then deep into the heavily wooded rolling hills and canyons south of Southeast Deverell Road. Here and there a dropped scrap of food or an empty wine bottle marked their path. Dan's watch read seven-fifteen. An hour and a half more of daylight.

"Hey, look," Kyle said. "The footprints are pointing in all directions here. Plus, look! The ground is matted down, like people were sleeping."

"Okay, let's all do a wide perimeter check, see if we pick up the trail," Dan said.

"Yuck. They definitely camped here. Lots of you-know-what on the ground over there, like they used that spot as their latrine," Kyle said.

"Here it is, a garbage dump, barely hidden. There's a couple of Harger's blueberry wine bottles: empty. These guys must've been hammered last night. No wonder they were still camping this late. But, they must've headed deeper east," Rigo said.

"Yeah, not too long ago. Look here. Some of their poop appears fresh, like, just dropped," Kyle said. "Take a peek."

"I'll take your word for it, Kyle," Rigo said.

"Where, exactly? Let me see," Dan said, and Rigo followed.

"There," Kyle said, pointing at the ground.

"Yup, like it was just made," Dan agreed, as he stared at the ground near his feet.

"What? You guys're experts at this?" Rigo asked.

"Simple forensics, Rigo," Dan replied.

"Are you sayin', are you tellin' us, that you aren't using night soil?" Kyle jokingly asked Rigo.

"Yeah, we all do … but I can't tell one hour poop from ten hour poop," Rigo replied.

"Very funny, Rigo," Kyle replied, as Dan walked head down through the field latrine with a short, broken branch, looking here, poking there, while ignoring their short, private conversation.

"Hey, you guys think they saw us and split?" Rigo asked the other two.

"It's possible. If they did, it means they have perimeter patrols, men constantly observing and reporting, like we do around town, except on a smaller scale," Dan said.

"That means they could be out there right now," Kyle suggested.

"So what? We're the ones with the assault rifles. They're the ones with the knives and bows. They're cro-mags. Cave men. Let's make 'em go extinct, again," Dan dismissively replied.

Chapter Thirty-Four

"Joe, I hear something," Buck said.

"Me too, voices, men talking," Joe replied.

"Yup, they're trying to talk quiet, but there's too many of 'em. It carries," Buck said.

"Yeah, I hear 'em, but can't pin down exactly where they are. Can you tell exactly where they're coming from?" Joe asked.

"It's from that way," Buck said, pointing to the south, deeper into the woods.

"Yeah, wanna move closer, just to be sure it isn't our response team?" Joe asked.

"And what if it isn't?" Buck said.

"Thirty or forty men with bows against us two. I'd say we're about even," Joe said.

"Yeah, well, in war soldiers are told to never fight unless you're at a clear advantage," Buck warned.

"Okay, cool, but let's at least move closer, just a little bit," Joe said. "That way we know exactly what we're up against."

"I'll be right behind you, Joe. I don't feel like picking up any more arrow holes," Buck joked. Then, the two men moved down the hill, closer to where the paved portion of the road ended.

Chapter Thirty-Five

The three kept moving. The sun set far to the west. It would get dark soon. Knowing they were closing the gap, getting closer to the ferals, they kept moving.

"It's gotten quiet," Rigo said, as he stopped dead in his tracks.

"Yup. Quiet. We're not alone," Dan quietly replied.

"Like someone hit the mute button on the woods," Kyle said.

"High search position, boys," Dan said, as the three rifles shifted in unison, away from their casual shoulder slung position to the aggressive, combat-ready two-handed position, all three aiming low, covering all directions at once.

"Follow the prints," Dan said. "Keep moving. Sun'll be setting soon. Then we'll get moonlight, lots of moon again tonight, just like last night. We're not going back 'til we find 'em."

The men kept walking, Rigo out front, all three occasionally glancing down at the dozens of clear footprints, all aimed east, while studying and memorizing every shadow, every shifting hue, as they gazed into the darkening silence.

Chapter Thirty-Six

"Uh-oh, Joe, listen. They're getting closer."

"They just turned west. They're heading up the dirt road, getting closer to the paved part."

"Oh, crap, now whadda we do?" Buck asked.

"Let's just stay low, a few dozen yards north of the road, across from our bikes," Joe said, while the two scruffy-looking men emerged from the forest and quietly walked past the "END COUNTY MAINTAINED ROAD" sign. They walked past Joe and Buck, quietly moving west, toward the center of Corbett, whispering now and then to each other, each carrying bows and what appeared to be empty packs, plus quivers.

"Only two? Where's the rest of 'em?" Buck asked.

"There! Look!" Joe replied, pointing at what appeared to be about thirty men, all following about a hundred yards behind the first two.

After the dozens of men had passed, and were about a hundred yards away, Joe broke the silence and whispered to Buck, "Did you see that? They were wearing Ebi and Harger's clothes."

"Yeah, I saw they were wearing nice clothes," Buck replied, "and they're probably out looking for more food. I bet they ate everything they took last night, feasted, and now they're gonna try to raid another farm for more."

"You recognize the guys who shot you?" Joe asked.

"No. It's too dark, plus I didn't get that good a look at 'em," Buck replied.

"We won't be able to ride the bikes for help. If we ride out, we'll bump smack into 'em. We're trapped."

"Yup, this is a dead end road. It's back about two miles until this road joins Larch Mountain Road," Joe said.

"So what do we do? We can't just let 'em go. They're gonna kill someone," Buck asked.

"We don't have any choice," Joe replied. "We go after 'em on foot, through the woods alongside the road. We change their plans."

"Just the two of us?" Buck asked.

"Yup. Me and you," Joe replied. "We nail 'em. Listen, we have three hundred rounds of AK ammo. I bet the best they do is bows and arrows. I remember about a mile and a half ahead there's an 'S' turn. Let's see if we can cut through, get ahead of 'em, find a good place a few yards off the road, let the first two walk by and then nail the rest as they pass by the second sharp bend."

"The moon'll be up by then, too. We'll be able to see 'em, but they won't see us," Buck said, as he quietly stood up. "I'm in. My third deployment finally started."

"Third?"

"Yeah. Army. One year in Afghanistan, one year in Yemen. Yemen was a disaster. The president gave up, pulled everyone out. Most went to Iraq when that war started up again, but I was rotated back to Georgia for thirty days. I was a few days from going to Iraq when it all fell apart. Then Corbett's my third."

"So, you're used to this, too?"

"Yup, bring it on. You?"

"Same. Three tours. SEALs," Joe said, telling Buck what he told anyone else who asked about his military experiences: almost nothing.

"SEALs?"

"Yup."

"Is that how you hurt your leg?"

"My leg's fine."

"Okay."

"It's my walking, that's all. A nerve thing. It'll get better."

"Okay."

"Okay, enough of that. Let's go," Joe said.

Chapter Thirty-Seven

Rigo suddenly stopped walking. "Look. The footprints've shifted. They're all heading north now," Rigo said, a bit too loud, turning his head toward Dan and Kyle.

Dan stepped alongside Rigo and placed his right index finger to his lips, urging silence in the universal way.

Kyle leaned an inch from Dan's right ear and whispered, "I can barely see the footprints. The three other groups don't know. Where are they? How will we let 'em know?"

Dan turned his head ninety degrees to his right. He whispered back to Kyle while Rigo placed his head close, "Forget it. Let's move after 'em now. If all twelve of us roll through the woods together we'll create a wave of our presence throughout the forest. It'll let 'em know we're following. Right now I don't believe they know we're here. We would've seen the prints shift, telling us they stopped. We gotta move after 'em fast, right now."

"I can't hear you in that ear. Try the other one," Kyle said.

Dan walked around Kyle and repeated what he'd just said, whispering an inch from Kyle's other ear.

It was now dark. The soft glow from the nearly full moon lit up the horizon to the east like a distant city, but it had yet to show over the hills and it cast little light. The three followed the footprints, then lost them in the darkness as they reached a dirt road aiming east and west.

"Crap," Kyle quietly said. "Which way did they go? East or west?"

"They're hungry. I bet they're heading back west, circling back for another hit like we thought they would," Dan said.

"I suggest we follow the road, but hug the side, near the trees," Rigo said.

"Sounds good," Dan replied.

They followed the dirt road until it became paved. "What road is this?" Dan asked.

"I dunno," Rigo replied. "I've never been out this far. Remember, I stuck close to home for a good reason."

"Kyle?" Dan asked.

"I think it's called Donahue Road, but I'm not sure. I've only been down this road a few times, and it's been years. But, I know it heads back to town," Kyle said, as they stood a moment, feet away from the well-hidden bikes stashed earlier by Joe and Buck.

"Back to town?" Dan asked.

"Yup, it hits Larch Mountain Road in about two miles. Then left into town. They just paved it a few months before the collapse."

"I've never been out this far, ever," Rigo said. "But they're probably looking for another easy score. Then, I bet they'll fade east again and hide ... and then they'll either hit some houses again, or leave."

"They think it's easy pickin's here. They aren't leaving on their own," Dan said.

"I agree with Dan. They're lookin' for another easy score," Kyle said.

"Where're they going to hit next?" Rigo asked.

"No telling. An outlying place, probably," Dan replied.

"They'll nail the first house they find tonight," Kyle said.

"I agree. We gotta beat 'em to it," Dan said.

"Or catch 'em," Kyle said.

"Wanna jog awhile?" Dan asked, grinning at Rigo.

"Yeah, great idea, Dan," Kyle replied. "Let's jog, close the distance."

"No way," Rigo replied, thinking of the high explosives stuffed into his backpack. "I am not running with that crazy old man's bombs in my backpack. You guys go ahead and jog. I'll be walking far behind you."

"We could stash the explosives," Kyle suggested.

"No way. They could come in handy," Dan said.

"Seriously, I don't feel good about running with this pack," Rigo said.

"How about we walk faster?" Dan suggested. "It's almost ten. I'd like to finish this up soon so I can get a decent night's sleep."

"Yeah, I could use a solid night's rest in my own bed, too," Kyle replied.

"The bombs, guys. Can we talk about sleep later?" Rigo pleaded.

"Okay, Rigo. We'll never reach em just walkin'," Kyle said. "Plus, it takes a lot more than a little shakin' to make 'em explode."

"Well, how about you carry the pack?" Rigo suggested.

"Good idea. I'll carry it and jog gently," Kyle said.

"Fine," Rigo replied. "You do it. But, I wanna jog ahead, if you guys don't mind."

Just as Rigo began to remove his pack, six gunshots exploded not very far ahead, followed by a pause. "That's some of us shooting!" Rigo said. The short pause in the gunshots was broken when dozens more gunshots rocked the west slope of Larch Mountain.

"Let's go!" shouted Dan, and the three took off running directly toward the gunfire.

Chapter Thirty-Eight

Tweedy, Corey and Don tried to stay a quarter-mile behind Dan's group, but when darkness arrived, it became impossible.

"I can't tell where they are anymore," Don said, in his usual serious manner.

"It wasn't clear how long we were supposed to stay on this track," Corey said.

"I can't even see the tracks anymore. Maybe when the moon rises higher, which should be soon," Tweedy said.

"So what should we do?" Don asked.

"I suggest we maintain a straight line east unless we see a sign telling us different," Corey suggested.

"Smart," Don replied.

"Okay, eventually we'll see or hear something. Until then, let's keep moving," Tweedy agreed.

"Wait, how about we stop a few, maybe have a quick snack. I'm feeling weak. Maybe a few hundred calories would do us some good," Corey suggested.

"I'm in," Don said.

"Okay, we gobble some fruit down, then move out," Tweedy said.

They rested briefly then headed out once more, walking another few miles at a slightly faster pace. They observed and listened carefully as they walked through the forest but somehow missed the change in the direction of the footprints.

"The moon's shining nice, now," Corey said. "Let's try to find the footprints. I can't see 'em any more."

"We can't see 'em cuz they're gone. We lost 'em," Don added, a slight nervous edge to his usual calm, even voice.

"Well, we better find 'em fast," Tweedy said.

"Any ideas?" Corey asked his good friend.

"Nope."

"How about you, Don?" Corey asked.

"Well, it's getting late and if we keep walking straight ahead we'll be on top of Larch Mountain by sunrise. It's pretty this time of year, but we don't want that right now. So, I suggest we head back, walk slower, and try to see where the footprints turned off. And, as soon as we find 'em, we run like crazy."

"That's a go!" Tweedy said, and the three reversed direction and headed back the way they came just as the unmistakable racket of semi-automatic assault rifle ammunition rocked and echoed across the hillside.

"How far away?" Don asked.

"Maybe a half mile, maybe less," Corey said.

"Let's move!" Tweedy said as he led the charge directly at the gunfire.

Chapter Thirty-Nine

As Joe and Buck hiked through the shortcut, another unseen, deadly war was taking place inside Buck's chest. Infection had been spreading outward from deep within his wound. The bacteria were multiplying fast. The cleaning Denise performed was thorough, nearly putting an end to the infection, leaving the wounds clean and eager to heal. A few years earlier, antibiotics would have easily killed the rest and Buck could have walked out of the hospital in days.

The attack inside his chest was slow to get moving, offering Buck a false sense of well-being as the day wore on. He felt his strength gain and his other wounds were healing nicely, especially his eye and the wound on his head. However, as the evening wore on, the infection started growing like wild. Had he looked, he would have seen redness under his bandages. It was spreading, front and back. The sweating he experienced was ignored, at first, passed off as due to their fast pace. His body temperature was increasing, now over one hundred. By midnight, he would be unable to stand and it would threaten his life. It was a battle Buck would fight alone: the most violent battle he had ever fought was well underway.

"Dude, you're sweating," Joe said, as they paused a moment while they tore through the trees and bushes scrambling to pass the line of ferals walking single file west on Donahue Road.

"I'm okay. It's just the exercise," He replied.

"Let me feel your head," Joe asked, placing a hand on Buck's forehead.

"I'm tellin' ya, it's nothing," Buck said.

"Whoa! You have a fever. You're sick."

"I'll be fine."

"Why didn't you say something? We gotta get you to the clinic," Joe said.

"We gotta pass through them to get to the clinic. I'll make it," Buck said, starting to slur his speech a bit.

"Okay, let's keep moving. We're almost to the road anyhow. They should be coming by soon," Joe said. They moved up the hill another few hundred yards and stopped when they hit pavement.

"It's too dangerous for us to take positions on each side of the road. We're the ones with guns and we could hit each other with crossfire. Let's set up right here, we'll fire at 'em as they approach," Buck said, hoping they would arrive soon, knowing he wouldn't last long. "Joe, you get the first three, I'll get the next. Then, we'll open it up, nail as many of the rest as possible. Okay?"

"Yeah. That's what I was thinkin', too. Hey, Buck. How you feeling?"

"Really, Joe, I'm fine. This is normal after a chest wound like mine."

"Look at the moon. I wanna see your eyes," Joe asked.

Buck turned east.

"Whoa! They're red. The swollen one's pointing the wrong direction a bit, too."

"Joe, really, I'm doing just fine."

"You're having trouble standing," Joe said.

"It's the hill, the uneven ground," Buck slurred, wobbling on his legs a bit more, struggling to maintain balance.

"There they are, the first two. Down!" Joe said. Buck was about to drop anyhow, so "down" was an easy command for him to follow. His face smacked the dirt as he went down hard. Joe glanced at Buck without a word. Buck shook his head and grinned back.

Moments later, the two men walked by. Buck and Joe were flat on the dirt, peering at them from behind bushes, rifles aimed at the center of the road. Buck had found the last of his energy, adrenaline pouring through his body in preparation for the coming battle. They heard the two ferals chatting quietly, but couldn't make out what was said. They disappeared around the final bend just as the rest appeared.

"Ready?" Joe asked.

"Yup. My spare magazines are ready, too," Buck replied. "The pockets in these deerskin pants are perfect."

Joe whispered, "Wait until they get close. Fire when the sixth man is even with us. I'll take the first three. You take the second three. Then we move to the road and nail the rest."

Chapter Forty

"I hear 'em," Rigo excitedly said. "Vamos! Let's go!"

Without the constant hum of distant internal combustion engines and overhead aircraft, the natural nighttime life in the forest was revealed. The wind brushed trees and leaves together. Small animals scurried about. Owls hooted now and then. Coyotes cried. A deer moved past, brushing through the foliage with its unique sound. The ever-present white noises of the past civilization were absent, revealing subtle sounds only heard far from cities and towns during the now-extinguished oil-burning era. Thirty men quietly moving on pavement made a unique sound too, even when three hundred yards away. The three moved toward them.

"Not too close. We need to find 'em all in one place. If they hear us, they might scatter like rats," Dan said, sneaking a glance at his watch out of an old habit: nine fifty-three.

"Let's hang back, follow from about two hundred yards, maybe. Let's be patient. We'll get our chance," Kyle said, just as the all-too-familiar sounds of semi-automatic rifle fire crawled into his brain through his one good ear. In a split-second it triggered a counterintuitive instinct buried in his spirit to make his legs run toward, rather than away from, the gunfire.

Chapter Forty-One

Meanwhile Pat O'Malley's group had become hopelessly entangled in a field of blackberry bushes a half mile south of Donahue Road. In their effort to stay parallel with Dan and his group, they decided it would be wiser to head straight through rather than around what they believed to be a narrow patch of the nasty vines. All of them knew the area well, having hiked and explored these hills since they were kids. But blackberry fields grow fast and spread out quickly, plus, it had been a long time since they had hiked in this particular area.

After getting sliced and jabbed by thorns, they thought they had finally made it through, only to find themselves standing at the edge of a thirty-foot, rock cliff. There were only three ways out: climb down the cliff, backtrack the way they came, or try their luck heading north, skirting the cliff and climbing over and through the vines dangling over the edge. They chose the latter, which only made matters worse. The true scope of their predicament only became apparent when the moon rose above the distant hills.

The nicked and bleeding threesome finally stopped. "We're trapped," Pat said, after they had struggled along the edge of the cliff for a while.

"No we're not. All we gotta do is jump down that cliff," Blake said. "Then, we're home free."

"Cute, Blake. Don't you ever say anything seriously?" Pat asked.

"Once, long ago, just to see what it was like," Blake replied, as Conner snickered quietly.

"I can't possibly climb down that cliff," Pat said. "I can't grab those rocks, especially in the dark."

When he was in his mid-forties, Pat developed the disfiguring symptoms of a rare genetic disorder called Dupuytrens contracture, also known as Viking claw. Unique to northern Europeans, like Pat, it slowly deforms the victim's hands. It caused the fingers on Pat's left hand to curl grotesquely inward, allowing him to grip the neck of a whiskey bottle just fine, but grasping and reaching small objects with that hand was more than just clumsy; it was impossible. The little and ring fingers of his right hand were recently curling inward, too, allowing him to practice pulling a trigger with his right index finger just fine, but flat-handed push-ups were out. Unfortunately, many other tasks were proving difficult, too, such as night cliff climbing. Since the collapse, Pat had transformed himself into superb physical shape, jogging regularly and working his butt off each day much like almost everyone else in town. However, stretching his fingers out and gripping half-inch ledges while scampering down a nearly sheer cliff-face was just too much to ask, but he tried it anyhow.

"Well, how about if I carry your rifle down, and then climb back up and help guide you down?" Conner said.

"Okay. Fine. I'm tired of getting cut up," Pat said, handing Conner his rifle.

Conner slung Pat's rifle over his back alongside his own and scampered down the nearly perpendicular cliff, finding handholds and footholds here and there. When he reached the bottom, he placed his rifle on the ground alongside Pat's and quickly scaled back up the cliff, but not quite to the top.

"Okay, Pat, this is easy," Conner said. "First, slide your feet over the edge while you face the cliff. Good! Now, put your left foot there and your right foot here, then grab the lip of the cliff here and here, but watch out for that rock there. Don't grab it, it's loose!" Conner tapped a narrow moonlit ledge with an outstretched hand while rattling off a series of convoluted instructions.

"Relax, Pat. It'll all be over with soon," Blake Raymond added, his contagious smile eerily illuminated in the moonlight.

"Gee, thanks, Blake," Pat scowled, attempting to follow Conner's precise, yet indecipherable, instructions.

"Remember, never look down," Blake added, leering over the edge, grinning down at Pat from six-feet, seven inches above the very lip of the cliff as if leaning over from the bucket of a cherry picker.

Pat glared up at him while Conner down below fought like crazy to extinguish a giggle.

Conner then rattled off another string of unintelligible instructions intended to help while Pat nervously clung to the cliff face with his curled fingers. "Great! You're doing great," Conner said, as he reached the bottom. Pat had moved about halfway down. Conner tipped his head back and looked straight up. "Now, Pat, grab that ledge there … no, not that one, THAT one … now, put your other foot here and, no, not there, on the other rock … careful, that ledge is too small for your foot … LOOK OUT!"

The one-inch ledge Pat entrusted with his life broke away, sending him sliding down the remaining twenty feet. He landed in a crumpled heap of sixty-something-year-old man alongside the two rifles just as a torrent of distant gunshots rocked and echoed across the nearby hills.

Chapter Forty-Two

All afternoon and into dusk, Bill Hartigan, Kelly Lee and Kevin Sakai had kept Dan's group in their constant line of sight, easily pacing them from a few hundred yards to their north, much like Pat's group had tried to do to the south. Then, it turned dark and it became impossible to maintain visual contact.

"Now what?" Kelly asked the other two. "Do we just keep moving east, or do we fall in behind, maybe hook up with Tweedy and his crew?"

"We stick to the plan," Bill said.

"But we have no idea where they are," Kelly continued.

"It doesn't matter. We'll just keep covering our line of march," Bill said.

"Kelly has a point. We're just stumbling around out here," Kevin said.

"Look. The moon's up now. Soon we'll catch sight of 'em. Let's just keep at it. My watch says nine twenty-five. Let's keep going until ten, then decide. Okay?" Bill said, wanting to compromise to avoid a possible mutiny among his friends.

They moved on. They were about to reach Donohue Road, a rarely used, dead-end spur, when Bill glanced at his watch again. It read precisely nine fifty-one.

"Footsteps," Bill said, as he froze in his tracks.

"Yup, only a few. Wonder who?" Kelly said, as the footsteps faded west then could no longer be heard.

"Must be a few locals out patrolling. We have people crawling all over town tonight," Bill added.

"Yeah, that's what it must be," Kelly said, as the group continued walking.

"Uh-oh. More. Lots more," Kevin whispered, moments later, standing motionless near his friends.

"Yup, we're close to a road. Like, thirty or forty yards away. Anyone know what road that is?" Kelly asked.

"It's Donohue Road," Bill said. "I expected us to have crossed it by now. It's the only road out here."

"None of our patrol groups have that many people," Kevin added, as his heart rate skyrocketed.

Suddenly, the silence was shattered when six AK-47 rounds broke the nighttime silence. A brief silence returned followed by dozens of gunshots, then it stopped. Then, they heard the distinctive footsteps of men running directly at them.

Chapter Forty-Three

The first shot is sometimes said to be the most difficult, but not for Joe and Buck. Not today. The first six men they saw as they peered through the drying grass and roadside weeds were armed with rifles. In the semi-darkness it wasn't possible to determine what kind of guns they carried, but what could be determined with certainty was that they were the same group that had shot Buck and slaughtered the Ebis.

Joe and Buck had their first six shots planned before the men began to pass. Joe had the first three, Buck the next three. Adrenalin gushed through their bodies, as they looked straight ahead yet were clearly aware of everything around them. Their minds were on overload, yet their hearts continued to beat at a steady seventy-five beats per minute. In the split-second before firing the first round, the former soldiers, over and over again, visualized what was about to occur in the next three seconds. It would be a simple matter of lining up the front and rear sights, squeezing the trigger and, once again, lining up the sights for the next shot and repeating the process over and over and over as fast as they could.

The field of fire was nicely illuminated by the bright moon, causing the men to appear to flicker as they walked into and out of the shadows of the trees lining the road. Joe and Buck intended to commence firing when the sixth man passed but, reading each other's thoughts, they waited until the fourth was in front of them. Joe and Buck fired three shots each. He and the five around him were dead within the first three seconds. They hit the pavement forming six streams of blood, which flowed on and around the stately row of pretty yellow flowers lined up, still softly glowing in the moonlight, peeking skyward from the middle of the road.

The rest of the ferals barely had time to flinch. Some stood motionless, in shock, while others dropped instinctively as their minds wasted precious milliseconds processing what had just occurred to their buddies. Some reached for arrows, while others turned to flee into the woods or back down the road.

Before the sixth one had fallen on the pavement, Joe and Buck were on their feet, moving fast past the graveled shoulder to the thin, already crumbling asphalt as they fired a few quick close-up rounds into the six as they ran. Then, side-by-side, feet squarely planted alongside the yellow centerline, they again opened fire. Puffs of dirty smoke spoiled the clear night air. Each time their barrels rose and fell the cloud grew angrier. The noise was incredible. Hidden in the constant explosions of the AK-47 ammunition, an empty magazine smacked against the pavement, then another, then another as they reloaded again and again, pouring ammunition down Donohue Road and into the forest at the scattering attackers.

The rest of the enemy had disappeared. Only the twelve dead and three wounded remained in the road. Joe ran straight into the slippery carnage, silencing all three of the wounded while they moaned with one quick, no-questions-asked bullet each. A smoky, terrifying silence gripped Joe as he cautiously backed his way to where he, moments earlier, had left Buck standing.

"The rest ran down the road or into the woods. I counted fifteen dead," Joe excitedly said. "If they were thirty, that means fifteen got away. Most ran back down the road, only a few into the trees. We need to hide out. They could re-group, come after us."

He glanced to his left for a response as Buck collapsed flat on his face in the middle of the road.

Chapter Forty-Four

Rigo saw them running straight at him from the west. He stopped and went down low into a kneeling shooter's position, one knee grinding into the roadside gravel, the other foot flat on the ground. A small clump of grass and some tall common weeds concealed his position but offered no cover protection. He aimed down the road at them with his AK and patiently waited, as invisible as a ghost.

Dan and Kyle, meanwhile, scooted back in the woods a short distance.

"That must be Bill, Kelly and Kevin we just heard shooting," Dan said.

"No doubt. It came from about where they should be by now," Kyle said.

"Those scumbag ferals are coming right at us," Dan said, aiming his words at Kyle's good ear.

"They'll be here in less than a minute. Quick, I need the explosives," Kyle said, a hint of frantic hugging in his soft voice. "How many of those freaks are there?"

"Ten, fifteen, maybe. Can't tell. Lots. Let me take your pack off," Dan said.

Kyle turned, allowing Dan to easily remove the bomb-filled pack and place it on the ground. Kyle crouched down and opened it, rooting through the contents as if reaching for a card in a random drawing.

"You're the bomb guy, not me," Dan said.

"Huh?" Kyle said, preoccupied with the contents of his pack.

"Never mind," Dan said.

"Ahh, these are the ones for close-in work. Here, Dan, hold these two for me. Oh, and this and ... uh ... this one, too," Kyle said, filling Dan's arms with small packages before securing the pack's cover flap.

"Any more?"

"No, I'll take 'em now," Kyle said, and he filled up a small, dark, nondescript canvas shoulder-slung pouch with the explosives. "I can reach 'em easy now."

"Okay, they're coming close. Rigo's by the road. He'll hit quite a few, others'll scatter into the woods. Let's get the ones who scatter our way," Dan said.

"The ones who matter?" Kyle asked, Dan's voice too far and too soft for him. As soon as Kyle spoke, Rigo opened fire, again filling the night with ear-splitting explosions.

There were ten men running straight at Rigo, yet none knew he was there. When they were even with him, he emptied one magazine into the mob as fast as his finger could pull the trigger. He pressed the magazine release when he thought he was almost empty, sending the magazine with two rounds remaining to the road and snapping in a fresh one, immediately firing into the forest where he saw the few survivors flee. Rigo then walked straight into the moonlit carnage displayed in the road near his feet. He scanned, counting six men shot. He quickly inspected each of them. He ignored the dead, but fired a round into the head of each of the two wounded.

"Six dead here, about four heading your way!" Rigo yelled, as he ran into the woods chasing after the remaining ferals.

"Six? Nice shooting. How many comin' at us?" Kyle quietly asked Dan.

"I dunno for sure. I think he said four."

"Any second now," Kyle said, rifle slung over his back, eyes straight ahead while he fingered a small package held near his belt.

"There's two," Dan said, squeezing his trigger twice, then, moving closer, twice more.

Kyle tossed a small package at them just for good measure. He knew what to expect, but the explosion shocked Dan.

"Wow!"

"Welcome to war, bro. One more, behind that tree," Kyle said, tossing another small package into the forest. He and Dan ducked behind a log, covering their ears. The package bounced once, then ferociously exploded, sending two severed legs spinning skyward. They flipped around among low hanging branches, then fell to the forest floor with two thumps, leaving behind a burgundy pinwheel shower which ever-so-slowly descended back to earth through the filtered moonlight, giving that passing yellow celestial body a bizarre reddish tint.

"Three. No need to check him," Dan stoically said.

Kyle gazed up, toward some low hung branches. "Dan, look. Check out the moon and that burgundy mist hanging in the moonlight. Wow! You don't see a pattern like that every day," Kyle said, mesmerized by the odd burgundy appearance of the overhead moon. "It's really beautiful!"

Dan glanced up at the moon. Then, he turned his gaze toward Kyle a moment, much in the same manner that a scientist might gaze at the world's first captured alien. "Man, you might look into a psych-eval."

"What?" Kyle asked.

A shadow suddenly moved. "Another!" Dan said, turning to his left, dropping low and popping off three quick random cover rounds at that barely visible shadow as it moved from one tree to another. Kyle moved behind a tree and reached for another small package, fiddling with it briefly.

"HEY! IT'S ME!" Rigo shouted from behind a thick evergreen tree less than ten feet away from Dan.

"Oops, sorry about that," Dan said.

"That's why we call you invisible, cuz sometimes you are," Kyle joked, as Dan looked back at him, briefly resuming his private psychiatric examination of Kyle.

"About four got away," Rigo said. "They all went this way."

"We heard you yell. We nailed three. That means one more out here, somewhere. Let's hunt him down," Dan said.

The men separated some and moved out in a westerly direction, unaware there were no ferals left alive nearby.

"Hey, guys?"

"What?" Rigo asked.

"I got a live one in my hand," Kyle said.

"Well, make it not-so-live," Dan suggested.

"I can't re-set it safely once I've readied it. It's impossible. Maybe, you guys should cover your ears."

"What are you going to do?" Dan asked.

"I'm gonna toss it behind that log." Kyle then gave it a quick underhanded toss and stood looking at the log with his head inquisitively tilted while the other two men dove for cover.

The forest rocked once more and Kyle lost a bit more of his hearing.

Chapter Forty-Five

"Gotcha," Kelly thought to herself, her heart suddenly racing when she saw the man hiding behind a thick tree. She was alone, dozens of yards from her friends, as they all continued the search for the fleeing ferals. Bill and Kevin had fanned out on either side of her, each combing the forest hoping to find the men they heard heading into the woods toward them. She believed Dan, Kyle and Rigo must have somehow crossed north of her group and bumped into the ferals, shooting many, but not all of them. With her rifle aimed head high she cautiously approached the man.

"Kelly! Look out!" Bill shouted from a distance.

When she was three feet away, the feral leaped at her, grabbing the end of her rifle's barrel. Kelly violently yanked back on her rifle, breaking his grip and slicing his hand open on the end sight. But he kept coming at her, knocking the barrel aside with his wet bloody hand, reaching angrily for Kelly's face while he growled like a rabid German Shepherd. She didn't have the proper angle to fire so she focused seventeen years of her martial arts training with her karate instructor, Sifu Rick Cropper, into one swift movement. She kicked him on the very tip of his chin, hard, shattering his jaw with her well-worn Danner boot and snapping his neck back at a sickening angle. He clutched at his throat with bloody fingers in a final futile gesture as his eyes rolled back one heartbeat before he died.

Bill and Kevin ran toward her from the shadows of the forest.

Bill asked her, "What happened? I heard a loud crack."

"Wow!" Kelly said, pointing at the man. "I kicked him. This is freaky. I broke his neck."

"Those kicks really friggin' work! Girl! That's gross," Kevin said, standing next to the obviously dead man, his bloody fingers wrapped around his own twisted neck, which was bent back and to the side in an unnatural, bizarre manner. His eyes remained wide open, staring into nothing.

"There're probably a few more," Bill added. "Let's look around a bit, maybe reduce their numbers to zero."

"Wait. Let's find out who shot all those rounds. We're heading that way anyhow," Kevin suggested, just as the nearby forest was once again rocked by dozens of rifle shots.

"We'll do both," Bill said. They searched the forest for a short time.

"Who, or what, was that?" Kevin asked, somewhat bewildered. Bill and Kelly looked at each other, shrugging. "The first bullets we heard were from the west, but those are from the east. Which way should we go?"

"Let's just keep going straight. We know more of those freaks are near us. Then we'll be at the road and we'll find out who's waging war where," Bill suggested, just as a loud explosion thundered a few hundred yards to the east.

"Damn, that was Kyle! Charlie's stuff really works!" Kevin excitedly said, jumping up and punching a fist in the air.

"Yup, but let's all calm down, forget all that. For now, let's just focus on those we hear coming at us," Bill said.

Chapter Forty-Six

"Wow! What was that?" Corey asked, suddenly turning in the direction of the nearby explosion. "I bet that was Kyle."

"Yup," Don said.

"I hope it was Kyle. Let's go!" Tweedy said as the three men ran even faster toward the battle. They ran and ran until they hit the dark pavement.

"This road should be dirt. Where are we?" Corey asked.

"Donahue Road," Don said. "They just paved it a month before the shut down. Look, it's already cracking, weeds growing in the pavement. Man, it sure fell apart quick."

The Mershon family had lived in the Corbett area for over a century. Don, as well as the rest of his family, knew every tree, stump, rock and road in Corbett. Since anyone could remember, Donahue Road was a privately owned dead-end dirt two-track leading past the Corbett water purification plant to a few nearby logging operations. Corey and Tweedy didn't know, but when the lumber market collapsed in the months prior to the collapse, the logging company couldn't afford to maintain it so they gave the road to the county. The Corbett Water District workers were the only ones who used it. Soon thereafter, the water district put down a thin, narrow layer of asphalt, which was already falling into disrepair.

"Let's go!" Don said. "It hits Larch Mountain Road in about two miles, but the gunshots were way closer."

Each of them could run five miles at an eight-minute-per-mile pace, which they did several times a week to stay fit, but tonight they ran that one mile in six and a half.

"Check it out," Tweedy said, as they arrived at the scene of Rigo's one-sided battle. "Bodies. Six of 'em. I think we found it."

"Nope. We heard dozens of rounds and an explosion. There's more," Corey said.

"Yup," Don said.

"Okay, let's check around," Tweedy suggested.

"Hey, here's another one. Dead," Don said, pointing to the side of the road at a hairy, unkempt, smelly corpse, bleeding out face down in the roadside gravel, a bullet hole in his head and another in his neck. "Any more?"

"Don't anyone get near him," Corey said, searching along the road and nearby woods with Tweedy for others.

"Let's keep moving down the road," Tweedy said, not realizing that Rigo, Dan and Kyle were fifty yards south of them, searching through the woods just like they were. "There's no one around and nothing we can do here."

"I hear someone running down the road, maybe two or three," Corey said. "They're running right at us!"

"Into the trees. Go!" Tweedy said.

"We'll nail 'em when they run past us," Corey said, peering through his rifle sights from behind an ancient fallen tree alongside his kneeling buddies. "Ready. Any minute now."

Chapter Forty-Seven

Bill, Kevin and Kelly cleared the forest, not finding the two fleeing ferals. They continued walking until they reached a gruesome bloody carnage displayed in the road.

"Damn," Kevin said in amazement. "Look at 'em all."

"Must be a dozen bodies," Kelly said. "The stink is terrible!"

"Yup. Terrible. Make that fifteen," Bill said. "Let's check 'em. You never know."

"Don't touch any of them!" Kelly warned. "Stay at least ten feet away. There's blood running all over the road. Don't get any on your shoes!"

"Someone walked through 'em and finished off a few. Point blank. Forehead. Look," Kevin said, as he checked each corpse one-by-one from a safe distance. Many of the bodies looked disease-ridden, with dozens of tiny pus-sores on their faces and exposed arms. "They're diseased. Don't get near them!"

"What do they have?" Kelly asked. "Measles? Staph? They certainly have something nasty, that's for sure."

"Hey, I'm over here," a lone voice called out from the woods just north of the road. "It's me, Joe."

"Joe Hancock?" Kelly shouted, in disbelief.

"Yeah, me and Buck. He's hurt really bad. We gotta get him to the clinic. I was afraid to carry him 'cuz two of those bastards went up that way, toward town. They got away."

Kelly ran up the hill to where Joe was standing. She gestured toward the road. "You did this?"

"Well, yeah. Me and Buck. We got most of 'em. But a bunch got away. Two kept going toward town, a few into the woods, and some more ran back down the road."

"You guys shot fifteen?" Kelly asked.

"Yup, but look at Buck!"

"Oh no. Joe-Joe. Ah, crap! Not again! Not another arrow. Let me look," Kelly said, assessing the damage done by the arrow that pierced his thigh.

"A bunch of 'em fought back, shot arrows at us, but we kept shooting, Buck, too. Then he fell unconscious. I carried him up here so we'd be safe."

"We heard the shots."

"It's sticking out. He's still unconscious. Barely breathing. I'm scared for him," Joe said, cradling Buck like a baby in his massive arms while gently caressing his hair.

"We'll fix him up, Joe-Joe. It missed his femoral artery, or he would've been dead by now."

Joe had a reputation for getting emotional after a fight and he started choking up when she said that.

"Let me see it," Kelly said. She looked close, trying to estimate how deep the arrow went. "Not too deep. I'll get it out, then I'll wrap the wound, pack it with blackberry leaves."

"I don't know. I'm really scared for him," Joe said, as he started crying more, tears dripping on Buck's face. "I wish we had better medicine."

"Well, these leaves really work. Plus, they're everywhere." Kelly dug through her medical kit. She could tell Joe had been crying for quite a while. "It's a long hike back to town, Joe-Joe. Miles. It'll take us two hours or more to get him back to the clinic if you carry him," Kelly said. She wrapped a protective cloth around the arrow, then gently pulled straight back on it with her bare right hand. It slid straight out. Blood seeped out the two-inch-deep hole in Buck's leg. Kelly tossed the arrow aside.

"Good thing he's out cold," Joe said.

"Did you handle the arrow?"

"No. I was afraid of hurting him more," Joe said.

"Good. It might have their disease on it."

"Disease?" Joe asked.

"Yeah. Some of them have sores on their faces and hands. It's probably contagious."

"That means Buck might have caught a disease, too, from the arrow," Joe said.

"Well, it's possible. A small chance. We'll have to limit the number of people who get near him. Just me, you, Chris and Denise."

"Hey, it isn't bleeding too bad," Joe said, a hint of encouragement in his voice.

"It's still critical. We need to have Denise look at him right away," Kelly said, assessing the dire situation.

"We have bikes. We stashed 'em near the sign at the end of the road. It's only about a mile down the road from here," Joe said. "I can lay him on my back and ride him into town faster than carrying him on foot. He doesn't weigh much. That's nothing for me!"

"I can pedal alongside and help balance you," Kelly quickly said. "Kevin! Bill! Will you guys go get Joe-Joe and Buck's bikes?"

"They're about a mile from here, in the bushes next to the 'END COUNTY MAINTAINED ROAD' sign," Joe shouted.

"Sure," Bill said.

"Right now? Leave you here?" Kevin asked, raising his arms some as people do when they argue, deeply concerned about leaving Kelly and Joe alone with Buck while a few ferals were still running loose nearby.

"We'll be fine. Go! Go now! Buck's hurt! He's been shot! We gotta get him to town! I'll wait here with 'em until you're back!" Kelly said.

"Okay, we'll be quick," Kevin said.

Bill and Kevin took off running, rifles in hand while Kelly waited, hidden alongside the road with Joe and Buck.

"Joe-Joe?" Bill asked, after they had run a distance. "It's been a long time since I've heard Kelly call him that."

"I don't get it," Kevin said, the two men running side-by-side at the same pace.

"I guess ya had to be there," Bill replied.

Chapter Forty-Eight

"Hey. Don, Corey. Here they come," whispered Tweedy.

"Ready to fire ... three ... two ... one ... STOP! It's Bill and Kevin!" Corey yelled.

Bill and Kevin stopped running, rifles ready, dead in their tracks. "Who's that? Is that you, Tweedy?"

"Yeah, it's us," Tweedy said. "Why're you guys running so fast?"

"Nice to see you guys, but we're in a big hurry. Buck's down, hurt really bad. Shot by an arrow. Again. Don't know exactly what happened," Bill said, panting to catch his breath. "Him and Joe nailed fifteen of 'em! A few got away. They're hiding in the woods back up the road a half-mile or so. Be careful. If you find any ferals, take 'em out, but stay clear, they've got some disease, probably contagious. They've got open sores on their faces, but we still gotta get all of 'em."

"Go! They could use help. It's just Joe and Kelly with Buck. They're in the trees near the bodies. You can't miss them," Kevin said. "And, don't walk in the blood. It's all over the road up there!"

"We're on our way," Tweedy said, catching up with Corey and Don, who had already started running up the road.

"We gotta get the bikes they stashed, get Buck back to town way faster on 'em. See you guys in a few," Kevin said, as the two men ran the other direction down the road.

Bill and Kevin ran another few minutes and saw the sign.

"This is the place. Joe said they're around here somewhere," Kevin said.

"Found 'em!" Bill said.

"We'll be back in no time," Kevin said.

"Yup,"

The two climbed on the bikes and pedaled frantically for a few minutes.

"Kevin, stop. Now," Bill said, slowing down. He hopped off and walked his borrowed bike to the side of the road. He pointed south. "Over there. I hear someone in the trees, right over there."

"Ah, crap. Buck's probably dying. We don't have time for this," Kevin replied, as he gently placed his borrowed bike on its side in the gravel and dodged into the low roadside weeds next to Bill.

"Rifles ready," Bill said, but Kevin already had his rifle aimed straight ahead, scanning the forest.

"I can barely hear 'em. Two, maybe three. Twenty yards south," Kevin said, remembering Bill's hearing was about half shot.

"Can you understand 'em? What are they sayin'?" Bill asked.

"Yup."

"Yup? Yup, what?"

"Yup, I can barely understand 'em."

"Well, what are they sayin'?"

"One of 'em just said something about Kyle's explosives."

"Dan, Kyle, Rigo! Is that you?" Bill shouted into the forest.

"Yeah!" a voice called out.

"Hey! It's us, Bill and Kevin!"

"Who?" Kyle asked.

"Us! Bill and Kevin!" Kevin said.

"Yeah, it's us, too," Dan said. The three walked out of the woods clumped together, then all five quickly chattered away, bringing each group up to date on the situation.

"Any word from Pat and his crew?" Dan asked.

"Nope," Bill said.

"Probably lost our trail in the dark," Dan said.

"Yup," Bill said.

"Pat's the best out in the woods. He'll be fine," Dan said.

"Yup," Bill replied.

"Plus, it's warm outside and they have rifles," Dan said.

"Yup," Bill said.

"Okay, then. Ride! Go!" Dan said. "We'll walk behind, clear the forest some near the road. We might get lucky, but we can't do it all."

"It's a big forest for three men to clear," Bill agreed, sitting on his bike alongside Kevin.

"That's for sure," Dan said. "But we'll catch up soon. Right behind Tweedy, Corey and Don. Wait for us!"

Chapter Forty-Nine

Bill and Kevin rode past Tweedy, Corey and Don reaching Kelly, Joe and Buck a few minutes before them. Dan, Kyle and Rigo arrived a few minutes later. Joe was just straddling his bike, back bent over flat when the last three arrived.

Kelly carefully straightened Buck after Joe had hoisted him up on his back, alone.

"How's that, Joe?" Kelly asked.

"Wobbly."

"Okay. Let me try something else," Kelly said, reaching around Joe, fumbling with the belt, and even more with Buck's leather waist strap.

"What are you doing?" Joe asked.

"You'll see. It'll just take a minute. Gonna make you two tight and snug."

"Okay, here's what I suggest," Dan said, during the pause created by Kelly messing around with Buck and Joe's belts. "Me and Kevin'll jog alongside Kelly, Joe and Buck. There're still at least two of those freaks out there, maybe as many as four or five. Riding into town alone they're vulnerable, so they'll need escorts. The rest of you stay and scour the forest. It'll be light all night under this full moon."

"Hey, man, I'm a better runner. Me and Kyle should run with 'em instead," Corey said.

"What if we need to use the explosives? Kyle's best at that. He should stay," Dan said.

"Okay, then how about me and Tweedy? He's almost as fast as me," Corey said.

"Almost?" Tweedy asked.

"Fine. You guys do it, then," Dan said, while Bill stepped back, admiring Kelly's strap work.

"How's that?"

"Fine," Joe said.

"Kelly. What do you think?" Bill asked.

Kelly walked over and tugged here, pulled there, shifted Buck a bit, side to side. "He's strapped tight. Joe, just stay bent over all the way back," she said.

"Ride close beside me. Keep an eye on Buck all the time," Joe said.

"Are you sure he'll stay on your back?" Bill asked.

"I won't let him fall, but he's still a bit wobbly," Joe replied.

"Okay, let me hook his belt to yours and then I'll tie my belt to him, too," Bill said.

"Good idea," Joe said.

"Don't touch him. Let me do it," Kelly said. "He may have been exposed to their disease."

"Fine, you do it, then," Bill happily agreed, handing Kelly his belt.

"Here, this should do it," Kelly said, hooking Bill's belt around Buck, then fixing it snug around Joe's belt.

"Much better. Thanks," Joe said.

"Fine. Since I'll need both hands free to hold my pants up, now I've gotta put my handgun and holster in my pack instead of carrying it. Don't crash, Joe. I don't want Ng Ling Cheow's bike to get scratched," Bill joked, smiling and winking at Joe in an attempt to cheer him up for his long bike ride.

"Bill, you just smiled. You haven't done that in two days. All this time I thought your face had gotten permanently stuck on serious," Kelly said.

"Maybe more like two years," Kevin replied.

"Yeah, you should smile more. Maybe grow a short beard. When you smile you look kinda like the most interesting man in the world from those old Dos Equis commercials long ago." Corey said.

"I'm way better looking than him," Bill said.

"Hey, Bill, did you really punch a magician?" Tweedy asked.

"Yes." Bill's smile disappeared. "However, it was a musician, not a magician."

"You did not," Kelly said.

"I did. I once had an uncomfortable moment, too, just to see what it was like," Bill said.

"One?" Kelly asked.

"Yes, only one. It was a very long time ago, before I quit drinking."

"Oh, sure. You've had way more than one of those," Kelly said.

"Drinks?"

"No, embarrassing moments."

"I can only remember that one."

"What happened that one time?" Tweedy asked.

"I can't remember," Bill jokingly replied.

"How about when you spilled fuel all over yourself?" Kelly asked. "You reeked of gasoline for days!"

Bill cracked a narrow smile. "That doesn't count. Anyhow, stay thirsty, my friends."

"If Bryan from Dancing Roots can properly wave his magic wand at the hops and barley he's growing we just might have a cure for that thirst," Kevin said.

"That's what I'm talkin' about!" Tweedy said.

"Oh, yeah!" Corey said.

"Yeah! That'll keep everyone happy!" Kelly joked, as Bill's smile returned again. She shifted Buck's hips slightly. "Enough nonsense! Are you ready, Joe?"

"Yup."

"Runners?"

"Yup," Corey said.

"Yup," Tweedy said.

"Let's get this show on the road," Kelly said.

The two bikes pushed off. Tweedy reached over a moment to steady Joe until he got up to speed, careful to avoid touching Buck. The two running escorts, jogging with the bikes between them, held their AR-15s at the same forty-five degree angle across their chests. They were dressed identically in black Danner Acadia boots, faded, patched blue jeans and weathered black t-shirts. They would have looked like identical twins if not for the fact that Tweedy was white and Corey was black.

Chapter Fifty

Blake scampered down the cliff with his rifle on his back. As soon as he made it down, Conner kneeled next to Pat. "Are you hurt?"

Pat remained motionless. Then groaned as Blake leaned near.

"He's alive," Blake excitedly said.

"Of course I'm alive, you clown. I just got the wind knocked out of me, that's all."

"Let's see if you can stand. I'm hoping you didn't sprain your leg, or something," Conner said, one arm reaching down to Pat.

"Arghh," Pat said as he stood.

"Well?" Conner asked.

"Any parts malfunctioning?" Blake asked.

"Just sore, scraped up. Might have broke a rib or two. Can't breathe hard."

"Glad you're not hurt bad. Man, you really scared me," Blake deadpanned. "I thought you were gonna land on your rifle and break it."

Pat looked around excitedly, ignoring his pains. "My Dragunov! Where is it?"

"Relax. It's right here. I just picked it up. Not even a scratch," Blake said, holding the ungainly-looking sniper rifle in the moonlight.

"Did either of you two touch the scope? If one of you touched the scope, I'll kill ya," Pat warned.

"No. I set it down so the scope wasn't touching anything," Conner said.

"See? No scope touchee!" Blake said.

"Ahh, nice," Pat said, reaching over, gripping the rifle in his good right hand. Everything in the world was well, once again.

"Nice landing, but let's get moving. Those shots are calling us," Blake said.

"What shots?" Pat asked.

"Man, you really were knocked out. When you landed, we heard gunshots, lots of 'em. From over there," Conner said, pointing almost due north.

"Let's roll, then," Pat said.

"Are you sure you're okay?" Blake asked.

"My right ankle's sore. As long as it stays flat and I don't have to run, I'll be fine. No more blackberry bushes here, thank goodness. Just forest. There's an old logging road just ahead maybe a thousand yards. It goes to the water plant. I bet that's near where the shooting was from," Pat said.

"We better walk quietly, and stop talking. If some of the bad guys got away ..." Conner suggested.

The three headed north. Before they made it a hundred yards gunshots rang out once more, followed a few moments later by an explosion.

"Kyle?" Blake asked, smiling.

"Yup," Pat agreed, smiling at Conner and Blake as they picked up their pace, Pat limping along a bit out front as they headed toward the battle.

Chapter Fifty-One

The two men ran like scared deer, straight through bushes while leaping over logs without pausing. They remained filled with terror after seeing the two armed men suddenly appear in the middle of the road and open fire with their rifles. It had shocked them out of their minds. They saw their buddies get shot and fall on the asphalt. The two men were lucky to have escaped and they intended to run and run and keep running until they were far from Corbett, maybe all the way back to California. They fled straight south in the moonlit near-darkness heading into the unknown, heading straight at Pat O'Malley and his incredible accuracy.

Conner suddenly stopped. "Pat, Blake, stop!" he said, after the three men had walked a few hundred yards.

"I don't see anything," Pat said.

"Me neither, can't hear it either," Blake said, as all three ducked down, partially concealed by low, nondescript bushes.

"I hear something, or someone, coming. Something's moving north of us. It's moving fast, straight at us."

"Maybe a deer?" said Pat.

"There! Doesn't look like a deer to me," Blake said.

"Two, maybe three men. I can just barely see 'em, far off. Maybe two hundred yards away. Coming at us," Conner said. "See the moonlight flash on 'em when they run. There! See that?"

"Yup. Let's see if this old rifle still works." Pat raised it and prepared to fire. Since the ferocious battles along Gordon Creek Road two years earlier, he had fired only five rounds, needed to precisely sight-in his prized, black, Dragunov SVDS sniper rifle. Once satisfied, he gently placed it in its custom-built hard case where it remained ever since, until the day before.

"If you miss, we'll get 'em," Blake said.

"I won't miss," Pat replied, deadpan, as the two feral men moved closer.

"They're definitely not from here," Conner said, sharing his perfect vision with Pat while holding his rifle at the ready. "Look, they're carrying bows."

"Damn!" Pat said, as he aimed at the one farthest away. The sudden jolt from dozens of freshly scabbing blackberry thorn wounds on his arms and the awakening cliff rash on his chest made him realize that he was very much alive.

"You got him?" Blake asked.

"Yup. Arghh, wow! That really, really stings!" Pat said, wincing at all the cuts and scrapes on his body. Then, ignoring his pains, he went to a standing shooter's position and froze. His right index finger slowly pulled back on the trigger.

Chapter Fifty-Two

"Hey, man, check it out. The gate's gone," Corey said, when he and the others arrived at Larch Mountain Road.

"They took it out when Donahue Road was paved. That was two years ago," Tweedy said, with more than a dash of sarcasm. "You've been up here since the crash."

"Yeah, once or twice, only. I guess I just didn't notice."

"Dude, we've been past here at least six times," Tweedy said.

"No way, I would've seen it," Corey said.

"We hiked by here hunting three times just since winter. We carried all that deer meat back, hiked right by here. Make that twelve times, twice each trip, six up and six back."

"Well, the road's hidden behind those trees. Who looks there?" Corey responded.

"You going blind, or what?"

"Look, I ain't on no gate patrol," Corey said, still jogging along beside Kelly.

"Well, maybe if you ..."

"Okay! Enough! Can you two guys argue later?" Kelly asked, wondering how such good friends as Corey and Tweedy could constantly squabble over such small things. "You're just like an old married couple, sheesh."

"Now, what exactly do you mean by that?" Corey asked, indignantly.

"Forget it, Corey. Let's not go there. Let's change the subject. How ya doing now, Joe?" Tweedy asked, a little red-faced from jogging and a bit redder still from Kelly's annoying wisecrack. "Hey! You're really sweating!"

"I'm fine. How's Buck look?"

"Let me see." Tweedy jogged closer, looking at Buck, still securely strapped on while Joe sweated buckets from carrying the extra weight of Buck after pedaling to Larch Mountain Road. "He's still breathing. Unconscious, though."

"Okay. You and Corey stay real close to us. It's still five miles to the clinic and we'll need protection. The first two feral bastards got away and could be anywhere up here. They both have bows, too."

"Man, I bet they took off running and won't stop running until they keel over," Corey said.

"Yeah, or run off the bluff, into the Columbia River," Tweedy added.

"I hope so," Joe said. "But don't forget the others. A few more ran off, too."

"The ones that ran the other way, they're probably in Eugene by now," Corey said.

"I saw the bodies. They hardly look human. Like some kind of Neanderthals," Kelly said. "Remember, don't get close, they're diseased."

"Does that mean I don't get to use my American Lawman knife this time?" Corey asked.

"If you get close enough to use that thing, you'll probably catch whatever they have," Kelly replied. "So, no."

"If someone else finds 'em first we'll know because of the gunshots," Tweedy said, Corey laughing along with him.

"Hey guys, maybe we shouldn't chat so much, just in case," Kelly suggested, and they all quieted, running and biking for a time. The only sounds in the forest were from their breathing and the soft slapping of their shoes on the pavement. Then two distant gunshots broke the silence.

Chapter Fifty-Three

The two running men had no idea they were being watched as they fled south through the woods. They ran and ran, the cooling summer air flowing by their faces as they moved inhumanly fast, bobcat fast, through the woods. They dodged trees, leaped over logs and sprinted past occasional boulders. A rusting logging truck seemed to pass them, they ran by it so quickly. They had placed so much distance between themselves and the two men with the rifles that they started to calm down, slowing to a fast jog. Soon, they could slow to an easy jog and then stop and make a plan.

The faster of the two ferals found out differently when a gunshot flashed ahead of him. First he saw the flash. Then a split-second later, he heard the explosion. He thought the distant, hidden shooter had missed him, unaware he wasn't the target for that first round. He glanced back at his companion and saw him collapse, revealing a gaping exit wound in the center of his back. He stopped momentarily, then started to duck, just as he saw another distant flash.

Pat aimed at his center of mass, but the feral man ducked, taking the round in the middle of his face rather than the center of his chest.

"Hot damn, Pat!" Blake shouted. "Two at once!"

"Pat O'Malley, you are absolutely unbelievable! They were at least two hundred yards away! BAM! BAM! Two of 'em, one second apart," Conner said.

"A hundred fifty," Pat corrected him.

"Fine. A hundred and fifty," Conner replied, still grinning ear to ear.

"Don't get too excited. We still have to check 'em," Pat warned. "They might be wounded, or I may have missed."

"I doubt if you missed," Blake said.

"Yeah, remember what happened to Kyle two years ago? He found a dozen in the road still alive," Conner said.

"They weren't alive for long," Blake added, recalling that battle two years earlier when Kyle had dispatched the wounded with his knife.

"Neither were their buddies," Blake added, referring to the hundred or more who had scattered into the woods.

"After taking out the wounded, Kyle ran straight down the road and cut the rest of 'em off. Those animals were all tangled up in the blackberries, climbing over logs and boulders. Then you came at 'em, Pat," Conner said.

"I remember every second," Pat replied.

"Kyle got way ahead of 'em, waited behind a log, and nailed some more," Conner said.

"That was a hell of a battle," Blake said, while they walked toward the fallen men.

"Okay, be careful, guys. Spread out. Rifles ready. Let's just see what we have," Pat said.

They made it to the bodies, then gathered around one another.

"Scumbag number one is dead. Most of his head's missing," Blake said. "What happened, Pat? You missed his chest."

"No way, it wasn't a miss. I saw the guy duck at the last second," Conner said.

"Yup," Pat said.

"Guy must have been surprised. Look at them. They look like zombies. It makes ya wonder what the last thing that went through this animal's mind was," Conner asked.

"Probably Pat's bullet," Blake said.

"That's cute, Blake. The second guy's also dead. Hole in the chest. Right where I aimed."

"Hey, look. These guys are wearing Ebi's shirts. I remember he always wore this black, button down dress shirt at funerals. Remember when we had twenty a week for awhile?" Blake said.

"Yup. Each week," Pat said. "I'd just as soon forget that first winter."

"The other guy's not wearing Ebi's shirt. He's wearing his wife's shirt. See? It's a blouse. He's got on her jeans, too," Conner said. "Look."

"See? They're newer, clean denim. She always kept them nice, for special occasions. These two guys are so skinny. They have nothing. They're very unhealthy looking. Notice the condition of his skin," Pat said, pointing at the first man he shot, the moon shining unkindly on his diseased face.

"Yeah, nasty. Like, maybe a vitamin deficiency or something worse," Blake said.

"Or some freaky disease. Let's not get near 'em in case it's contagious. These guys couldn't go on living like this for too much longer," Conner said.

"Look at his hair. It's falling out in places," Pat added.

"Yeah, especially where your bullet took half his head off," Blake said.

"Now, Blake. You know what else this means?" Pat asked.

"No," Blake said.

"What?" Conner asked.

"It means that people living like this are a dying breed. It means we'll probably never see another group like this again. Look, no women, no kids, no possessions, either. Buck mentioned he hadn't seen a group of wandering people in a long time. Their numbers have been dropping steadily, and they're not recruiting. See what they did to Buck? They could have invited him into their group. But they didn't. No, to me, this is a very happy moment. Unreal. Yeah, I think I've shot a man for the last time."

"I doubt it. Corbett's just too tempting a target. We'll always need people to defend us," Connor said.

"Hey, this one has a small pack on his back. He fell on it. We should look inside," Blake suggested.

"How do we do that without touching him?" Conner asked.

"We could use a branch, lever him over," Blake suggested.

"Okay," Pat said. Blake and Conner found a few suitable strong branches on the forest floor.

"Okay, let's flip him over," Conner said. They turned him over and Blake carefully removed the pack. It was light, nearly empty. Blake unhooked the snaps with his fingertips, dumping the contents on the forest floor.

"Two knives and a thick book. That's all," Blake said.

"Better leave that stuff," Conner said.

"A book? I can't believe it." Pat said. "It looks as tattered as him."

"What's the title, Blake?" Conner asked.

"Let me see, I gotta hold it to the light. It's a dictionary."

"A dictionary?" Pat asked, unable to believe what he'd just heard.

"Yup, a dictionary," Blake said.

"I can't believe it," Pat said. "A tool of words, a reflection of man's collective minds. His thoughts, all found in one book. All that's needed is to arrange the words in that book in creative, thoughtful ways and one can express any idea, any concept in the entire universe. And this simple animal was carrying one. Imagine, of all the books to carry. This is unreal."

"Okay, enough philosophy. What do you wanna do with the two bodies," Blake asked, pointing the dictionary at the bodies with his left hand, rifle in the other.

"Leave 'em for the forest. It has to eat, too," Pat said, sprinkling a bit more of his somewhat crude, yet common sense wisdom on the younger men.

"How about the dictionary?" Blake asked.

Pat thought a while. "Hm. Maybe we should bury it. It's a book of our language. It should be treated to a proper burial, unlike these two animals."

"Well, it's kinda moldy, really beat up. Some pages are missing. In fact, if you look you'll notice about a fourth of 'em are torn out. Gone," Blake said.

"I wonder why?" Conner asked both of them, all three pondering this dilemma a moment, standing alongside the two bodies.

"Oh man. I get it," Blake said, and he started laughing. "Dude, it's his toilet paper."

"You should drop it. I mean, on the ground, like, right now," Pat said.

"That guy hasn't washed his hands in ages ... and look again at those sores on his face," Conner said.

"And his hands," Pat added.

Blake released the dictionary, letting it fall on the ground.

"Their skin. It's almost falling off in places. They were all slowly dying. Let's get out of here, see if the others need any help. And be ready. There might be more of 'em. Our job is to get 'em all before they get us," Pat said, "like they did to the Ebis."

Chapter Fifty-Four

The two remaining ferals were armed with deadly handmade bows. Both men had twenty arrows snugly grouped into their quivers. When the shooting started they panicked and ran in the opposite direction, eventually turning left on Larch Mountain Road, running straight west into town.

They moved along the roadside, not the middle. They had to duck into the trees three times to avoid passing patrols, including one with two bikes, two joggers and an injured man tied on the back of a muscular bike rider.

Those patrolling the eastern half of Corbett heard the gunshots and explosions that had just rocked the western slope of Larch Mountain. They were eager to help, but the disciplined guards continued patrolling their areas or remained at their assigned positions, as good soldiers always will.

"You hear that? Another two shots," Alison said.

"That makes about two hundred, plus all those explosions. We're missing the war," JP said.

"My sister's out there. How about me and Vladimir go out a ways, just to the Vista House turnout," Alison said.

"You know the deal. The second response team stays right here."

"JP, let me explain," Vladimir said. "Our team has twelve, plus you, plus all those guys hanging out at the fire station. That makes about fifty armed people along this two-mile stretch of the highway. You won't miss two of us. Plus, we'll only be out for a while. We'll go out there, watch and listen for a while, then come straight back."

"You'll both be back by midnight?"

"Not a minute later," Vladimir said.

"Yup. JP, sitting here on the soccer field waiting while Kelly's out there is driving me nuts! But I know I belong here, too, with my team. Just 'til midnight. Two hours. We'll be back. Promise."

"Okay, but take Dave Smith with you. And grab three bikes. If you see something get back here fast. If the Chief or anyone asks, I'll say the three of you are on an inner town patrol. Dave's gonna make sure you don't get lost, you know, maybe come back late for some reason."

"Lost?" Alison asked.

"Just kidding. Three is stronger. Safer."

"Thanks, JP," Alison said, and gave him a nice wrap-around hug.

"C'mon, Alison, knock it off. You're gonna get Dave and Vladimir jealous. Everyone knows your heart belongs to them," JP joked.

Dave worked for the Bonneville Power Administration and knew the area by heart. The redheaded, ruddy-faced, scholarly-looking man of slender build had an incredible vocabulary. People said his thick, bushy hair, his red afro, sprouted larger as his vocabulary increased. He kept a word-a-day study going right through the disaster and up until this very day. "In this life I would like to memorize the entire English language," he would sometimes say. Medical terms were a recent favorite.

"What's the word, Dave?" Vladimir asked, as the three walked east along the highway.

"Trust."

"Trust?" Vladimir asked.

"Yup, trust. That's the word."

"That's an easy one."

"Yup. JP gave it to all of us. Let's not lose it. The turn-off, wait an hour, then return. That's it."

"Well, it's better with three, anyhow," Alison said. The three enjoyed the moonlit bike ride, making it to the turnoff in no time.

"Hey, let's wait over there, behind that guardrail. That way, if any of the ferals come we'll see them first," Alison said.

"It's past the turnoff," Dave said.

"Yeah, but only by a hundred yards or so," Alison replied.

"It's the best place. Nice and dark. The moonlight is on the road, but behind the guardrail it's dark. Perfect," Vladimir added.

The three moved up Larch Mountain Road and hopped the guardrail. They stashed the bikes in the trees and sat in the gravel and waited. They didn't wait long.

Chapter Fifty-Five

Pat and his crew eventually made it to Donahue Road. They saw the seven dead men in the road near the water plant, inspected them briefly from a safe distance, and kept walking. They eventually met up with the six others who had just gathered near the fifteen dead still staining the asphalt where Buck had just been shot by another arrow.

"Pat! Blake! Conner! Damn good to see you," Dan said. Bill, Dan, Kyle, Kevin, Rigo and Don were standing in the road just after carefully checking the dead for anything of value. They found eleven excellent quality bows, two ratty-looking ones, several dozen knives, six rifles and two battered old revolvers, but didn't handle any of the newfound weapons. The dead had no food in their possession. True scavengers.

"Stay away from these bodies. They've all got some sick-looking skin thing," Dan said. "We found a few things worth keeping, as you see, but in the morning we'll have to dig a shallow pit and somehow drag 'em there and dump 'em in it. The river's too far to move 'em all."

"Why bother? The two Pat just shot are on the forest floor. Animals will clean their carcasses in no time," Conner added.

Blake jumped in. "You should've seen Pat's shots, too! Unbelievable! Two hundred yards away he ..."

"A hundred and fifty ..." Pat corrected.

"We heard the shots," Kevin excitedly said.

"Two shots, two dead. Typical Pat O'Malley excellence!" Conner added. Pat blushed some but in the moonlight no one noticed.

"Hey, wait a minute, I'm telling the story," Blake said looking down from half a foot above most of the others, a foot above a few. And he did tell the story, sparing no detail. After a few years had passed, the story grew. It became two, five-hundred-yard shots in total darkness, but by then everyone had heard the real story dozens of times so they just listened, enjoying Blake's friendly humor.

"The others took Buck back. He's got a fever. Infection from the earlier arrow wound. He was just now shot in the thigh, not deadly, but still a nasty wound. He was unconscious when Kelly strapped him to Joe's back for the bike ride to town," Bill said. "Kelly's with him now, riding side-by-side, and Tweedy and Corey are jogging with them, too. Joe said two got away, down the road toward town. The forest here is as cleared as we can get it tonight," Bill said.

"We counted twenty-eight killed. Fifteen here, seven in the road a mile back, two I shot in the woods, one Kyle blew apart, the two Pat shot and one Kelly kicked," Dan said.

"Kelly kicked someone?" Blake asked.

"Yeah, the one Kelly kicked," Dan said.

"Whadda ya mean by that? I don't get it," Blake asked.

"Yeah, me neither," Conner added.

"She kicked a guy and he died?" Pat asked, wondering along with the others what the real story was.

"Yeah. Exactly what I said," Dan replied.

"How many times?" Blake asked.

"Once," Kevin said.

"Once?" Pat asked, wondering where this story was headed.

"How do you kick someone once and kill them?" Pat asked.

"Hit 'em in the right spot," Dan said.

"Okay, okay, how did number twenty-eight bite it?" Blake asked, tired of hearing the explanation go around in silly circles.

"Okay, here's what happened. The guy tried to steal her dad's AR-15. So Kelly kicked him in the chin. That's all."

"She kicked him in the shin?" Kyle asked.

"No, the chin, right here," Dan said, pointing at his chin.

"Oh."

"That's all?" Pat asked.

"Yup," Dan answered.

"Hey, any one of us would have done the exact same thing if some scumbag was trying to steal our dad's AR," Blake said.

"Yeah, but only Kelly could've made one kick deadly," Dan added.

"Well, there's one other person," Bill said.

"Who?" Blake asked.

"The only person in town that can kick her butt, that's who!"

"No one kicks Kelly's butt. She's totally bad-ass," Blake said. "I sparred with her once, just fooling around. Never do that again."

"No one can guess who I'm talking about?" Bill asked. "C'mon!"

"Oh! I get it. You're talking about Alison, her sister. Yeah. Oh yeah. My money would be on Alison, too," Blake said. "Alison's not as tall, not as strong, but she's way faster."

"Yup," Bill said, as the others nodded in agreement.

Chapter Fifty-Six

"Look! It's Kelly! And Joe!" Alison said, hopping the guardrail and waving her arms. "Sister!"

"Alison! What are you doing out here?" Kelly asked.

"Vladimir, Dave and I heard the shots and explosions. Probably everyone did. We, me and Vladimir, we talked JP into letting us wait here, in case we heard or saw anything," Alison said. "Dave came along, too."

"We'll talk later. I gotta get moving. Buck's shot. Sorry Alison, but we really gotta go," Joe said. Tweedy and Corey arrived a moment later, exhausted, glad to know they were almost to the clinic.

"Okay, hurry!"

"Listen, there're still a few of them wackos running loose. You be careful," Joe said.

"The road's clear the remainder of the way to town," Dave said. "Get moving!"

They took off, Joe and Kelly pedaling hard, leaving the runners jogging behind.

"Well, your sister's safe. Wanna head back?" Vladimir asked.

"Well, since we're out and about anyhow, why not remain for our allotted time. We might get fortunate and apprehend a few bad guys," Dave said, grinning like a wild haired, mad scientist.

"Well, why not? Let's chill out behind the south guardrail," Vladimir said.

"It's a nice evening, we might as well," Alison said. They waited, whispering to one another now and then while all three stared in an easterly direction, down the road and into the nearby forest. It was a stunningly beautiful evening. It was still warm as midnight drew near, the moon shone bright, and the air remained windless.

"I hope Buck's okay," Alison said.

"I'm sure Denise and Kelly will have him good as new by morning. Buck looks like a really tough guy, with a strong will to live from what I heard," Dave said. "Remember, it's the will to live that carries many back to health, not the medicine. If I had to select one or the other, I'd grant myself a strong will to live over all the pre-collapse medicine in the world."

"I don't know. He looked like a corpse tied to Joe's back," Vladimir said. "I mean, they better hurry up and do something."

"Quiet. There's something. Don't move," Vladimir said.

"What?" Alison replied.

"Light footsteps, not too far off. It's coming from the side of the road, the gravel. Listen."

"Footsteps," Dave said.

"Yup," Alison said. "Two people. Maybe fifty yards away."

"Rifles ready," Dave said, but he didn't have to say it. The three rifles were already lined up, motionless, raised just below the rusty "S" curved guardrail.

"It's them," Alison said.

The crunching of gravel grew louder as they approached the east end of the guardrail.

"If they walk on our side of the guardrail, they'll walk right into us," Vladimir said to Alison, so quietly Dave was unable to hear him.

Alison nodded.

The two men edged right, walking right at them on the asphalt. The three rifles were a foot apart, rock-steady, pointing straight down the road, an inch under the top of the rail. It was nearly pitch dark in the shade behind the guardrail, but the road remained illuminated with moonlight. The Carhartt label on Fred Ebi's jacket was clearly visible when Dave stood suddenly and shouted, "Freeze!"

One of the ferals hopped the guardrail and bolted toward the woods. Alison and Vladimir opened fire at the same time, dropping him dead, while Dave's rifle remained fixed on the center of the other man's chest.

"On the pavement, arms out. Move!" Dave shouted.

Without speaking a word, the nervous and jittery man flattened out on the asphalt, arms and legs far apart.

"Vladimir, search him," Dave said.

"No way. I'm not getting near him. He has sores. Nasty-looking ones," Vladimir said.

While Alison and Dave pointed their rifles at the man, Vladimir ordered the man to sit and remove the stolen jacket, and toss it aside.

"Take your boots off, scumbag. Toss 'em," Vladimir ordered.

"Pants, too," Dave added.

"Even from twenty feet away, this guy reeks something awful!" Vladimir said, turning away briefly for air.

"The pants, asshole. Off now," Dave ordered.

"Dave! Such language!" Alison said.

"Sorry. I forgot you don't like people swearing. I was thinking of words much worse," Dave said.

"Why his pants?" Alison asked.

"In case he runs," Vladimir replied, for Dave.

"We need to interview him, find out if there are more threats," Dave said.

"Dave's right," Alison said.

"I say we dust this animal right now," Vladimir suggested.

"Later. First we'll take him to town, see what he knows," Dave said.

The man was barefoot. All he was wearing now was a filthy t-shirt, which hung discreetly to his thighs when they made him stand.

"Walk!" Dave commanded the man. He did.

"I wish I had some rope," Alison said.

"Yeah, we could hang him off the Vista House," Vladimir replied.

"No, I mean to tie his hands."

"Then you'd have to put your hands on him. I just hope he runs," Vladimir said, jabbing the end of his rifle into the man's back.

Since it was a gentle slope nearly all the way, it would have been easier riding the bikes back to the fire station, but still, they made it there in a short time.

Chapter Fifty-Seven

"Look what we have," Dave shouted out to the Chief while approaching the fire station. "A prisoner!"

"What do you mean?" The Chief asked. "We don't have anywhere to put him. What the hell you bring him here for?"

Dave walked through the open bay door and stood next to the Chief, who was standing with a small group of men alongside the still-gleaming yet permanently parked red fire truck. "To quiz him. We might learn something," Dave replied.

"Let me look at him," the Chief said, walking through the tall door. Others were gathering in the highway near the smelly spectacle.

Alison and Vladimir stood guard a safe distance from the man.

"He's sick. Everyone, stay far away from him!" Alison shouted.

"He's really sick, no one get near him," someone yelled. The small crowd of curious onlookers backed away.

"I believe he has staphylococcus aureus," Dave said.

"What's that?" the Chief asked.

"A sometimes deadly skin disease. Small, open, pus-filled sores on the skin. It's very contagious. A small percentage of people have it. A few spread it. Some of us in town may, too. But his sores look ugly. He's very contagious."

"He knows we're going to kill him, too," Vladimir said. "He understands English, but he isn't talking."

"Well, we still have a prisoner," Dave said. The smelly captive sat in the middle of the highway. Harger stood under the tall sliding door. Alison and Vladimir still had their rifles casually pointing at the man even though he was no longer a flight risk with a dozen or more men gathered around a safe distance away. There was still the chance he might bolt and run into someone, spreading his disease, so eyes remained aimed at him.

"Why didn't you just shoot him?" Harger asked.

"I still could," Dave suggested.

"Fine. You do it. Take him out in the woods so he doesn't bleed on the asphalt," The Chief said. He was often rough with words, yet exceptionally compassionate when caring for people of the town and still strangely fastidious about the cleanliness of his volunteer fire station and the nearby highway.

"No, wait. We can't do it that way. Let's give the man a fair trial," Reverend Golphenee suggested. "Tomorrow morning, just before sunrise."

"Fine. First thing in the morning, then."

"I'll see you guys then. Right now, I'm going to the clinic, see how Buck's doing. See you all there, or in the morning right here," Scott said.

Most said goodbye to Scott, but a few others tagged along, interested in checking on Buck's progress.

"Well, maybe some value can come of keeping him alive a few hours. We'll interview him, find out more about the outside," the Chief said.

"Good idea, but he isn't talking. We tried," Alison said.

"Oh, I bet we could get him to talk. Look at him. He's dying of hunger. If we set food in front of him, he'd talk," The Chief said.

"Good idea, but a waste of food," Dave said. "But first, can we hose him down? He really stinks."

"Good idea." The Chief waved his hand toward the group of men gathered from some distance around the prisoner. "Could a few of you take this guy near the driveway and power-wash him? If you take off a layer of skin, I doubt the Ebi boys would mind. He was wearing their dad's coat. I know I wouldn't mind if you hosed it all off."

"Stand over there," someone said. The man walked to the place he pointed, then stopped, standing in the highway where he was told.

None of the men wanted to get near the prisoner, so a human traffic jam formed near the truck as the man was ordered to stand in the road near the driveway, just within reach of the hose. No one dared get close for fear of catching whatever caused the open, tiny, reddish, puss-filled sores on his face and arms.

After he was thoroughly hosed down, the shivering man stood outside, dripping water and who-knows-what-else all over the highway. "Don't breathe near him. He might be contagious," Dave said.

"You know what? I wanna talk to him," the Chief said.

"Down," several men ordered. The man sat.

"I'll go get some delicious smoked salmon," someone said, loud enough for the prisoner to hear.

He returned. "Here's the salmon, let me put some on the road, maybe slide it closer to him so he sees it better, smells it, too."

"I'll start with an easy question," The Chief said. "What's your name?"

The man sat quietly, unmoving, staring at the salmon.

Chapter Fifty-Eight

It was uncanny how quickly news spread without automobiles and telephones. Fast pedaling bicyclists and runners often carried news this way and that. This evening, bicyclists and runners fanned out across town going from house to house with the good news that the attack was nearly over, and all but one of the attackers had apparently been killed.

Within no time at all, nearly everyone in town, and most people in outlying areas, had heard about the twenty-nine ferals killed and the one captured alive. They had heard that the attackers numbered thirty, yet no one knew for sure how many there were. But, when the tally hit thirty, a cloud of fear lifted.

The celebratory mood was tarnished by the sad news that the stranger, Buck, who had risked his life fighting valiantly for their community, had been wounded in battle and that he was at the clinic near death.

Although he had only been in town two days, the story of his amazing walk across the continent and his life-threatening chest wound was known by nearly everyone. The few who had the good fortune to meet him told others of his captivating kind manner and of his gentle, genuine personality. People he had met only briefly considered him their friend. Those who only heard of him felt an odd growing kinship with him. When they found out he had been shot again, carried unconscious on a bicycle to the clinic on the back of Joe Hancock, they were heartbroken and couldn't just sit at home doing nothing. The community mobilized.

When they heard about Buck, they got out of bed, laced up their boots and moccasins and headed to the clinic, where a crowd was forming in the warm summer night.

When the two Ebi sons found out that one killer had been captured alive, parked in the highway in front of the fire station, they too got out of bed. They also grabbed their guns and saddled up, literally. But they didn't have Buck on their minds. They were focused on revenge and had already started galloping to the fire station just when the Chief was about to give up asking questions.

"He won't talk, I tell ya," Dave said.

"Oh, eventually he will," the Chief replied.

"We've been sitting a long time and he still won't say a word, just keeps staring at that scrap of salmon," Dave said.

"Horses. I hear horses," someone said.

Rocky Ebi rode up to the fire station, "Is that him?" Rocky asked, as he got off the horse. Andy, his brother, rode up a moment later and got off his horse, tying both to the speed limit sign in front.

"Don't do anything stupid," The Chief said.

"Oh, I won't. I'm just gonna slit his throat, like he did to my mom and dad."

"Don't go near him. He's diseased," Alison warned.

"Can't you wait 'til morning?" the Chief suggested.

"Why? He killed my mom and dad."

"Because we're going to have a trial in the morning, right before sunrise. We're not gonna become scumbags like them. We'll have due process around here as long as I'm president of the town council. You can slit his throat after that. Or shoot him, if you prefer. He isn't going anywhere. You can wait a few hours. Both of you."

"What's the difference? Why wait?"

"Find someone else to argue with. Go over to the clinic. See Scott. If he doesn't convince you guys to wait, come back, we'll talk. Maybe we can speed the trial up some."

"We'll be back shortly," Rocky said.

Then, as he and Andy walked past their horses, Andy looked at the man sitting at the end of the driveway, not twenty feet from their impromptu hitching post. "Don't go anywhere, we'll be right back. While we're gone, think of that one bullet and where you'd like to get it."

Andy and Rocky walked to the clinic and saw the crowd. "What's this?" Andy asked someone.

"It's that stranger, Buck. He was shot by another arrow when he was fighting the attackers with Big Joe. He might die."

"We heard," Andy said.

"He's on his death bed. We're praying for him," the man said.

"All of you?"

"Not all, but lots. More in the back, too. Some of the Buddhists are chanting there, by his window. Buck risked his life for us. We all want to do what we can to help him. You should join us."

"Maybe later. We have something to do, first. Where's Scott?" Rocky asked.

"In the front, on the footpath by the porch. See him?" The man pointed through the crowd.

"Yeah, thanks," Rocky said, and he and his brother snaked their way through the crowd.

Chapter Fifty-Nine

"How's he look, Denise?" Joe asked. Denise and Kelly had been working on Buck for thirty minutes before they allowed the two men inside the examination room.

"Horrible. The wound in his leg isn't bad at all. It'll heal if he lives long enough. It's the infection. It's eating him up from the inside."

"How's his fever?" Joe asked, while Denise's husband, Chris, Tweedy and Corey all stood by.

"One-oh-three point five," Kelly said. "He's no longer burning up, but he's still very hot. That's why we took all his clothes off, except for that extra-large yellow tank-top so he could have some decency."

"How's a guy have any decency in a yellow tank-top?" Tweedy asked.

"Joe Tweedy!" Corey said.

"Denise thinks she was able to isolate some salicylic acid from birch bark," Chris said.

"What's that?" Tweedy asked.

"Aspirin … well, almost aspirin. It's from birch bark. Reduces fever, stops inflammation and reduces pain. It does all sorts of things. Denise's been trying to produce some for months now. Just experimenting. But now she says she has it."

"We also have some really old antibiotics. One of the guys found them in that abandoned farmhouse, the one the ferals tore through last night. They're expired long ago. Some are missing but I'll try anything," Denise said.

"He's out cold. How do you plan to get the medicine inside him?" Tweedy asked.

"There's only one way when someone's unconscious. Corey, Tweedy, Joe and Chris, would you guys mind waiting outside while Kelly and I do this? In fact, he may be contagious. All of you should stay out, except Joe and Chris. If Buck's caught the feral disease, it's too late for them. Too late for me and Kelly, too."

"Huh?" Tweedy said.

"I'll explain it to him outside," Corey said, and the men left the room, giving Buck some privacy for what was soon coming his way.

Kelly dribbled shots of cold tap water on Buck's head while Denise crushed up two of the tiny white pills.

"I'm going to give him some more salicylic acid, then two crushed antibiotic pills at once now, then one every eight hours until they're gone," Denise said.

She and Kelly gently rolled Buck on his right side, folding his knees as near to his chest as possible so they could easily administer the medicine.

"Now we wait. We just stay here and wait," Denise said.

Kelly stepped out of the examination room to share the news with the men, all of whom were standing near the front door looking outside. "What are you staring at?"

"Look," Joe said and he started crying, softly. "Look at the front of the clinic."

Kelly walked between the men and looked outside. It was after midnight, yet a huge crowd had gathered in front of the clinic. "Hi everyone. What's this all about?"

"We heard about what Buck and Joe did," a voice from the crowd said.

"We heard he was dying," another said.

"We heard he was shot, again. We all want to help him," yet another said.

Kelly stepped into the front of the porch and explained to them the facts of Buck's dire condition. Then she went back inside.

The Reverend had arrived earlier and addressed a new group just joining the crowd. More townspeople were constantly arriving, many carrying weapons. Some rode horses, including the Ebi boys, who were just then passing by on their way to the fire station.

Jimmy and Deborah Lee arrived, too. "How's Buck?" Jimmy asked Scott, after stepping through the growing crowd.

After hearing about his condition, Jimmy asked, "Which room is he in? I would like to stand near his room and chant a while, if it would be okay."

"Some others beat you to it. They're already by his window, chanting," Scott said.

He joined Deborah as they walked around the building, stood in a small group in the back and quietly began chanting in Pali. It was an ancient language, which carried through time an even more ancient prayer for the sick and injured.

"Chanting?" someone asked. "How long will they do that?"

"Until sunrise," Kelly said. "Maybe longer. I'll join them soon, but from inside. Ng Ling Cheow is back there. Anyone's welcome."

The crowd continued to grow. And then it grew some more. Soon there were hundreds of people in front of the clinic, many in small groups, quietly praying together for Buck. The crowd, larger then the one on election day, reached the highway in front of the clinic. A group of twelve sat cross-legged in the back, under Buck's window, softly chanting in that ancient, but not forgotten, language.

Just as Scott was about to lead the crowd in a special prayer two men walked up to him. "Scott? Me and Andy need to talk to you," Rocky said.

"I know what you want from me. You want my blessing for your revenge. Well, that's perfectly understandable. If I was in your shoes I might feel the exact same way. But that animal isn't going anywhere. We'll have a trial in a few hours. It'll be fast. A jury decides a case like this pretty quickly. Remember, we won't decay to their level. We'll follow the rules, our six laws. Murder is only punishable by permanent banishment. That won't work in this case. We could also charge him with trespassing into town, which is punishable by death. He'll have a chance to defend himself."

"My mom and dad didn't have a chance to defend themselves," Andy said.

Scott drew very near Andy and Rocky and spoke softly, so others couldn't eavesdrop. "I understand your anguish. But we're above the crude and simple savages on the outside. Please abandon your quest for revenge, just for the time being, and join us now in a prayer for Buck. He's dying. One or two more of us praying can make a mighty big difference right now."

"When it's near dawn, we'll draw a jury and get this finished?" Andy asked.

"That's exactly what'll happen," Scott replied.

When the pre-dawn light began to chase the night away, the crowd thinned some, but the majority was still there, keeping the vigil going for Buck.

Chapter Sixty

Denise had managed to grab three or four short naps during the night. Buck's fever had dropped to one-oh-two, and she thought she heard him mumbling while he slept.

Chris and Joe had been on the floor in the main room, near the front door, trying to keep their prayers for Buck going, but after such a long, strenuous day, they had reached their physical limits. They were now flat on their backs, alongside each other near the door, sound asleep. Corey and Tweedy were sitting on the front porch, leaning against each other, backs to the horizontal siding, sleeping.

In the crowd, people stood around in small groups. Some sat in the grass. A few slept. Most of the people in Corbett lived within a few miles of the clinic, so it was a short walk. Without lights, television, Internet and cell phones, there was very little to do after dark, so generally people slept. But on this warm summer night, with the moon full and a powerful reason to gather, they came out by the hundreds and they stayed.

A soft, melodious chanting could be heard in the backyard. A constant murmur of the talking and praying from hundreds drifted through the open front door.

Bill, Dan, Pat, Kyle and the rest of the first response team had arrived during the night and had joined in the vigil for Buck. Vladimir and Dave were in the back of the crowd talking to Eddie Cho, who, despite his pleas to visit with Kelly, was not allowed in the clinic. She would only speak to him from a safe distance. Kelly and Denise didn't want any more people exposed to the staph infection. Alison was with her parents, out back. The prisoner still sat in the road, guarded by Mike Walker, Mason Scharfe and Brad Sharp, three of the volunteer firefighters gathered at the fire station. He remained silent, staring at the now-withering scrap of salmon.

Most of the town's perimeter patrols remained in effect, but, although many in the crowd had gone home, others were arriving as their patrol shifts ended. It seemed like everyone in Corbett was still gathered at the clinic. It was no doubt the largest gathering the town had ever had. A third of the adult population of Corbett, maybe six hundred people, had been there at one time or another through the night. Three hundred were still there as the sky started to glow in the pre-dawn. Most were still awake.

Denise stepped over Joe and Chris and walked to the front porch. "Everyone! Listen! His fever is dropping some. He spoke during his sleep. The arrow wound from last night is healing fine, no swelling, no infection, yet.

The one from three days ago still looks bad, but it's not getting worse. We're changing the blackberry leaf coverings regularly. The birch bark is working on his fever and swelling. I'll give him more soon. For now, each breath he takes is a miracle. Please, stay. All of you. He really needs your help. Please, stay."

"We aren't going anywhere," a voice called out.

"None of us are leaving," said another.

Denise went back inside.

"Scott, it's time we picked a jury," Rocky said.

Scott was well respected and trusted by all. He was responsible for choosing the jurors. This was the third time a jury had been assembled.

"Okay. I agree. We can't leave that unresolved any longer."

"Attention! Everyone! I need volunteers. Seven citizens are needed for a jury. Right now. You all know what this is about. If you find the scumbag guilty of trespassing, he'll face the death penalty. You'll all have to serve on the firing squad. Seven rifles, only one with a live round. Alison, Vladimir, Dave, you three are witnesses. Since you caught him, you'll need to come, too." Dozens of hands shot up.

Harger had dozed off on the drying grass in the clinic's front yard. He felt a gentle kick to his ribs. "Get up. Get up. We need to go to the fire station. Right now. It's time for the trial," Kimberly Cho said. "Ed Rainier and Bill Hartigan are there waiting for us. The Chief, too. The trial starts well before sunrise. That's very soon, now. Go out back and get Alison. She's needed as a witness."

The seven jurors were quickly selected. The first seven adults Scott saw with their hands raised were picked. Scott briefed them, like he had done with different jurors two times before. The group walked to the fire station, trailed by a few dozen curious onlookers. The doomed man sat in the highway. Three rifles were aimed at him from a safe distance.

Most of the crowd trusted that justice would be delivered and remained at the clinic. Praying for Buck was more important.

Chapter Sixty-One

The Chief stood in the highway facing the accused with Harger and Kimberly on his left and Ed and Bill on his right. Three men with rifles stood twenty feet from the man. No one had been near him.

"The People's Court of the Town of Corbett is now in session. Jurors, please stand near the rest of us. We have before us a man accused of murder and trespassing. If he's found guilty of murder, the penalty is permanent banishment. If he's found guilty of trespassing into town, the penalty is death. Jurors, are you ready?"

"Yes," they all said, almost in unison.

"Witnesses, are you ready?"

"Yes," Alison, Vladimir and Dave replied.

Since there was no need for public defenders or prosecuting attorneys, the Chief and the other four members of the town council stood a safe distance away and interviewed the suspect while he sat cross-legged in the highway, nude other than the loose-fitting t-shirt.

"What's your name?" Harger asked the man.

Silence.

"Okay. It's John Doe, then. John Doe, how to you plead? Guilty or not guilty?"

Silence.

"Okay, we'll call it a not guilty plea," Harger continued. "Next councilmember, your question."

"Were you in the group that killed the Ebis?" Kimberly asked.

Silence.

Are you intending to defend yourself at all?" Kimberly asked.

Silence.

"Next councilmember," Kimberly said.

"Were you a member of the group that raided three farmhouses two days ago?" Bill asked.

Silence.

"This isn't getting anywhere. I'd like to interview the three who caught this piece of garbage," Ed said.

Alison, Vladimir and Dave drew closer.

"Alison, could you describe the clothing this man was wearing when you caught him last night?"

"Yes. He had on baggy blue jeans and Fred Ebi's Carhartt jacket. He was wearing newer boots, too. They're right over there, by the jacket and jeans," Alison said.

"Vladimir, is what Alison's saying correct?"

"Yes."

"Dave?"

"Yes."

"Alison, was the man alone?"

"No, he was with another guy."

"Where is he?"

"Dead, along the road by the Vista House turnoff."

"What was he wearing?"

"He had on Marilyn Ebi's jeans and shirt. They fit him, he was really skinny."

"That's enough. Next councilmember?"

"I wanna ask Rocky and Andy a few questions. Have either of you seen his clothing or the clothing worn by the one Alison and Vladimir shot?" Bill asked.

"No."

"The clothes are still in the middle of the road. The body is a few feet away," Alison said.

"Okay, I see the sun's rising soon. Would it be possible for you two to bike up there and take a peek, then come back and let us know if the clothes they were wearing belong to your parents?" the Chief asked.

"Yeah, we'll take the horses. It'll just take us a few minutes," Rocky replied. He and Andy untied their horses and mounted.

"Remember, don't get near the dead guy. He's got some skin disease," Alison said.

"We're gonna look, then come straight back," Rocky replied.

"Well, I don't see a need to question this animal any longer. Jurors, are you ready to meet?"

"Yes," they replied nearly in one voice.

One juror spoke up. "But we'll decide when Rocky and Andy get back. If Rocky and Andy come back and say the clothes on the dead guy belong to someone else, we should maybe question him more."

The jury met in the front of Rueben Moreland's house, just across the highway from the fire station. They stood and waited.

Meanwhile, Rocky and Andy returned, sullen, heads down. Andy was crying. They rode up to the jury. "Dad's clothes are in the road. The dead guy's wearing mom's clothes," Rocky said.

A moment later, one member of the jury crossed the highway, "Chief, we've reached a verdict. It's unanimous, too."

"What have you decided?"

"Guilty on both charges. Punishment: death. Could someone get the seven rifles ready? We don't want this piece of trash to see the sunrise."

"I think we have them ready now. Rueben, didn't you say you would prepare seven rifles? You got 'em ready?"

"Yup. While you guys were conducting the trial, I set 'em up against the fire truck. Only one has a bullet. Six of them are unloaded. But I must say, I'm not too happy about wasting a bullet on this guy. Wasting ammunition is still punishable by banishment."

"Good point, Rueben. Me neither," said the Chief. "We really don't have a rule specifying how we implement the penalty phase of a trespassing conviction. All the others shot first, or at least threatened to. Anyone wanna offer a suggestion?"

"Arrow!" Harger shouted.

"Arrow!" Ed agreed.

Then, more people started to shout, "Arrow! Arrow! Arrow!"

"Okay, does anyone have a bow with arrows handy?"

"Yup," Rueben said. "I have four bows, but one's not safe to pull. I'll get the three good ones right now. Could someone help me carry them?"

Rueben had recently expanded his home craft shop to include bow making. Yew, alder and black locust trees grew wild in and around Corbett and after a few initial rookie mistakes he was now cranking out a five or six foot long bow each week. He fashioned the arrows out of split fir and cedar. The feathers came from goose or turkey wings. He charged one silver coin for each bow. Most people saw no value whatsoever in silver or gold coins so they gladly paid. If he lived long enough, he would have nearly every silver coin in town buried in his backyard.

A few guys volunteered, quickly returning with the three new bows. Rueben set an arrow in his favorite and pulled it back, testing the string, aiming it at the man in the highway. "Nice."

Four other bows appeared from among the men at the fire station. One of the men set an arrow, casually testing its pull. Another joined in. A few jurors stepped up and started to fiddle with a few bows. The man sitting in the road looked around nervously, fingers fidgeting, eyes darting this way and that.

"Jurors, if any of you are unprepared to fire your arrows, say so now."

Silence.

"Okay. Line up. Let's get this done." The Chief ordered.

"He's getting up! He's gonna start runnin'!" someone yelled.

The three men with the rifles prepared to fire.

"Don't shoot him! Save the ammo!" Rueben yelled, as he pulled back on the string and aimed his bow. The man turned and ran just as Rueben released the arrow. It sailed at the man just as he started to gain speed. The arrow struck the man, piercing his lower back, but he kept running east, away from the gathered crowd.

Another arrow flew at him, shot by a juror. It missed. Then another juror shot an arrow, penetrating his upper torso and he fell into the gravel alongside the road, moaning and slowly flexing his arms and legs in the dirt and small rocks.

Another juror walked up near the man and stood about fifteen feet away. Another juror joined him. They pulled back their strings, carefully aimed, and shot two arrows into the man's neck, killing him instantly.

One turned to the crowd. "This jury of the town of Corbett has carried out its sentence."

Chapter Sixty-Two

"Denise, what is it?" Kelly asked, while Chris once again wrapped a clean t-shirt around Buck's thigh and listened.

"No doubt, it's staphylococcus aureus."

"What's that, exactly?" Chris asked.

"Well, it's a vicious staph infection of the skin. Eventually the skin decays, then it falls off. It's a horrible condition."

"How come so many of them had it?" Kelly asked.

"My guess, one of them caught it attacking a person who had it. It could have been days, weeks or months ago. Impossible to tell. Plus, not everyone gets sick from it, though it's highly contagious. Some are just carriers. Remember, these guys liked using knives. That's very close contact. Since these guys lived like a pack of dogs, they were in regular skin-to-skin contact with each other. If one catches it, most will get it, even though they may not show symptoms," Denise explained.

"Is that why some of 'em didn't have the ugly sores?" Chris asked.

"Exactly," Denise replied. "Remember, those without sores probably carry the disease."

"We need to monitor everyone who had any contact with them," Denise suggested.

"We may be lucky. No one reported actually touching them. A few touched their clothes, briefly. Blake held a book, a dictionary that one of them was using for toilet paper. That was gross," Kelly said.

"Hey, look! There he is now, out front. I gotta talk to him," Denise said. Kelly and Chris stayed by Buck while Denise went outside, near the crowd, careful not to get too close to anyone.

"Hey Blake, come here. I gotta talk to you," Denise said. "Don't get too close to me. I'm quarantined."

"I understand you handled a book belonging to one of the ferals, is that correct?"

"Yeah, but it was only for a minute."

"Did you handle the body?"

"No, well, yes, sort of. When I rolled him over to get to his pack, I shoved on his shirt. Why?"

"Well, I believe many of them had a type of staph infection that may be incurable. It's highly contagious and could be deadly."

I need you to go home and stay there for a few weeks. Right now. It's too risky having you walking around. Have you touched anyone since then?"

"No, no one," Blake said.

"Good. We may get lucky," Denise said.

Denise and Blake both looked over at an approaching head looming high over all the others. It was moving through the crowd, bobbing up and down in their direction. "It's my dad. He looks mad about something."

"Did you tell my son he was restricted to our house and farm for two weeks?"

"You have good hearing, John Raymond," Denise said. "Yes, you heard correctly. Blake needs to go home right now and stay there for two weeks. He can't be near anyone."

"You can't tell us what to do," Blake's dad said, as a mountain of a man, Joseph Hancock, moved closer to see what the commotion was all about.

"I believe I just did. He could be exposed to a deadly staph infection. He had contact with the clothing and property of one of the ferals. If he catches it he may die. There's nothing I can do about it. Have you touched Blake?"

"No. This is the first time I've seen him in two days. And it's not your business if I do. No one tells my kid where he can and can't go," Blake's dad said, moving closer to Denise, threatening her personal space.

"Look, John, stay away from me. I'm quarantined, too."

"What's this about? Are you giving Denise a hard time?" Joseph Hancock asked. Joseph, Joe Hancock's dad, was the sweetest man who ever walked the face of the Earth until someone screwed with him, or a friend of his. Then, a Doctor Jekyll and Mister Hyde style change would occur. His Mister Hyde side would sometimes take over and guide his actions. Over the years, people got hurt when this happened. Some people got hurt really bad.

"It's none of your business," John said.

Joseph Hancock's face and neck started changing color. He went from a weathered tan to an angry red. He then activated his massive twenty-two inch arms. They started twitching and rippling. Veins could be seen pumping blood down toward his thick, massive hands. Denise stared a moment at one of his arms and silently started counting off his pulse, "Sixty-six," she thought to herself. "One healthy guy."

People stepped away. All stared. Some had seen this transformation before. When it happened, nothing could be done to bring him back to normal until it had run its course.

"She told Blake he's under house arrest. No one tells my kid where he can and can't go. This is a farming area. We do what we want here."

"Listen," Joseph said, struggling with all his might to maintain self-control. "If Denise says he's restricted to his house, then that's exactly where he'll stay until she says he can leave," Joseph said. "If he's infected, he could kill everyone he touches. I'm sure you understand."

People standing nearby heard Joseph and moved away from Blake, who now stood alone, isolated with a wide empty space surrounding him.

"So she's the town veterinarian. Big deal. What's she know about human skin infections? Probably nothing. I'm not taking orders from her and neither's my son."

Someone swore they saw a small puff of white smoke emit from one of Joseph's ears.

"Okay. Fine. Let me explain it this way." Joseph moved closer, near enough so he was almost, but not quite, eye-level with the protruding adam's apple on the six-foot eight-inch John Raymond's throat. "If I hear of or see your kid step off your property or if he gets close to anyone except you, I'll rip your intestines out with my bare hands. Is that simple enough for you to understand?"

"You can't talk to me like that!"

Joseph's aimed all five fingers on his right hand at the tall man's stomach. They looked like five cruise missiles aimed directly at the man's guts. If he fired them fast enough he could probably blast right through him and halfway through a nearby tree trunk. A few people gasped. Parents' hands covered their children's eyes. "Oh, please try me. It's been twenty years since I've ripped someone's guts out. I could use a quick refresher course. You have the count of three to get you and your kid moving home or I swear I'll rip your guts out right here. One. Two. Thr ..."

"Dad! Hold it. They're right. If I caught this disease I could spread it around. Joseph, Denise, I'll stay home 'til we're sure I don't have it. C'mon, dad. Let's go."

His dad backed away from Joseph, glaring down at him but not saying a word. He walked over to Blake and placed his arm around him. "Let's get out of here, son."

"John Raymond. That quarantine now includes you, too. You're both quarantined," Denise said. "Neither of you can get close to anyone. That means no one!"

"Both of you, get. Go home. Stay home," Joseph added.

"Thanks, Joseph," Denise said, as Kelly stepped outside.

"What's going on?" Kelly asked.

"Nothing. I just quarantined a few people. They aren't too happy about it and I can't really blame them."

"Can we make them?" Kelly asked.

"I don't know. We might need to add another law. If people don't take the quarantine seriously we could have a big outbreak," Denise said. "People could die. Lots of us."

"If they spread it and people die, it'll be murder. That means banishment," Kelly said. "We need to talk to the council about having a vote to add one more law."

Kelly thought a moment. "Bill, Dan, Rigo, Kyle, Joe, Kevin, Tweedy, Corey and a bunch of other guys just took off to bury the dead. They'll be back later. I hope none of our guys gets the disease," Kelly said.

"We're lucky to have people willing to volunteer for that job," Denise said. "I really have no idea how contagious it is, but if every one of the dead ferals had it, then it obviously jumps from person to person easily," Denise said. "We should stay on the safe side. Maybe tell the Chief and the council we should avoid large public gatherings for a while."

"What about this vigil for Buck? It's not losing steam at all!"

"In a few minutes I'll go make another announcement reminding everyone to not get close to anyone who contacted the ferals. And, that anyone who touched one of them needs to stay home. That's a start."

"Good idea," Kelly said.

"Pat O'Malley wanted to go help dig the pit, too, but he and Conner had so many cuts on them from blackberry thorns that I wouldn't let either of them. A spore would find an easy entry point on either one of them. Plus, the poor guy, Pat, could barely move," Denise said. "He was walking like a man on stilts."

"Anyhow, I made it more than clear to them before they left how dangerous it was to touch the bodies. But burying them had to be done. We all know this. Those guys are brave, I tell ya. They'll dig pits next to the battles, then, they'll hook and drag the bodies with a long bent piece of sharpened re-bar. Pete Roth made one this morning so hooking and dragging the bodies into the pits without handling them should be safe and simple. They know to not touch them, or their clothing and things."

"What about the people who handled their weapons and clothing?"

"Same thing. All we can do is wait. The chances of exposure are much lower just handling bows and clothes, but there is a chance. If it spreads among us, though, it could wipe out a big percentage of our population. It would be a disaster. But, I really doubt anyone'll catch it," Denise said.

"What about Buck? Twice, he was shot by arrows they handled," Kelly asked.

"It might all depend on which strain of staph infection they caught. Some antibiotics work and some don't. All we can do is what we've done. I can't believe he's still alive, though. What's his blood pressure now?"

Kelly checked, "Normal."

"Well, at least his heart's fine."

"We still have hundreds of people out front. We haven't given them an update for quite a while," Kelly said.

"I'll do it," Denise said, suddenly gagging, bending over as if she was about to throw up.

"Denise! What's wrong?" Kelly asked.

"It started a few days ago, before Buck showed up."

Kelly smiled. "I saw you do that yesterday. I think I know what it could be."

"Morning sickness?"

"Maybe."

"Probably?"

"Definitely."

"Yeah, definitely."

"Congratulations, girl!" Kelly said and hugged Denise. "Chris know?"

"Not yet. There's no hurry. I'll tell him in a few weeks. I just want to be ... sure."

"Okay. I'll keep it to myself."

"Thanks. Well, can't let that stop me. It's almost midafternoon, time for Buck's antibiotics. Plus, we should give him some more birch bark aspirin," Denise said.

"Let's give him a complete check. Then make the status announcement," Kelly suggested.

The two women went to work on Buck.

Chapter Sixty-Three

"His temperature's ninety-nine point four!" Kelly excitedly noted.

"Can't be. Check it again, Kelly."

Kelly checked it once more. "Same thing."

"This is really strange. Kelly, his chest. It's not burning anymore. Plus, the circle of redness around his chest wound is shrinking. The infection is definitely backing off!" Denise said, grinning like a happy puppy.

"We need to get some fluids in him. At sundown it'll be a day since he had any fluids. We should try to wake him up soon," Kelly said.

"Hey, why don't you two let the people outside know what's up, and I'll stay with him," Chris said.

"Good, but first we have to give him his medicine. Chris, could you step outside, please?"

After giving Buck his antibiotics and aspirin, Kelly and Denise stepped out to the porch. They stood facing the crowd. It seemed like the whole town was there. In front they recognized familiar faces, many armed, including Bill Hartigan, Dan Long, Pat O'Malley, Kevin Sakai, Vladimir Zhalobovskaia and many of the others on the response teams, plus Rueben Moreland as well as Pete and Linda Roth. "Attention everyone! We have good news about Buck! His temperature has dropped nearly to normal, it's ninety-nine point four, and his redness from infection is fading away. His blood pressure is still normal. He still hasn't had any fluids or eaten in a long time. Chris is in with him now. Any questions?"

"We love you, Buck! You too, Denise!" a woman's voice called out from the back of the crowd. It was Mary Lou Rainier. She'd been waiting in front of the clinic with her husband, Ed, since midnight. Staying awake all night praying had left the couple exhausted both physically and emotionally.

The screen door suddenly flew open, smacking Kelly in the back. "Hey!" Kelly said.

"Denise! Kelly! He woke up! Come quick!" Chris said, stumbling out the door, nearly tripping and falling as he ran to the porch.

Denise and Kelly turned and ran through the doorway, back into the clinic, heading straight to Buck's room. "Chris, go get some water ready. We need to get fluids in him, now! Some blueberry juice, too!"

"Kelly, get some of that energy mix Alison made, let's get some of that in him. A few pieces of salmon, too!" Denise said, excitedly running into the room.

"Buck! Are you awake?" Denise asked, approaching the heavy wooden examination table.

"Arghhhh."

"Buck! It's me, Denise. Kelly and Chris are here, too!"

"Water," Buck slurred.

"Here, Buck. Water," Kelly said, pouring a few ounces into his mouth. "Ready for some blueberry juice?"

"Where am I?"

"Back in Denise's examination room. Do you know why you're here?" Kelly asked.

"Yeah, infection. My chest was hurting like crazy. I was with Joe. I remember I could barely stand up."

"Do you remember the battle?" Denise asked.

"No. All I remember is hiding in the bushes with Joe. We saw the ferals walk by. Then, nothing after that."

"That's amazing," Kelly said. "You don't remember the shooting?"

"No."

"Do you remember getting shot?" Denise asked.

"Shot? Was I shot again?"

"Yeah, in the thigh. You didn't know?"

"Not until just now," Buck said, reaching down toward his leg.

"Leave it alone, Buck. It's packed and wrapped," Denise said, then she and Kelly filled Buck in on all the details of the one-sided battles, including the one he was in.

"You had a fever of one-oh-four. Now you're almost normal. It's flat-out incredible," Kelly said.

"Hey, what's that strange noise outside?"

"Chanting," Kelly said. "In Pali. It's an ancient language. A small group has been chanting for your health since midnight. My mom and dad. The Sakais. Alison, me and a few others dropped in now and then, too. Your buddy Ng Ling Cheow, too. He's there now. Even Joe's mom tried chanting last night."

"What time is it now?"

"We don't tell time like we used to, anymore, but it's midafternoon," Kelly said. "Getting close to dinnertime."

"We had lots of people out front, many of them praying for you, Buck," Denise said. "I couldn't believe it. Five hundred or so, last night around midnight. Fewer now because there's so much work to do. But still, there're several hundred camped out front. Looks like their prayers and all that chanting worked."

"We should let 'em know he's awake," Denise said.

"I'll stay and feed him. You two go back outside and let everyone know," Chris said.

"Okay," Kelly replied. "We'll only be out a short while."

Denise and Kelly walked back out of the clinic and stood on the broad porch. "We have even better news! He's awake and talking. I do believe he'll pull through!"

"It's a miracle! It's an absolute miracle!" Mary Lou said, loud enough for everyone to hear, tears of joy starting to form under her eyes.

Denise and Kelly spoke some more, answered a few questions and went inside to care for Buck, making sure he ate well and stayed flat on his back.

"This is really crazy," Kevin said to Pat. "Guy's been here only three days and the whole town adopts him like a wandering saint."

"He's acted like one since he got here. Everyone he meets likes him. The way he talks and moves, waves of calm emanate around him. Plus, we haven't had someone to rally around in two years. No one's been allowed in since Stan and Karen Bohnstedt walked up the highway a few days after the war. Getting a dentist was the best news we could've had. He's now installing gold fillings, free! Remember, we turned away hundreds, maybe even a thousand people back then, in the weeks after it hit. Had to shoot a few hundred, too. But lately it's been just us, all isolated like we've been stranded on an island. I believe we were missing something very important, something to unify us. We've been missing contact from outside. More important than that, we've needed something outside of ourselves and our community to focus our good thoughts and our compassion," Pat replied, staring in the distance in his well-known, thoughtful manner.

"Yeah, he is our very first contact with the outside," Bill said. "I can't wait to hear him tell his story, when he's better."

"It's almost like it's not an accident that he appeared here," Pat said.

"What do you mean?" Kevin asked.

"What he means is there are no such things as coincidences," Bill said, speaking like a former cop.

"Yes, that. But we've been missing a connection with those who remain, too. Now, we have one," Pat said.

"He wants to go to Portland, soon. He'll need protection for a trip like that. Last winter from the Vista House we had a view of smoke from a few chimneys that direction," Bill said. "Where there're people, there's always danger."

"Buck's from Portland. He's tough. He'll get better, soon. Plus, he's a soldier. He sure fought like one, from what Joe said. He's one more town hero, now," Pat said.

"Boy howdy," Bill said.

"I still can't believe he got up and around after that chest wound," Kevin said.

"I've seen that before," Bill said. "When I was a cop I saw people get hurt really bad, rest awhile, then they get a weird second wind."

"It's a survival instinct," Dan added. "I was on duty one night when a guy with a broken femur climbed out the windshield of his crashed car. It happened two hours after he went off the road and down into a ravine. He woke up and limped two miles to get to a phone. He finally made it to a gas station and passed out by the pumps. That's when I saw him. He damn near died. Getting hit in the chest with a skinny arrow, missing vital organs, I can see how Buck might feel better after two days even though serious infection was slowly eating away inside him."

"Well, this time he stays at the clinic until he's properly healed. When he's better, and the quarantine's over, he'll get to work on a farm," Kevin said.

"We gotta get him voted into town, as a citizen, first, so he's not called an outsider anymore," Dan said.

"I'm sure the council and the Chief are already thinking of that. Right, Bill?" Kevin asked.

"Uh, yeah, right! It's the next order of business … today, in fact. We need a quarantine rule, too. I don't wanna see Joseph Hancock rip someone's guts out. He might get infected that way," Dan said, while Bill laughed and Kevin just looked at the two of them, missing the joke.

"I don't get it."

"Get what?" Bill said.

"Forget it. Must be your sick cop humor, or something," Kevin said.

"Or something," Dan said.

"Yup," Bill said.

Chapter Sixty-Four

The Chief spoke. "The Town Council meeting of July, and the first meeting of the year, is now in order. As a reminder, Year Three began five days ago, on July first, the second anniversary of the bank failures. Mary Lou, are you ready to take a few notes?"

Five simple, brown steel folding chairs sat close together in a row, elevated about two feet above the main worship hall in front of Reverend Golphenee's podium. The Chief sat in the center chair. Councilmembers Cho and Hartigan sat to his right, the other two to his left. Scott sat in the back row, near the center doors, to avoid the impression he was influencing the meeting. Robert's Rules of Order were not followed. The meetings generally went fast.

"Yes," Mary Lou replied. With paper in such short supply, the meeting notes were limited to half of one side of a sheet of paper. She wrote small, only summarizing key points.

"Okay," the Chief said. "Roll call. Councilmember Cho?"

"Present."

"Councilmember Hartigan?"

"Present."

"Councilmember Harger?"

"Present."

"Councilmember Rainier?"

"Present."

"That's five out of five. We're all present. We have two items on the agenda so far. Number one is the new quarantine law. Number two is citizenship for ..."

The crowd interrupted the Chief with piercing whistles, loud obnoxious country-style hoots and prolonged applause.

It had been four days since Buck washed up on that Sandy River beach. He was stuck in the clinic, busily pestering Denise and Kelly to let him get up and do some gardening to earn his keep. They kept threatening to have Joe and Chris tie him down on the platform if they caught him getting out of the makeshift bed arranged on the floor of the examination room. He didn't ask as often after Denise reminded him what happened to him the last time he was tied down on that platform.

"Okay, okay. We hear ya. We hear ya. Any other items from the council?"

They turned their heads back and forth, looking at each other, then turned in unison toward the Chief and said nothing. The monthly meetings of the Corbett Town Council were scheduled on the first Sunday of each month, after the Mount Hood Christian Church Sunday service, held every Sunday around midmorning. The council meeting was held around noon inside the church only because it was the largest meeting hall in town. Typically, a few dozen townspeople showed up. Sometimes fewer. This time, the place was jam-packed. People stood in the aisles. The shaded front porch, where Ng Ling Cheow did his clever bicycle repair, was elbow-to-elbow.

Since anyone could request an agenda item the Chief asked the huge crowd, "Okay, hearing no additional agenda requests from the council, are there any agenda requests from the citizens?"

The people in the massive crowd shifted their feet, looking around, no one asking to add another agenda item, but everyone eager to get to the second agenda item.

The Chief spoke loud so he could be heard over the inevitable whispered chitchat between friends. "Okay, let's get to number one. This rule would allow Denise or Kelly to order any one of us quarantined if they believe one of us has a contagious disease. We've always tried to stay away from outsiders. It's an old rule, not a law, but plain common sense. Everyone follows it because they don't want to get sick, then spread the sickness around town. We have almost no medicine left. A new kind of flu, or a new disease, like a skin disease, could decimate us. As you probably know, one of the response team members got a little too close to a feral. He didn't know the guy had a staph infection, and he rolled the guy over to search him and then handled his book, a dictionary the feral used for toilet paper. A few others got close, too. Kyle, for example, blew a guy up. The explosion caused leg parts to fly in the air and a red haze to form. They say none of it hit anyone on their team, thankfully. Then there's Buck. The ones who shot the two arrows that hit him were probably infected, too."

Buck didn't know it yet, but he was quarantined at the clinic. Denise, Kelly, Joe and Chris were confined to the clinic, too, because they were the only ones who had personal contact with Buck. Denise believed any symptoms should arise within a few days or weeks. She wasn't sure, so she chose the side of caution.

The Chief continued. "On the other hand, some might say freedom to do as we wish and not having others tell us what to do and where to go, is more important. Let's start the discussion. Is there anyone who would like to speak against adding this new rule?"

The discussion went fast. Most spoke in favor, arguing that it'd be rarely enforced and the only time there'd be a risk would be when outsiders arrived. Plus, most knew there was so much work to do on their own land restricting movement didn't really impact them, much. Like all town actions, a decision was made by voice vote among those present. It was overwhelmingly in favor. Law number seven had been passed. The punishment for violating the quarantine would be a one-year banishment.

"Agenda item number two is citizenship for Buck," the Chief said.

The crowd began cheering, a few whistling. The Chief waited a moment for the assembly to calm down.

"We all know the deal with Buck. We've only done this once before, with Stan and Karen Bohnstedt. It was unanimous in their case. Frankly, I like it better when we're in agreement on an issue instead of arguing each and every minor detail like we always do with the farming and school issues. First, councilmembers. Do any of you want to argue in favor or against?"

Kimberly Cho didn't bother asking for recognition and simply stood up from her chair. "We've all discussed this before the meeting. We're unanimously in favor."

"Okay, then. Townspeople, anyone wanna argue against the motion?" the Chief stood and yelled it out loud so everyone, even those outside, could hear.

The room fell silent. Hundreds of men, women and children stood still. A crying baby fell silent. Not even a whisper could be heard.

Scott Harger raised his hand.

"Yes, Harger?" the Chief said.

"I move we grant full unconditional citizenship to Buck and have an immediate town vote."

"I second that," said Bill, Ed and Kimberly at the same time.

"Okay. Let's skip the formalities. Everyone! All against, say no!"

Silence, once again.

"All in favor, say aye!"

The room went wild. Hundreds of people cheered, hats flew into the air, a few babies started crying. A man seated in a rear pew pulled out a bottle of raspberry wine and took a hefty congratulatory chug, passing the bottle to his friend seated next to him, who also took a long pull on the bottle. Two scruffy young men sat in one of the forward pews, one whispering to the other, "Hey, man. I feel like celebrating. Let's go out behind the church and burn a fat one."

An elderly woman overheard the comment and shrieked and started banging her cane on the back of the pew in front of her, "They're going to set someone on fire!" It was so loud in the church few heard her and none of them took her seriously. The two young men rose, headed to the aisle, then they went out back.

Pete Roth had arrived earlier in a mule-drawn wagon he constructed out of the bed of a fifty-year-old Chevy pick-up. He placed a knee-high wooden table on the asphalt. A car battery went next to it, on the pavement. The battery had a few small gizmos attached to it by copper wires.

"No one touch that battery!" Pete commanded. He placed an old turntable on the table. A few tall speakers were lifted out of the wagon and placed near the table. Next, he somehow rigged up the solar charged car battery to the ancient turntable without getting electrocuted. A tangle of wires went here and there, including some snaking to the speakers. He flipped open a box, then turned to his old friend, Peter Coonradt, "Hmm. Which album first?"

"Nice collection. How about I just grab one at random. Does it really matter which one we play first?" Peter replied.

"It does. Let's pick something that signifies getting the world restarted again," Pete Roth said.

"How about 'Start Me Up,' from The Rolling Stones. Got that in your box?" Peter asked. "We could all use a restart."

"Yup, you can say that again," Pete said, as he flipped through the vertically stacked album sleeves. "Here it is.

The Rolling Stones' 'Tattoo You' album. This should set the proper tone."

"Will that old turntable work?" Peter asked.

"It did last night when Alison Lee figured out how to get the electricity flowing from the solar charged battery to the record player. She's in my garage working on another project or she would be here doing this herself."

"She did that?"

"Yup," Pete said. "Don't ask me how."

"We're getting a lot of use out of the remains of the past civilization," Peter joked.

"Let's enjoy it. It won't last long," Pete said.

"I hear ya. Each window we break needs to be replaced by salvaged plywood. We're living off the carcass. Forget windows. It gets harder and harder to find plumbing supplies."

"I just hope the batteries last a little longer," Pete said.

"It's like that with everything. The roofs, too," Peter said.

"Yup, mine's leaked this winter. I had to borrow roofing shingles from an abandoned house. Can't do that for long," Pete said.

"Hey! Where's Alison? She's missing the party," Peter asked.

"She'd rather be tinkering with electricity. Her sister's missing it, too," Pete said, then, a sly grin appeared on his face. "Kelly's stuck at the clinic for a week or two ... with Big Joe. Eddie Cho's not too happy about that. Denise won't let Eddie near Kelly."

"Yeah, who would be happy about that? On the other hand, a lot of women wouldn't mind getting stuck somewhere with Big Joe for a few weeks. Everyone's gossiping about it."

"Yup, everyone," Pete said.

"They're sayin' Kelly's not too upset about it."

"That's what I hear, too."

"Wouldn't wanna be in Eddie's shoes right now," Peter said.

"Nope."

"Hey, Gretchen Simkovic's here, with her kids. I haven't seen her in ages. Excuse me, I've got to say hello to her," Peter said.

"See ya! Nice talking to you, Peter!"

Peter crossed the parking lot while Pete pulled the precious disc out of its jacket and gently placed it on the turntable. He set the needle to play the first song, "Start Me Up." "It's been a long time since I've heard that album," he said, to himself.

Suddenly, the loud, nineteen eighties rock music filled the air in front of the church. It was very loud. Everyone turned toward the sound, shocked, as if a bomb had just exploded. Applause broke out. For most, it was the first recorded music they had heard in two years. People of all ages started dancing in the parking lot. Many had yet to eat breakfast. None had eaten lunch.

"Son-of-a-gun, it works!" Pete said.

Chapter Sixty-Five

The screaming coming from within the light green, two-story house filled the air in the highway where Buck stood. He walked in the sunshine down the concrete driveway toward the screams of the woman. It took him twenty paces to walk past the dozens of tomato plants growing in the front yard. None of them were ready to pick. He stepped onto the small covered porch and paused a moment. Another scream smashed into him, louder this time. He knocked on the four-inch-wide wooden frame of the screen door. He waited. Then, he knocked again, but a little louder.

A beautiful, slender, forty-something woman with short brown hair soon appeared. She was dressed in the standard Corbett style: faded denim jeans and a dark blue t-shirt. Her unpainted toenails poked out of a pair of large tire-tread flip-flops, probably made by Rueben. "Hi, my name is Michael Baccellieri," Buck said. "Is this the dental clinic?"

"Yes."

"I'm here to see the dentist, Stan Bohnstedt."

"You've come to the right place," she said, opening the door. She moved aside to make room so Buck could walk past her. "Come inside, he'll see you soon. It's nice to meet you, Michael. I'm Karen, his wife and assistant. I've heard a lot about you." Her voice was pleasant.

"Please call me Buck. I've heard about you and the dentist, too."

"Silly question, but I bet you're here to have a tooth looked at. Am I right?" Karen asked.

"Yup. I've had a problem with a few molars. It's been a long time since I've been to a dentist."

Another scream was heard. This one was muffled, as if a rag was being held over her face.

"No Novocaine," Karen said. She shrugged. "It only hurts while he's working. After that, it's okay. Have a seat."

Buck sat on the small, armless wooden chair. It was near the door, back to the window. Karen walked out of the entry room and disappeared around the corner to the dark, unlit hallway. A stack of old, well-read car magazines sat on a short, heavy wooden lamp table. The lamp was missing. He picked up the top magazine and started thumbing through it when another, much louder scream blasted from down the hall, this time followed by an unusually creative string of shouted cussing. Buck thought he counted all seven of the worst swear words. He turned another page. Then another.

After a wait, a young woman, around twenty, walked into the entry room from the hallway. She was tall and, even with the crooked, shallow scar running from her left eyebrow past her hairline, she was stunningly beautiful. Her medium brown hair was tied back in a single braided ponytail. If she were wearing makeup it would have been running down her face because she had been crying. The bottom of the black cloth eye patch over her left eye remained dry, as did that side of her face. "Thanks, Doctor," it sounded like she said, turning back to face the hall.

A man's voice was heard behind her. "Those two should be the last ones. You're a tough girl. Two wisdom teeth at once. Wow! I am so proud of you, Mandy," he said. "It would have been easier if they hadn't been impacted, you know, in there sideways. No food for a day. Drink lots of that blackberry and lavender tea I gave you! Keep those cloths in the holes until I look at you again in the morning."

"Miss Winters, you forgot your bag. Your tea's inside," Karen said, appearing from the hallway, holding a dark green canvas purse.

She took it and mumbled what sounded like, "Thanks. See you tomorrow morning."

"Early," the man's voice replied.

"Early," Mandy said, then she turned toward Buck. "Hey, are you Buck?"

"Yes." Buck stood. "Pleased to meet you." He absentmindedly extended his right hand, and slowly withdrew it, as if he wanted it to stay near her.

Mandy smiled at Buck, mumbling some more. "I've heard all about you. I hope you can find time to tell me more about your journey."

"I'd love to."

"Drop by the berry farm. That's where I work."

"I will."

"Well, bye, now. Hope to see you soon."

Buck sat in the chair. "She certainly fits nicely into her deerskin skirt and dark green t-shirt," Buck thought to himself as she went out the door and walked toward the road in a head-turning, loose-jointed stride. He stared out the window until his neck wouldn't turn any more.

Someone coughed. "Hi, Buck. I'm Stan Bohnstedt."

Buck jolted upright, standing as if at attention. "Oh. Hi. I'm Michael Baccellieri." Neither moved to shake hands.

"Michael Baccellieri. I knew a guy in Portland with that exact name. Sold coffee. Longbottom Coffee and Tea, I believe it was called. Are you related?" Stan asked, pronouncing the last name perfectly.

"The guy you knew is my dad. That's why I came here in the first place, to get to Portland and find out if my family's okay."

"He is a good man," Stan said, careful to use the present tense of the verb. "What can I do for you today?"

"I thought I had a few bad molars. But, uh, I think they're okay now. Maybe I'll just go, come back some other time."

"Let me take a look. Trust me, they never get better. Come with me back to the examination room." They went down the dark hall and into a large, white-painted, well-lit converted bedroom, the sun shining brightly through a large window.

"Rueben Moreland said I should offer you this," Buck said, pulling a small silver coin out of his front pouch.

Stan stared at the small coin like it was the Hope Diamond. "Nope. The first one's going to be free, for you. But you can bring that coin next time. Have a seat."

"I'll keep it with me," Buck said, placing the coin back in the sewn-in pouch. He sat in the elevated reclining chair. It was a typical living room chair, basic brown fake leather, a handle on the side, much like the ones millions once sat in to watch football games. It was set on a sturdy, wooden, two-foot high platform, so the dentist could work better.

Karen stood on one side of the chair, the dentist on the other. "I'm ready," Karen said.

"Hey, I heard what you did. And, I heard you got citizenship. Congratulations! Welcome to Corbett, Mister Baccellieri. Open up, please."

"Ahh."

"Wider."

"Arghh?"

"Better. That's right. Ah hah! I see them. On the upper left." He poked and jabbed, causing moderate pain.

"Arghh!"

"Yup. One's gotta go. Wider, please." Stanley reached for a shiny metal tool of some sort and placed it in Buck's mouth. Then asked Karen for another slender rod of cold steel. "Elevator, please."

"Elevator."

It, too, went in Buck's mouth.

Stanley twisted on something. Then dug and scraped some.

Buck screamed. Stan and Karen continued working. He screamed again.

"That might have hurt a little," Karen said, smiling. "He's just getting started. You're a soldier. You can take it."

"Arghh! Arghh?"

Stan somehow understood Buck's mumbling. Dentists have a special knack for that. "Yeah, it'll hurt. Tooth pain is a strange thing, though. Once it's out, it won't hurt anymore." A frightening set of steel forceps went in. Karen retracted Buck's cheek with the fingers of one hand and pressed down on his forehead with the other.

"Arghh aht?"

"Forceps. That's right, out. Ready? Don't move."

"Arghh."

Stan grabbed the handle of the forceps in his fist. Karen held Buck's head firmly to the chair. "This'll only hurt for a few minutes, but you might wanna grab the arms of the chair real tight because it's going to hurt like crazy!"

Chapter Sixty-Six

John Raymond headed over to Joseph Hancock's berry farm. The quarantine was over and he now had a matter to settle. When he was halfway there he saw Joseph walking toward him in the distance. He kept walking. So did Joseph. They were on a collision course. The two big men stopped six feet away from one another in the middle of the road. The hot sun was high overhead. It was so quiet their breathing was the only sound in the air. No one else was around. They stared at each other a moment, hands hanging by their sides. Loose-fitting tattered flannel shirts covered their handguns.

They both said each other's names at once.

"Joseph ..."

"John ..."

They both successfully fought to suppress grins, but continued staring into each other's eyes, Joseph's head angled up and John's down.

"You got somethin' to say to me?" John asked, looking down at Joseph from somewhere near the tops of the roadside telephone poles.

"Yup, and you?"

"Yup. You first," John said.

"No, I insist. After you," Joseph said, his arms starting to throb once again, blood flowing toward his hands.

"Okay," John said. "I'll speak first. I'm sorry I got in your face last week. Denise says we're all lucky. No one's shown any symptoms and therefore the quarantine is over. I was on my way to your house to apologize."

"Well, funny thing. I was headed over to your place to apologize to you. Right now. You see, I'm a bit of a hothead sometimes and I simply lost my stupid temper. I apologize, too," Joseph said.

Both men stepped forward, gently tapping each other's knuckles with both fists, rather than shake hands. It was a simple precaution Denise had suggested everyone do for a while rather than shake hands in the traditional manner.

An uncomfortable moment passed, each man staring at each other. Then Joseph threw his arms around John's waist, which was as high as he could reach, placing the side of his head on tall John's chest. John did the same to Joseph, wrapping his arms around Joseph's bald head. They hugged a while right there in the middle of Evans Road. A tear fell out of Joseph's left eye. Another from his right wet John's shirt. "Just like my boy," Joseph said.

"My kid, Blake, I should listen to him more," John said, as they backed away from each other, resuming their more comfortable six-foot, conversational distance. "He has a lot of common sense, that boy. By the time we got home that day he'd convinced me that the quarantine was the best idea, for everyone's good. I've been itching to apologize to you ever since. Thanks for coming over to meet with me."

"My wife, Mary Kay, you know her, right?"

"Yup."

"Well, before I even got home she'd heard what I said to you. I can't believe how fast word spreads around here. Anyhow, she asked if it was true. I told her it was. She told me she'd talk to me again after I apologized to you. Would you mind walking over to the berry farm with me and tell her I've apologized to you? It would mean a great deal to me."

John laughed. "Of course. Let's do it now."

"I'll fix you a cup of some blueberry wine. When's the last time you had any of that?" Joseph asked.

"About a mile ago. Needed a bracer before I saw you," John replied.

"Yeah, me too," Joseph said. "Got a bottle stashed in the garage. Wanna split the rest of it?"

"Sure!"

They walked for a time, back along Evans Road toward the Hancock farm and saw a wobbling bicycle approach in the distance. "Hey! I think that's Buck!" Joseph said.

"Denise finally let him out?"

Joseph smiled, knowing the quarantine had been lifted for everyone. "I guess so."

Buck stopped in the road, as nearly everyone did these days when they passed by someone else. It was one of the nice social changes brought about by the death of the automobile. "Hey, guys. What's up?"

"Not much. Heading to my house. What about you?" Joseph asked.

"Denise said I need exercise, so she told me to ride a bike … slow, easier on my leg. Plus, she said to stay off hills. She says I'm accident prone."

"Well, you're apparently freed from custody," John said.

"What happened to your mouth?" Joseph asked. "It looks swollen."

"Went to the dentist. He had to pull one."

"Oh. That's not as fun as it used to be, is it?" Joseph said.

"It hurt. Next week he'll do a filling."

"Ouch," John said.

"Congratulations on getting citizenship, by the way. You're only the third to get it, you and the dentist, Stan Bohnstedt and his wife, Karen." Joseph said. "Well, plus the Lees, but they came in just before the wall dropped. We're really glad they came in, too, by the way."

"Yeah, I've met all of 'em, Kelly, mostly. They're a fine family."

"They chanted all night when you were near death," Joseph said.

"Denise and Kelly told me all about that during the quarantine," Buck said.

"All night?" John asked. He apparently still hadn't heard the details of the overnight vigil since he had been quarantined almost as soon as he arrived.

"Yup, all night and into the next day, too. That's why the big crowd was there. It was a non-stop prayer vigil. If you missed it, it's okay. Not everyone could make it. Plus, not everyone believes in that sort of thing," Joseph said, implying that he didn't believe in praying or in prayer.

"Hey, hold on," Buck said. "If it might help and it doesn't hurt, why not give it a try? Heck, I might not be standing here today!"

"Hmm," Joseph said.

"At least consider it," Buck said.

"Well, I haven't been in church since I was married, well, except for some of the town meetings. They're held in the church. But I'll give it some thought. I must admit it's a mighty strong coincidence, you getting better so fast. So, Buck, have any plans?"

"My first plan is to see my parents' house. My journey won't be finished until I do."

"Lately, quite a few of us have been talking about taking an exploration trip into town," John said. "We don't see lines of smoke rising up anymore. It might be safe, if we go with a large force. I ain't going, but my kid, Blake, he can't wait."

"It'll have to wait until after the planting and harvest is over. Remember, winter comes early and it hits hard around here, especially up near the Columbia River bluff. We work all summer to get ready for that. Preparing food, chopping wood, repairing roofs and windows, plus, getting winter clothing made," Joseph said.

"And hunting. It's all done with arrows now. The bullets are saved for war. You ever shoot a bow, Buck?"

"Nope, but I'll learn."

"You sure will," John said.

"So, now that you're out of the clinic, where are you going to be staying?" Joseph asked.

"Joe just asked me this afternoon if I'd stay at the berry farm. I told him to make sure you and your wife approve, first. I guess he hasn't asked you yet."

"Nope. He hasn't asked but you just did and it's great! I approve! In a bit Mary Kay'll be talking again, and I'll ask her, but you're a town hero! I know she'll be happy and honored to have you stay with us. We have lots of work to do, too. No end to it, in fact. The Lees are over all the time, working on the berry farm and cooking."

"I met a girl when I was at the dentist. Her name is Mandy. She said she works at the berry farm," Buck said.

"Mandy Winters is there almost every day. You'll like her. She got in an ugly fight there two years ago. Did you hear about it?"

"Joe mentioned it," Buck said.

"It was big news around here. Some guy was constantly bullying her. Every day this eighteen-year-old boy kept calling Mandy fat and lazy," Joseph said. "One day he went too far and smacked her on the butt with his shovel. Some kids laughed. It happened right on our farm. Mandy finally got fed up with it and hit him back. Then they fought. He hit her in the face. Then she drove her shovel through his neck. Everyone, including the boy's family, called it self-defense."

"Frontier justice. We don't have repeat offenders," John said.

"Mandy lost an eye, but the boy? Well, let's just say no one teases Mandy any more. In fact, after that, we're all very respectful toward women around here," Joseph said.

"That's what Joe told me a few weeks ago and I think it's wonderful! Well, not the fight, but the respect," Buck said.

"It was strange. All the crude comments, the old culture ghetto trash talking about women, all of that crap suddenly ended when they went at each other with shovels. He lost his life and the women of Corbett won their respect," Joseph said.

"I remember people used to listen to music with lyrics calling women all kinds of nasty names," Buck said.

"No more," Joseph said.

"Some good comes out of everything," John said, then he nodded at Joseph.

Joseph returned the nod.

"Why would someone bother her about being fat? She ain't fat," Buck asked. "Not even close."

"Like most of us, she looks a lot different now," John said.

"Yup," Joseph agreed.

"Maybe I'll get to meet everyone on your farm tomorrow," Buck said, mostly looking forward to meeting Mandy again.

"Deborah Lee comes over and cooks with my wife, Mary Kay, at least once a week. Hey! I even have a bench press, but you better not try that for a few months. Anyhow, there's lots of work to do making sure the berries stay watered and keeping weeds out of the garden and all that. The berries'll be ready soon, too. Then it's berries, berries and more berries. It's sunrise to sunset, every day, Sundays, too. You ever garden or farm, Buck?"

"Nope. Never," Buck said. "Did I hear you say Mary Kay isn't talking? Is she sick?"

"It's a long story, but she's fine. I'll explain some day, or maybe you'll find out yourself, with a local woman."

"Huh?"

"Forget it," John said, laughing along with Joseph.

"Are you staying at the clinic tonight?" Joseph asked.

"I don't know. It's the only place I've spent the night since I got here. I'm ready for a room of my own."

"We got a room waiting for you. Get your things and come over."

"I have nothing."

"You're like a monk or a priest. No possessions," John said.

"Why don't you drop off the bike at the clinic and walk over later?" Joseph asked.

"Okay."

"We'll have dinner ready."

"Then tomorrow you get to start learning all about farming," John said.

"I'm a city boy. Only had one job. Been in the army all my adult life. I don't know the first thing about growing things, just destroying things."

"Well, that's about to change," John said.

"Yup," Joseph added.